CATHERINE COOKSON

Kate Hannigan's Girl

A NOVEL

SIMON & SCHUSTER

New York   London   Toronto   Sydney   Singapore

SIMON & SCHUSTER
Rockefeller Center
1230 Avenue of the Americas
New York, NY 10020

Originally published in 2000 in Great Britain by Bantam Press

Manufactured in the United States of America

1 3 5 7 9 10 8 6 4 2

Cookson, Catherine.
Kate Hannigan's girl: a novel/Catherine Cookson.
p.cm.
1. England, Northern—Fiction. I. Title.

PR6053.0525 K38 2001
823'.914—dc21   00-066173

ISBN 0-7432-1252-5

KATE HANNIGAN'S GIRL

1

Annie stood gripping her bicycle and staring wide-eyed at the tall, auburn-haired boy leaning nonchalantly across his saddle.

'What did Cathleen Davidson tell you?' she asked.

'Well, if I tell you you'll jump down my throat.'

'No I won't.' Without taking her eyes from his she flicked her head from side to side, throwing the long silvery plaits over her shoulders.

'Your hair's marvellous,' he said.

'What did Cathleen say about me?' Annie asked again, a nervous tremor passing over her face.

'Well, if I tell you, will you promise to go with me?'

'Go with you? Oh, I can't.' Annie stared at him, aghast. 'You're nearly sixteen. And . . . and there's Cathleen.'

'Oh, very well.' He shrugged his shoulders and ran his hand through his wavy hair.

'Yes I will. All right, then, Brian.' The words came with a rush.

'Well . . .' His eyes moving over her face, from the fringe above the wide green eyes to the large, curving mouth, Brian was savouring the effect of his coming words: 'Well, she said your mother and stepfather aren't really married.'

'What!' This was new; she hadn't expected to hear this.

'That's what she said.'

'Oh, the wicked thing. They *are* married; I was there when they were married. It was the day after New Year's Day, nearly four months ago.'

'Were you really there?'

'Yes, I was!' she said with emphasis.

'Well, don't get so mad, you asked me to tell you. She said it wasn't a real marriage because you are Catholics, and it was in a registry office, and the priest said that in the sight of God and all Catholics they are living in sin. That's what she said.'

'Oh, she's wicked . . . wicked, wicked! They *are* married. What else did she say?' Annie demanded, her eyes wide.

'She said . . . Oh, it doesn't matter.'

'It does! It does! What did she say?' There was the urgency of self-torture in her voice; she knew quite well what Cathleen had said, but she must hear it aloud.

'Well, it doesn't matter two hoots to me, you know, but she said you hadn't got a da either. She said Kate – your mother – had never been married.'

Annie had never ridden so hard in her life, and when she reached the gate to the wood the perspiration was running down her face. When Brian had attempted to ride with her she had pushed him so hard that he saved himself from falling only by dismounting, and she had pedalled away like a wild thing.

Inside the gate and out of sight of the road, she flung her cycle on to the grass and ran, stumbling and crying, along the path through the wood . . . Oh, Cathleen Davidson, you wicked, wicked thing! Oh, how could you tell Brian! That's why some of the girls in the convent school had cut her. And everybody would know now. The nuns would know . . . Sister

8

Ann . . . Sister Ann would know. Oh, Cathleen Davidson, I hate you! I don't care if it is a sin, I *do* hate her. And Mam is married, she is! . . . Why does Rodney like Cathleen? He can't like her, she's so wicked. Oh, if only Mam and Rodney had been married in a Catholic church, if only Mam would become a Catholic again! Oh, sweet Lady, make her a Catholic again and be married in the Catholic Church so they'll not be able to say that about her.

All the agony she had so recently experienced returned; the feeling of knowing she was a girl without a father weighed on her once more. For years she had prayed she would have a da like Rodney, and now, by marrying Kate, he was her da; but somehow, it would seem, it didn't alter the fact that she was still a girl without a real father. Nobody round here knew that Kate hadn't been married before. But four miles away, in Jarrow, they knew. Here was another world, a world of lovely houses and beautiful furniture, of grand meals and new clothes and . . . the convent. And now it was spoilt.

She started to run blindly on again, crying as she went: 'Oh, Cathleen Davidson, I wish you were dead. I do, I do. I don't care if it is a sin . . . Eeh! yes I do. Well, she's wicked and she's spoilt everything.'

Ever since Rodney married Kate, Cathleen had been horrible. She said Annie had taken her uncle away from her. But Rodney wasn't Cathleen's uncle, he was merely her father's friend. Perhaps she had done this latest injury because her father had told Rodney not to buy her any more expensive presents; he said she was being spoilt and had come to look upon them as her right. Annie had pricked up her ears when she heard Kate and Rodney discussing this: she had felt glad and sorry at the same time, for Cathleen's brother, Michael Davidson, would have to come under the same ban, and Michael was nice.

For the moment she wished she were back in Jarrow, in the

9

fifteen streets, among the dreariness and poverty she had grown up in and knew so well; it didn't seem to matter so much there who your father was. You lived so close to your next-door neighbours that you could hear the words of their fighting and laughter through the walls, and you could keep no secrets; yet out here, in these extensive grounds where you couldn't even see your nearest neighbour's house, it seemed imperative to bury the stigma of your birth. Up to four months ago she had known this area only as the place where the swanks lived, but now Shields seemed far removed, and Jarrow . . . oh, Jarrow was another world away. Yet at this moment she longed to be back in those familiar surroundings.

She went stumbling on, sniffing, blinded by her tears. Dazedly she felt she must find some place to hide and have her cry out, for she mustn't go into the house like this; Mam would ask too many questions.

Leaving the path, she zigzagged through the trees at the back of the house. If she went deep enough into the wood she would skirt the place Rodney was having cleared so that he might build his clinic for sick children: Mr Macbane might be there, and she was afraid of Mr Macbane. He helped around the grounds in his spare time and lived in the cottage by the woods, cycling past the house every morning on his way to the pit. Rodney liked Mr Macbane; he said he was a character, though he could well understand how sharp a thorn he had been in the previous owner's side. But Annie felt she would never like him.

Her jumbled thinking and mental pain seemed suddenly to be transferred to the physical as she felt her legs wrenched from beneath her, and a voice yelled, 'Look out there!' She was thrown into the air, and she turned a somersault before hitting the ground.

When she opened her eyes the trees were swimming all

about her, and as they steadied she found herself looking up into the angry face of a young man.

'I . . . I fell,' she murmured.

'You should look where you're going,' he said sharply. 'Running like a mad thing!' Then, more gently, he asked, 'Are you hurt?'

'No; I don't think so.' She got up slowly and brushed the dry leaves from her clothes. 'I tripped over something.'

He made no answer, but turned from her and busied himself tightening a rope which was strung from an iron stake in the ground to a tree some distance away. Feeling a little sick and dizzy, Annie stood watching him and wondering whether he noticed she had been crying and that her face was all wet. She supposed he hadn't. She hadn't seen him before, but she knew who he was. He was Mr Macbane's son whom Kate and Rodney had been talking about last night; they didn't know Mr Macbane had a son until he had said, 'Me lad's comin' home. Can you set him on with me, part-time, clearing the wood?' The Macbanes seemed to be forever working: Mr Macbane worked at the pit and between times cleared the wood, and still made time to tend a vegetable garden – there were no flowers in the Macbanes' garden – and Mrs Macbane went out each day to work in the village. And now this mysterious son had been pressed into work too.

She noticed he was very thin and that when he bent down his lank, black hair drooped over his forehead, and that although his face was thin his head was large . . .

Before her startled eyes, she saw it swelling until it blotted out the sky. The next she knew was that his hand was on the back of her head, which was being pressed between her knees.

'Take a deep breath,' he said, pulling her up straight again.

She tried, but found it impossible.

'Here, here,' he exclaimed; 'pull yourself together!'

Oh, he's snappy, just like his father, she thought. Then she fell down, down into the earth, to the sound of his voice pleading, 'Great Scott! Don't pass out; pull yourself together!'

As she came round she realized she was being carried. She blinked slowly at the face close to her own, and when she felt his arms sag she became panicky, thinking: He's too thin, he can't carry me.

He hitched her closer up against him, and she closed her eyes as the blackness threatened to engulf her again.

They were out of the wood now and crossing the little wooden bridge over the stream. She knew this, for faintly she heard the loose plank go *plop, plop!* She wanted to be sick, and wondered if she should ask him to stop so that she could be sick over the side of the bridge.

She didn't remember passing through the orchard, or through the belt of firs, but she knew they had reached the greenhouses below the cypress hedge which bordered the side lawn when she heard Steve's startled exclamation, 'God! What's happened?'

With relief she felt his big arms go round her and his broad chest pillow her head. She liked Steve: he was big and safe, and he let her sit next to him in the car and put her hands on the steering wheel and pretend she was driving it. She was borne swiftly and smoothly to the house.

There was a clamour of voices about her. Summy was saying, 'Is she killed? Oh, the bairn!' Summy was nice; she made lovely cream sponges with icing and nuts on the top . . . There was Rodney's voice, crying, 'What on earth's happened?' Oh, her beloved Rodney's voice! That was a nice word, 'beloved'. She had only learnt it in the past few months . . . beloved, darling, dearest, all lovely words; the house seemed full of them. Rodney was always calling, 'Where are you, darling?' and Kate would answer, 'Here, dearest.' Those were Kate's hands on her now, moving swiftly, tenderly over her. The comfort of being near Mam – she was putting one of Annie's lovely nighties on her. Now Rodney was saying, 'Don't worry, darling, it's just slight concussion.' She wondered vaguely what concussion was, but whatever it was Rodney would cure it, for he was a doctor.

The bed was warm and soft; she seemed to be adrift in it. Vaguely she was conscious of Kate and Rodney looking down on her. They would be standing close together and his good arm would be around her. He had two arms, but one of them wasn't much good since he had been wounded in France in 1917. It was the same with his legs: he had two of them, but one wasn't much good either. In fact, there wasn't any foot on that one. The first time she had seen the leg without the foot she had felt ill. One day she ran into their bedroom, and there was Kate helping to strap on the stiff boot to the leg that seemed to end in a post above the ankle. She had run out without speaking, and it was a long time before she could look at the trouser leg and forget what it hid.

Rodney's voice came to her, saying, 'I think I'll phone Peter. There's nothing wrong, but I'd like him to have a look at her anyway.'

For a moment, the name of Cathleen's father brought back with a painful leap the reason for her running, but she was suddenly too tired even to hate Cathleen. As she sank away, she was wishing vaguely that Rodney had never lived with the Davidsons for a year after he came back from the war, for then Cathleen wouldn't have such a claim on him.

How long had she been asleep? Annie didn't know, but it was night when she awoke. She opened her eyes slowly, to see Kate sitting by the shaded bedside lamp. Her face was half turned away and her eyes were downcast; she was reading. Still feeling too tired to speak, Annie lay watching her. Kate was wearing her rose-coloured dressing-gown which seemed to draw lights from her burnished brown hair. The skin of her cheek looked warm and creamy. Even in worn-out and threadbare clothes Kate had always appeared beautiful to Annie, but now, in the clothes that Rodney showered on her, she had taken on a beauty that Annie would never have believed possible. At times, Annie found herself watching Kate as if she were a new person, for the clothes gave her an air that was unfamiliar. She had need of Kate's arms about her, and to hear her voice and to see the kindness in her eyes, to be convinced that the wonderful clothes had made no difference. Years ago, when Kate worked at the Tolmaches' house, they had bought her a new set of clothes every Christmas. But they weren't like the clothes she wore now. These made her look . . . well . . . oh, she didn't know the word for that look, and anyway she still felt too tired to bother.

To the side of her, the door opened softly, and she closed her eyes: she didn't want to talk, or to be given anything to drink; all she wanted was to go to sleep again.

Rodney said, 'Come on, my love, you're not sitting here any longer. She's perfectly all right; she'll sleep until morning.'

Kate's answer vaguely puzzled Annie. She said, 'I've keyed myself up all day to tell her, and now this had to happen.'

Annie heard the merest whisper of a kiss, and smiled faintly to herself. It was no embarrassment to her to know that Mam and Rodney were kissing; rather, she experienced a feeling of joy for Kate, for she still remembered the long, long years after Kate had to leave the Tolmaches' to go home to look after her mother, who was sick, when her days were filled with work and washing and living in dread of her terrible father. The thought of her grandfather, although safely dead these two years and more, still had the power to make Annie shiver.

She was on the very border of sleep when further whispered words of Rodney's dragged her back, filling her with sharp envy and resentment. She listened, her body becoming stiff.

14

Mam's words no longer puzzled her, but they were like arrows piercing her mind: Mam was going to have a baby. They were wondering if Annie would like it, how she would take the news. Rodney was saying, 'Once she knows, she'll love it. It's better to tell her sooner than later.' Would she love it? How could she love it? For it would have a father: it would have Rodney for a real father. Oh, why hadn't Kate married Rodney years ago, before she was born, then all these years she wouldn't have dreaded with that sickening shame the words 'Annie Hannigan's got no da!'

On the fifth day of being in bed Annie felt quite well enough to be up, but Rodney's orders were that she was to stay there for a week. For the first two days it had been nice to lie still in a strange, untroubled state of mind, while Cathleen seemed no more real than a witch in a fairy story. As for the knowledge of the coming baby, strange even to herself was the fact that from the very morning after she had learnt of its existence, she liked the idea. But gradually the pain caused by Cathleen's treachery returned. Maybe it was not so poignant, but it was still a pain. And it stabbed anew when Kate, who was sitting by the window, said quietly, 'Who were you running away from, dear, when you fell? We found your bicycle just inside the wood gate.'

Annie answered haltingly, 'I wasn't running away from anyone, Mam.'

'But you had been crying such a lot. Your face was so swollen.'

Annie lay watching, through the bed rails, the fire dancing merrily. She still watched it when Kate came and sat on the bed and took her hand. 'Was it Brian Stannard?'

'No. No, not really.'

'Then who was it? Cathleen? Was it Cathleen Davidson? Did she say something to you?'

Annie stared at her. 'How do you know, Mam? Why do you ask?'

Kate smiled quietly down on her. 'Because Cathleen doesn't like either you or me, my dear. I've been waiting for some time for something like this to happen.'

Annie felt her body sink inches into the bed with a feeling of relief. It was like being in the deep end of the pool and knowing there was a good swimmer beside you.

'What did she say? Tell me, dear, and you won't feel it half so much. Was it something about me?'

Mam made things so easy; she seemed to simplify everything. Annie no longer felt alone against Cathleen, but she could tell her mother only part of what Cathleen had said. 'Cathleen . . . she told someone that you . . . well, she said you and Rodney aren't really married, because you weren't married in a Catholic church.'

It was evident to Annie that, like her, Kate had expected to hear something different, because for a moment she simply stared in surprise. Then she asked, 'Was that all?'

It wasn't all. But Annie could never put into words anything touching on the subject that, in her mind, took the form of a triangle, with Kate at one point, a man without a face at a second, and a formless thing labelled 'Shame' at the third.

This triangle had come into being on a Christmas Eve morning years ago when, realising she hadn't a father, she had decided to give herself one and picked on the doctor to fill this position.

She had told her best friend, Rosie Mullen, and Rosie had told Cissy Luck, and Cissy Luck had told her mother, and Mrs Luck had baited Kate in the street . . . That was a terrible Christmas Eve! No, she could never speak of this thing to Kate.

Kate was saying, 'You see, dear, Cathleen is very fond of

16

Rodney, and she blames us for taking him away from her. So you must try and take no notice of the things she says, because it would upset Rodney if he thought there was bad feeling between you. You understand?'

'Yes, Mam.'

'After all, it is we who have Rodney, isn't it?'

'Oh yes, yes!' Annie snuggled down in the bed. Yes, they had Rodney. He was theirs now and for ever; he wasn't just 'the doctor' any more, he belonged to them. Kate was Mrs Prince, no matter what Cathleen said. Oh, if only she was called Annie Prince instead of Annie Hannigan! But she would always be Annie Hannigan, nothing could alter that. Yet when she married her name would be altered, wouldn't it? Yes, of course, when she was married. How soon could she get married, and who would she marry? Oh no, not Brian; she didn't even want to be his girl, even if she had promised . . .

'There then,' said Kate, bending and kissing her; 'let nothing worry you. Just think of the nice long Easter holiday you have. And remember, Cathleen will be leaving the convent for the art school one of these days, and then you won't be troubled with her. And when she and her family come later, treat her as if nothing has happened, will you?'

'Yes, Mam.'

'And we'll say nothing to Rodney about this, will we? I mean, not being married in the Catholic Church; it would only upset him.'

Kate went out of the room, but did not immediately go downstairs. In her own room across the landing, she stood by the window, biting her lip . . . That little cat! To say such a thing! She had thought Annie was about to tell her that Cathleen was taunting her with not having a father; it was just the kind of thing she would do. But to say she and Rodney were not married because the ceremony was not performed

17

in a Catholic church was preposterous. Wasn't all the strife this subject aroused finished with yet?

She could hear again the old arguments, and Peggy Davidson saying, 'But Rodney, you can't ask Kate to be married in a registry office, she's a Catholic.'

She had tried to explain her changed views to both Peggy and Peter.

'But you don't attend any other church, do you?' Peggy said.

'No.'

'Well, then, you are still a Catholic. You know you're still a Catholic at heart, Kate, you know you are!'

No amount of talking had convinced Peggy that Kate was not still a Catholic at heart; that was the very spot where she was not a Catholic. But in her happiness Kate had allowed herself to be persuaded, and a dispensation was asked of the bishop for, Rodney not being a Catholic, this had to be granted before a mixed marriage could be solemnised in church.

It was not until she saw the revolt in Rodney, when he realised that the part required of him by the dispensation was the signing away of the spiritual liberty of any children of the marriage, that Kate knew she could not ask this of him; nor did she want it for herself. So they were married in a registry office.

Father Bailey fought to the last to make her see reason, as he put it. And he told her he was frankly amazed that she could be so unrelenting in her attitude towards the Church, yet quite willing to promise him she would do nothing to prevent Annie from remaining a Catholic. When she agreed with Annie's desire to attend the convent her decision made him scratch his head in bewilderment.

Kate had said, 'It may be the wrong religion for me, but I think it's the right one for Annie; we are not all made alike, father: we are individuals. She is happy in it, I never was; she loves the pageantry and the feeling of one large family, I never did. From an early age I rebelled against it. I cannot distribute my love or affection. I have found it must be all on one thing or person, or nothing. I must go direct to the source, so to speak, for I have found that intermediaries create a sense of frustration in me. And the Church is so full of intermediaries. But Annie seems to draw comfort and peace from them, and I'll never do anything, I promise you, to shatter that feeling. Although I sent her to a Protestant school when she was young, I never interfered with her going to church, and now she's set her heart on going to the convent I'll do nothing against it.'

Looking back on that conversation with Father Bailey, Kate felt the old sense of foreboding returning. Why was one not allowed to work out one's own salvation? Life had been hard enough, God knew, without having to fight the old battles over again. If she had chosen the wrong way, then she alone would suffer for it, for in making her choice she had not influenced Annie.

As she went downstairs she heard three hoots of a car horn from outside, and unconsciously she straightened her back and gave a lift to her chin. Mrs Summers was already at the front door, and the first person Kate saw was Cathleen. She had run up the path ahead of her mother and Michael.

Giving Kate a long stare that could have been insolent, she said, 'Hello. Where's Uncle Rodney?'

Before Kate could reply Cathleen ran past her on her way to the study. And as Kate went down the path to meet Peggy Davidson, she realised it would take a lot of self-control to prevent Cathleen from seeing just how much she annoyed her.

19

2

✍

They were all sitting round Annie's bed, and the Easter gifts
had been exchanged. But no real presents, as Cathleen
thought of them. She was perched now on Rodney's knee,
with one arm round his neck, a favourite position of hers
when subjecting him to teasing. From time to time she would
turn his face to her and say, 'Hello, pet. Know me?' and wait
for his eyes to twinkle and to hear him say, 'You minx!' or
'You little devil!' She used all the tricks she knew, for she was
aware of Annie watching her. She was also aware that on the
chest of drawers there were two large boxes, loosely covered
with tissue paper. These were most likely presents Uncle
Rodney had bought Annie. She wondered why he was so
long in giving her hers . . . He had bought that Kate a beautiful new wireless, while they at home still had stupid old
earphones. Everything at home was shabby. And look at
this place Uncle Rodney had bought! Twelve rooms with
beautiful furniture, and all the ground floor covered in the
same thick red carpet, and the paint all white and egg-shell
blue. And that Kate had a room just for herself, a rest room.
Huh! a rest room for her, when she'd lived all her life in the

fifteen streets! And look at her standing there with another new dress on, a yellow one, all soft and full.

She jerked her head, tossing her short black hair about her face in attractive disorder, and her dark, luminous eyes flashed around the room from one occupant to another.

She made her brother aware of her scorn as he sat looking adoringly at Annie; she put her own mother on tenterhooks, guessing what she would do next. As for Annie, that rabbit, she knew how to manage her. She thought, with satisfying glee, how she had already fixed her in a number of quarters. Her gaze came back to Kate and her feeling guided her in her desire to annoy this woman who now had all Rodney's attention. She turned to Rodney, pulling his head close to hers, and whispered in his ear.

Rodney listened; then with the slightest touch of sharpness said, 'Come! Don't be a silly girl.'

'Cathleen!' Peggy cut in, 'behave yourself.' It was as if she had been waiting ready to chastise her, so sharp was the exclamation following on Rodney's words. She was now ill at ease, and said to Kate, 'Do you think Steve will turn the car for me, Kate? I'm hopeless at turning it in that narrow lane, and we'll have to be getting back.'

Kate was saying, 'Certainly, Peggy. I'll go down and tell him,' when the sound of a kiss made them all turn towards Rodney and Cathleen.

Her arms wound tightly round Rodney's neck, Cathleen was kissing him full on the lips. And when, with an embarrassed laugh, he attempted to loosen her arms, she snuggled closer to him.

It was Peggy who pulled her to her feet, saying angrily, 'Behave yourself, girl!' Cathleen's rejoinder was a deep, impish laugh.

The room became very uncomfortable. Michael was

standing up, looking furiously at Cathleen. 'Why don't you do something with her, Mother?' he exclaimed.

His mother turned her baffled gaze from one to the other. She looked helpless, and said to no one in particular, 'I don't know what things are coming to.'

Kate felt that she must get out of the room at once, and she was glad of the excuse to go and find Steve. The feeling within her was not one of annoyance with a girl of fourteen, it was as if she were combating the personality of a grown woman. She suddenly felt that Cathleen, in some strange way, was threatening the happiness of them all.

Not finding Steve in the garage, she asked Mrs Summers where he was.

'I think he's in his room, ma'am. But if you're going down for him you'd better put your coat on – that wind's enough to cut you in two.' Kate slipped a coat over her shoulders and ran down the garden to the summer-house that had been converted into a bed-sitting-room for the chauffeur.

Her knock on the door was answered immediately. 'Steve,' she began, 'would you mind turning Mrs Davidson's car for her? I'm sorry to trouble you, but even with your expert tuition I don't think I'm capable of it yet.'

'Why certainly; I'll come right now.' He threw the book he had been reading back into the room, closed the door behind him and buttoned his coat as he walked beside her up the garden.

She said again, 'I'm sorry to disturb you, Steve, just when you're having a little time to yourself; we always seem to be needing you at odd hours. If it isn't the generator it's the boiler, and if it's not that it's—' A terrific gust of wind whirled her coat over her head and muffled the rest of her words.

His big hands clumsily coming to her aid, Steve said, 'That's what I'm here for, ma'am; I'm only too glad to be of use . . . I think you'd better put the coat on, this wind will tear it away.' He held the coat while she struggled into it. Then they went on again up the path.

They were almost in front of Rodney's study window when Kate noticed Cathleen standing there. Her eyes, dark and deep, were staring unblinking at them, and they looked full of curiosity; they held some quality that Kate could find no word to define. She's like the embodiment of a witch, she thought, a very old witch in a young body. With a startling certainty, she knew that this girl would have to be fought. She would have to fight both for herself and for Annie, and do it subtly if she wished to succeed.

With a word, she left Steve and walked directly to the french window of the study, opened it and went into the room. She closed the window with slow deliberation, and as she took off her coat she smiled down on Cathleen, who now stood by the side of the window, still staring at her. 'It's frightfully windy,' Kate remarked with a calmness she was far from feeling, for she had a great desire to slap that look from the dark, piquant face.

Cathleen made no rejoinder, merely continued to regard Kate coolly, and Kate's pose of calmness was slipping under this silence and unblinking stare when the door opened and Rodney came in, saying, 'Ah, there you are, darling. Is Steve seeing to the car?'

'Yes, dear; he's doing it now.'

Rodney turned to Cathleen. 'This is where you are, is it, you little imp? Your mother wants you to say goodbye to Annie; they're ready to go.'

Cathleen's demeanour had changed with the opening of the door. 'All right, Uncle Rodney, I'm going now,' she said, in a small-childish voice. She stood for a second smiling engagingly up at him, then ran from the room.

Rodney turned to Kate, taking her hand lovingly into his: 'She's a little monkey. Did you ever see anything like that exhibition up there? That was for Annie's benefit, don't you think? But there's really no harm in her. She's an attractive little thing in her way. You can't help liking her, can you?' Without waiting for a reply he went on, 'But she's not a bit like Peggy or Peter. Have you noticed that? I wonder who she does take after.'

I wonder, said Kate to herself. Aloud she said, 'I must go and see them off.'

'Here.' He pulled her towards him. 'What on earth's the matter, darling? Are you upset? Did she upset you?'

'No, of course not.'

'Sure?' He looked at her anxiously.

'Yes.'

'That's all right then. For the moment you looked . . . Oh, come here.' He buried his face in her hair. 'Darling, you're lovely; you look like the picture of spring in that dress. It's odd, you know,' he whispered: 'I like people to come, but I long for them to go so that I can have you to myself again. You get more beautiful every day.'

'They'll be coming in a minute.'

'Just one more.'

'Darling, the door's open!'

'What odds?' With his one arm he held her tightly to him: 'Do you love me?'

'Mmm . . .'

'How much?'

'I'll tell you later.' Laughing, she disengaged herself gently from his arm and went swiftly into the hall, only to pull up sharply, for there she saw Cathleen making hurriedly for the stairs, and knew that she had been listening and watching them through the crack between the door and the jamb.

As she slowly mounted the stairs behind Cathleen, she was assailed by a feeling of weariness, which blotted out the joy of a moment ago. Why should there be the necessity to fight this child, or anyone else? All her life she'd had to fight, first one thing, then another: poverty, shame, fear, drink, and things which could not be put into words. When she and Rodney had at long last come together she'd thought her fighting days were over, but now this girl seemed to be over-shadowing her life, and Annie's too. Perhaps, though, it was only the psychological effect of carrying a child that was making her magnify Cathleen's actions and turn them from acts of petty jealousy to the deeds of a dark power. Yes, perhaps that was it.

She followed Cathleen into the bedroom and was able to smile on her with greater serenity. This puzzled Cathleen not a little, but did nothing to minimise the rage that was tearing through her: they were going home, and she hadn't received a thing! Not even a small present – you couldn't call a clarty Easter egg a present. And Uncle Rodney kissing that Kate like that! And the chauffeur had put his arms about her. It was all right to pretend it was windy; she did that herself when she wanted the boys to touch her. She'd watch that man when-ever she got the chance. She would watch them both.

3

This was the fourth day Annie had come down to the wood to see the young man and to thank him for carrying her home. She knew he worked here in the grounds for part of the day, and there was always evidence of fresh work having been done, but she had not seen him. But today there he was, hacking away at the undergrowth.

On sighting him she started to run, but pulled herself up; she didn't want to fall again – he'd think she was doing it on purpose. She called, 'Hello!' and he straightened up and watched her coming towards him.

'I've been looking for you for the last three days,' she said. 'I wanted to thank you for bringing . . .' she didn't like to use the word 'carrying', 'bringing me home,' she ended.

'Are you better?' His voice sounded cold.

'Oh yes, thank you.'

'That's all right then.'

He turned once more to his hacking, and she stood with her hands behind her, watching him. She moved the toe of her shoe and made little ridges in the dark leaf-mould. Then she asked tentatively, 'What's your name?'

After a moment he replied, 'Terence.'

'Oh. Terence . . . it's a nice name. Mine's Annie,' she said. 'Wasn't it lucky, when I fell, we were only two days from breaking up. I should have hated being off school. I go to a convent school.' And she wondered why she was telling him this; he would think she was silly. And wasn't he stern? He looked as though he never smiled. She tried to imagine how he would look if he were to smile. He must be old, very old, eighteen or twenty.

She realised, as she watched him, that she felt sorry for him; he had to work when he was evidently on holiday. And he was so thin. Perhaps he didn't get enough to eat. That must be it; he didn't get enough to eat, poor thing, because his mother had to go out to work. She would be tactful, like Kate; she could say she was going to have her tea in the wood, and he could have some with her. As a lead-up to this, she said, 'Are you on holiday?'

He gave a little sigh and replied flatly, 'Yes.'

'Where do you work?'

He made no answer.

'Haven't you a job?'

'Yes.'

'Where, then?'

He hesitated, hunched his shoulders, then said, 'I'm going to Oxford to work.'

'Oh.' It wasn't Newcastle, or Whitley Bay, or any place she knew. She remarked quite brightly, 'I'm hungry. I'm going back to get my tea and bring it down here . . . Can I bring you some?'

'No thank you.'

'But aren't you hungry?'

'No.'

'Wouldn't you like . . . just a cup of tea and a cake?'

'No!' The word was heavy with finality.

'But your mother goes out to work and you haven't anyone to make your meals.'

27

She put her fingers to her lips as he turned and stared at her. His eyes were grey and cold and very like Mr Macbane's.

She stumbled on, 'You're sweating, and it would do you good.'

'Thank you; I don't want any tea.'

'But it wouldn't be any trouble—'

'I don't want any! I've told you I don't want any tea . . . Now run away!'

'There's no need to shout at me.' Her lips trembled, and her eyes started to burn. She stood still, tensed for flight.

'Well, you won't take a telling.'

'I was only thinking it . . . it might do you good.'

'I don't want doing good . . . Oh Lord,' he broke off, 'don't start howling! What on earth's up with you now?'

She hung her head and the tears streamed down her face. She made no sound, but stood shaking before him. He stared at her, his expression one of mingled surprise and horror. 'Don't! What have you got to cry for? Oh Lord!' he repeated, throwing down the billhook with an exasperated movement.

She couldn't tell him it was because she was sorry for him; he was so thin, and he wouldn't let her be kind to him. She wanted to fly away, but she seemed condemned to stand before him for ever.

'Don't! Will you stop it! Here, stop it!' he demanded, taking a step towards her. 'What have you got to cry for anyway? A big girl like you, crying!'

She looked up at him, her face awash with tears which glistened like rain: 'You're so . . . so snappy,' she sobbed.

He stared blankly at her.

'Just because I . . . I asked you to have some tea.' She groped for her handkerchief, but couldn't find it. 'I've lost my hankie now,' she finished pathetically, gathering her tears on the tip of her tongue.

His face slowly softened, and his voice and eyes held the slightest hint of laughter as he said, 'Here, use this.' He brought an extraordinarily white handkerchief from his back pocket and handed it to her. As she wiped her eyes, he said quietly, 'I'll have some tea.'

She gazed up at him, smiling through her tears. 'Oh, will you? All right then, I'll bring it down.'

'But only after you've had yours in the house,' he added; 'it's too cold for you to sit about down here.'

'Yes. All right then.' She thrust the handkerchief at him and dashed away, running and leaping through the trees. Oh, she was glad he had told her to have her tea indoors, for, now she came to think of it, Mam might not let her have it outside, because it was still very cold. And now she need only ask for some tea for him.

Twenty minutes later she was walking carefully back through the wood carrying a basket with a covered jug tucked in the middle. It had not been as easy getting the tea as she had imagined, for Summy had said, 'It's no use taking him tea; Steve went and asked him to have a cup the other day, and he wouldn't.' And Kate had added to this, 'Rodney told him to come up and have his dinner here, but he refused.'

Annie had not explained the scene that preceded the acceptance of her offer, but simply repeated, 'Well, I asked him, and he said yes, he'd have some.'

She put the basket on a log on the cleared ground and called into the thicket, 'I've brought it.'

She arranged the tea things first one way, then another. And when he stood beside her, she said, 'There!' with the air of a conjuror, then added, 'There's a hard-boiled egg and bread and butter, and a piece of pie, and a bit of cream sponge with nuts on. You'll like the cream sponge . . . I love it.'

He stood looking at the array in silence, then half turned as if to say something to her. But instead he stood staring down into her smiling face. Then, sitting down abruptly by the log, he began to eat.

When she took a seat on a nearby log and sat watching him in silence, he moved his hand quickly over his face as if to smooth away some expression. Annie thought he was about to laugh, but no, his face remained blank.

He was finishing the piece of pie when his father walked into the clearing. He stood up awkwardly, dusting his hands. Mr Macbane's grizzled eyebrows twitched as he looked in surprise at the remains of the meal. 'Yer not paid t'do that,' he said.

'They sent it down,' his son answered quietly.

'Yer should have told 'em.'

'I did.'

'Well, come on now an' make up for lost time.'

'What about the cream sponge!' cried Annie. 'It's lovely, and—'

'You eat the bit cake yerself,' said Mr Macbane, not unkindly; 'the lad's got work to do.'

'But I get plenty, Mr Macbane.'

'Well, d'you think he's starvin'?' Mr Macbane's eyebrows seemed to link at the top of his nose. 'His mother's a fine cook!'

'I . . . I didn't mean . . .' began Annie.

'Hold on,' said the young man aside to his father. Then he bundled the crockery into the basket, which he handed to Annie, saying, 'I enjoyed it very much . . . Thanks . . . and thank your mother.'

As she walked away she heard the young man say, 'You would have had her howling in a minute, she cries easily. I had to take the tea to stop her from howling.'

Oh, she thought indignantly, I *don't* cry easily! Oh, that isn't fair. I was crying the other day because of what Cathleen said, and *you* made me cry because you snapped, and I was sorry for you because you're so thin . . . I'll tell you about it tomorrow. Yes, I will.

The following morning there was evidence that the young man had already finished his work before Annie could manage to get down to the wood: a fresh bonfire was smouldering in the clearing. She was disappointed, for she wanted to make it quite clear to him that she didn't cry easily.

But her disappointment was quickly forgotten when Kate said, 'Would you like to go to the Mullens' for me, dear?' This meant a trip to the fifteen streets, and the pleasure of carrying nice things for the Mullens to eat, and she would see Rosie if she was home from her job.

She was in the kitchen helping Kate to pack the basket when Rodney came in from the garden. He was evidently excited. 'I say, darling. What do you think I've just learnt?' he said.

'What?' Kate smiled warmly at him across the table.

'I can't believe it,' he went on, 'but Steve has just told me that Macbane's son is going up to Oxford.'

Kate stopped her packing. 'Oxford? You don't mean to a college?'

'Yes, St Joseph's.'

'Well, how marvellous! How wonderful!'

'But fancy the old man not saying a word about it; Steve heard them talking in the village pub last night. Apparently the young fellow has won an open scholarship. It seems he was good at most things, but quite brilliant at maths. He's going up in October.'

'Oxford!' repeated Kate. She suddenly thought of Bernard Tolmache; he had been a lecturer at Oxford. Dear, dear Mr Bernard, who had shown her a new way of life. He had come into her kitchen and said, 'Stop polishing silver, Kate, and come and polish your mind; it will glow brighter than silver.'

And he certainly had polished her mind with the books he lent her and his conversation. She had never been to Oxford, but from him she had glimpsed a little of its magic. And now that boy down in the cottage was going there. 'That's why they all work so hard then,' she said to Rodney.

'Oh, my dear, what they work for will scarcely keep him in clothes and fares. He must be getting a grant of some sort besides his scholarship. But fancy that dour old devil not saying a word about it!'

'Oxford,' said Kate again. 'It seems like a fairy tale. Oh, I am so glad for him. But what a terrific struggle they must have had to get him this far.'

'You know,' said Rodney, 'I admire that old boy.'

'And the young one,' put in Kate.

'Yes, and certainly the young one.'

'And not forgetting the mother; she must have slaved for years with this in view. What an honour for them! But why haven't we seen him before, if he's still at school?'

'Apparently to be near the school he stays with an aunt in Newcastle,' said Rodney.

Annie stood looking from one to the other. Yes, she thought, he said he was going to work in Oxford. Oxford to her was linked with another name, Cambridge. They didn't appear as towns in her mind, but as remote islands, where people who were different went and learnt to talk swanky . . . Would he talk swanky? He didn't talk swanky now. Yet he didn't talk like his father either, did he? But he was so thin, and his clothes looked old. Perhaps he kept old ones just to work in . . . And they said he was clever at maths. Oh, and she had told him he was snappy!

She remained behind in the kitchen while Kate and Rodney went out, still talking . . . Was he a gentleman now, because he was going to Oxford? Could he be a gentleman when his father worked down the pit? And did gentlemen clear woods?

Well, Rodney worked in the greenhouses, and he was a gentleman. She was disappointed Terence was going to this Oxford; it stopped her feeling sorry for him, somehow. And she couldn't ask him to have any more tea now.

When Mrs Summers bustled in, Annie said, 'You know Mr Macbane's son, Summy? Well, he's going to Oxford.'

'Oxford? You must be mistaken, hinny . . . That lad!'

'He is. Steve told Rod . . . The doctor.'

'Well! he doesn't look as if he's got that much gumption.'

'He's very clever, and has passed a lot of exams.'

'Well, well! And his mother doing daily for Mrs Tawnley in the village. Ah!' Mrs Summers stopped in the process of loading a tray. 'Now I suppose that's why he refused to come up and have a cup of tea when Steve asked him. Feeling too big for his boots. You know the saying, hinny, "Put the Devil on horseback and he'll ride to . . ." Well, he'll ride somewhere,' she finished, 'and likely break his neck in getting there. His sort of get-ups generally do.'

Annie got out of the tram at Westoe Fountain and took another for Tyne Dock. The ride was a transition between two worlds. What green there was appeared darker; even the spring flowers and trees in the park all seemed to have a film over them: they weren't so new-looking as those about her new home. Nearing Tyne Dock, the houses became flatter and branched off in narrow streets from the main road. The tram ran down the bank, and as it passed the Catholic church Annie bowed her head reverently. It would have been nice to 'pay a visit', but the basket was too heavy to carry far. On past the station, then into Tyne Dock proper the tram rocked, past Bede Street, with Bob's, the pawnshop, seeming to reflect its black depths into the street. The glint of the brass balls caught her eye, and she remembered having to go there one time when Kate had a dreadful cold and her grandmother was lying upstairs dying. She was too young to pawn things, so paid a woman threepence to do it for her. Bob was kind, but it did not lessen the feeling of shame, and she crept out of the place by the back way, and so into the street, where the dock men were lined up on the other side of the road against the railings. They always watched everybody coming and going, and as she walked past them towards the dock gates she remembered thinking that this was why Kate walked into Shields to the pawn, rather than pass under the stares of these men. But now there would never be any more Bob's for Kate, or her . . . never, never.

Down the dock bank, past the line of public houses, and then the tram stopped opposite the high stone wall, with the iron bolts that went *clank! clank!* when the dock horses, which were stabled on the other side, moved.

As she got down, she saw the Jarrow tram disappearing through the first arch. She walked over to the corner opposite the dock gates and set the basket down near the railings. Then she stood watching the assortment of nationalities going in and out of the gates. She felt a strange stir of excitement within her. It was a long time since she had stood at the dock gates; she generally went swiftly past them in Rodney's car now . . . That was nice, but this was nice too: a sort of coming back to something that belonged to her.

A little boy was standing near her, his hands behind him gripping the iron railings which surrounded the dock offices. He let himself fall forward, then pulled himself back in a swinging movement. He smiled at her, and Annie smiled back, and she wondered where she had seen him before. His hair, in loose ringlets round his head, was jet black and shining like ebony, and his skin was pale and clear. He had large blue eyes that looked sad. 'Are you waiting for the tram?' she asked him.

'No, for me ma; she's across there.' He motioned with his

head to the line of public houses. 'I've got a penny,' he said, opening his palm and showing the penny pressed into the flesh by the iron railings.

'Oh, you're rich,' she said. 'Here's another. Now what will you buy?'

'Pork dip, or pie and peas,' he answered.

A man who was standing near, with a whippet on a lead, said, 'Aye, that's reet, look after yer belly, son. The Earl here likes his belly, and his drink.' He bent and patted the dog. 'Watch,' he said, and pulling a bottle from his pocket he poured some spirit down the dog's throat. The dog shivered and its bones could clearly be seen rippling under its skin.

The little boy laughed, but Annie didn't; she didn't like those dogs. She remembered going with Rosie one Saturday afternoon to the rabbit coursing at East Jarrow. The poor little rabbits had been kept in boxes and let out for the dogs to chase. When the gun went off she tumbled down the bank and fell into a ditch full of water. She was sick, and did not go again.

The little boy left the railings, crying, 'Here's me ma!' and ran straight into the road towards two women and a man who were coming across. One of the women, who looked enormous, even at a distance, clipped his head and shouted at him, and he turned and ran back to the pavement again.

Annie stared at the approaching woman, and felt her eyes widening in surprise. It was her cousin Connie – well, Kate's cousin Connie from Jarrow, who always smelt of scent, nasty scent. She hadn't seen her for years. Connie often used to visit their house when they lived in the fifteen streets, but after she married Pat Fawcett she came no more . . . Why hadn't she? Annie never found out, but she knew it was something to do with Pat, because Kate had been going to marry Pat. Pat was killed in France during the war, and now Connie was a widow, and oh, wasn't she fat! Could she be the boy's mother? Annie stared at the child again. Now she knew why she thought she had seen him before. He looked exactly like Pat, except that his face wasn't red.

The man and the women stood on the kerb, and it was evident they were drunk. The man kept leaning towards Connie, emphasising each word he was saying with a pat of his hand on her enormous breasts. Connie would throw back her head and laugh, and Annie was fascinated by the size of the cavity, all grey and wet, behind the blackened teeth. Annie stood behind the man with the whippet, for she didn't want Connie to see her; she was ashamed of her being drunk. If she hadn't been drunk, she would have spoken to her, for she liked the little boy. She could see him now, pulling at his mother's skirt. And she heard Connie say, 'Blast yer! What is it, eh? Who give yer a penny?'

The boy pointed, and the man with the whippet moved aside to speak to two iron ore men who had just come out of the docks, and Annie found herself looking into Connie's bloodshot eyes. A terror filled her. She felt a fluttering in her stomach; it was light and seemed full of wings. Her legs, too, became weak under her, and she could not have turned and run away even if she had not had the basket to carry.

'Huh! By God, if it isn't the Countess's daughter! Well!' Connie's eyes narrowed into slits that showed red glints as she looked Annie up and down. 'Jesus! That's what comes of marrying yer fancy man. Nellie! look' – she nudged the other woman – 'that's Kate Hannigan's bastard, y'know, the one I told yer about. That's her. She's got her up, ain't she? They're livin' among the toffs now. It's money yer want, Nellie . . . Yer can get off with any damn thing if yer pick one with money. Why ain't you got money, Jake?' She gave the man a punch in the ribs that sent him reeling. The three of them laughed. But Connie's laugh held no mirth, and she turned once again towards Annie.

Groups of men were standing by the dock gates, and people were gathering in twos and threes for the Jarrow tram; they seemed to Annie to have stopped talking and were listening to Connie Fawcett saying terrible things. Annie was burning with shame, it made her hot and sick. Why had she to be ashamed of so many things? There was always something of which to be ashamed: of her grandfather who had been wicked and bad, of not having a da, of the pawnshop, of Kate not being a Catholic, and now of Connie Fawcett.

'Look, Pat,' Connie was saying to the boy, 'that's yer cousin. Take a good dekko at her . . . Ain't she nice? I could dress you up to the eyes too if I had a mind. All yer want is a bit of education. That makes the tart business pay.'

'I never knew it mattered, Connie,' the man spluttered, his hand falling once again to her breast. 'That's a new un on me. By God! Ain't that funny, Nellie? Education for a tart! You can keep yer education, Connie; you just give me—'

'Here! I think that's enough o' that,' a woman standing near shouted towards them. 'You should be damn well ashamed of yersels . . . with bairns about.'

Annie felt faint. She kept her eyes on the pavement and clutched the railings behind her. Oh dear, dear Jesus, make her stop. Oh Holy Mary, make her go away. Please. Please.

'You mind yer own bloody business; this is a family matter,' Connie shouted back at the woman.

'I'll call the polis from over there,' said the woman, nodding angrily towards the dock policemen's cabin.

Annie's head dropped still further: Oh St Anthony, guide me. Oh St Anthony, guide me away from her. Dear, dear Lord, help me.

From under her downcast lids Annie saw two feet coming rapidly towards her. They stopped in front of her. A hand lifted the basket and another took hold of one of hers. Oh

37

thank you, St Anthony, she thought, before she looked up. Then she almost cried out aloud: Oh, why had you to send *him*? Oh, not him! Oh, the shame of it! He must have heard all Connie said. Oh St Anthony, why couldn't you have sent someone else? I'll never be able to look at him again.

She let him lead her through the scattered groups of people. They crossed the road and walked through the arches. Her head still drooped and she could think of nothing clearly, only that this was another shame to add to the many others, and that it was rather mean of St Anthony to send Terence Macbane, because now she was going to cry and she just couldn't help it.

He said gently, 'I shouldn't worry.'

She didn't answer, and they walked on in silence, he still holding her hand.

They had passed through the five arches before he spoke again: 'I have an aunt like her . . . In fact, she's worse than her.' Annie turned bright, burning eyes towards him. He went on: 'She's terrible. Everybody in . . . in Glasgow knows her. We're dreadfully ashamed of her, so I know how you feel. That woman . . . well, she isn't a patch on my aunt.' He smiled inwardly at the image of his creation, and added consolingly, 'There's nothing to be ashamed of . . . not a thing; everybody has relations like her.'

The dry brightness of Annie's eyes softened into a mist; the tight pain in her chest lifted into her throat and seemed to burst from there with a loud report. She turned, her hands covering her face, and leant against his chest. He stood taut for a moment, staring straight over her head. She had knocked off her hat, and it lay on the greasy pavement. He put the basket down, and slowly his arms went about her. They were standing in the deserted road leading to the sawmill; it stretched empty for half a mile ahead. He bent his face above the shining silver mass of her hair, and for a moment his lips hovered over it. Then he dropped his arms from her and stood stiff again.

His thoughts raced, tumbling and fighting each other . . . This was how things started between fellows and girls. Well, it wasn't going to happen to him, now or ever. She was only a child, but why had she to look like that? When she looked at you she made you feel . . . Oh Lord, he'd have to get away! He told himself vehemently: I've my work to think about. Nothing's going to touch that! Yet I've never felt like this before. It all started that blasted night a month ago that I saw her at the window . . . But how can it be? She's only a child. It doesn't matter, it won't start.

Sniffing and smiling apologetically, Annie picked up her hat, thinking: Oh, he's nice! And I don't care what Summy says, he's not one of those people who would ride to . . . you know where, if you put him on a horse.

4

Mr Macbane got up from the table and walked to the fire-side. He took a spill from the Toby-jug on the mantelpiece and a clay pipe from a pocket of his sleeveless cardigan, and sat down in the wooden armchair by the side of the fire. He sighed as he lit his pipe, and his wife and son exchanged smiling glances across the table.

'That was a good dinner, missis. I always do say the left-overs make a better meal than the beginnin's; there's always something about Boxing Day meals that's satisfyin' . . . What do yer say, lad?'

'All Mother's meals are satisfying.' Terence rose from the table and took the armchair on the other side of the hearth. He put his slippered feet on the fender and lit a cigarette.

'Aye,' went on his father, 'I don't suppose ye got any better up there.'

As so often in the last four years, Terence assured him he hadn't.

'I didn't tell yer that that Jimmy Toonsend an' Bill Swain were quizzing me about yer, did I?'

'No,' said Terence.

'"That lad o' yours is nearly finished at that Oxford,"

Jimmy Toonsend said. "What's he going to be? Prime Minister?"

'"No, man. Summat that needs brains," I said. But yer should have seen 'em with their lugs cocked when the under-manager came up to me. "I hear yer son's passed," he said. "Aye," I said; "he's got a first." Yer should have seen those two numskulls; they didn't know what a first meant. "And aye," I went on, "he does pure an' applied maths."'

Terence threw back his head and laughed. It was very funny, his father talking of pure and applied maths and firsts . . . No, it wasn't funny; it was pathetic. It was pathetic that men like his father could only bask in the reflection of the education of their offspring. They had to grub all their days, while some voice cried out from deep within them for a different way of life, for knowledge of the things that only the young could grasp. Let youth pass, and no matter what opportunities presented themselves, the capacity to build the broad base required to support the structure of learning was gone. He said gently to his father, 'What else did you say?'

'Well, I said, "He's going to take a teaching course now." "Really!" said the under-manager. "He must have a heed on his shoulders." "Aye," I said, "he has that. And he's got ideas, has my lad. He's going to teach lads like he was himself. He's going to show 'em that there's brains in the workin' class. Aye, more brains than among the moneyed lot. He's going to push lads on." "Good luck to him," said the under-manager to me. "He's a credit to yer." By, Terry lad! Yer should have seen Toonsend and Swain! That shut their gobs up.'

Mrs Macbane brought a chair from the table and sat down between them.

'Here, sit in the armchair.' Terence made to get up, but she pushed him back.

'Sit where y'are, lad, I'm all right here.'

41

'Yes, take it easy now you're home,' said his father.

Take it easy! Terence looked at his mother, and saw the grey hair, the wrinkled skin, the knotted hands, and he thought: She's never been able to take it easy; he's never spared her, or himself. From morning till night for as far back as I can remember she's been at it. He used to drive me too, but now when I do nothing all day he tells me to take it easy. It's a case of 'To him that hath shall be given.'

His mother said to him, 'Won't yer come down to Mrs Plum's with us, lad? They'll be so glad to see yer. Come on, just for a cup of tea.'

He shook his head. 'You go along; you know the Plum females terrify me.'

His father laughed boisterously, and his mother leant towards him and whispered, 'Won't yer go down to the house then? They've asked yer. Miss Annie's havin' her little bit party today.'

'Will yer stop calling the lass Miss Annie, as if she wor class!' Mr Macbane glared at his wife. 'You know,' he said to his son, 'she gets me goat. She always treats 'em as if they were blue blood, just 'cos they're rotten wi' money.'

''Tisn't that at all,' said his wife. 'You can go on how you like. I like 'em; they've always been nice to me.'

'Patronisin'!'

'No, they aren't, they're just kind.'

'So can anybody be, wi' money.'

'But everybody isn't. I should know, I've worked for some . . . Look at the money the doctor's spent on that clinic. And that place for the nurses. And he could have asked us to get out of here to make room for 'em. Don't you forget that.'

'I'd like to have seen him.'

'You couldn't have done anything.'

'Couldn't I? I would have told him a thing or two . . . And I'd have told him into the bargain he was a fool, at that, bringin' that lass up as if she was a duchess. Swimmin'-pool! Tennis court!'

'It hasn't done her any harm; she's grown into such a nice lass. It must be a year since you saw her.'

'About that,' Terence said.

'Yes, she was on holiday in the summer when you got back from that walkin' tour.' She nodded to herself, then turned to him again: 'Won't yer go down there, lad? I hate leaving you here alone.'

'Don't worry about me, there's piles of things I can do.'

'Aye. And where did he get his money?' Mr Macbane began again. 'Out of the poor steelworkers' sweat, durin' the war. They say he owns half the bloomin' steelworks now.'

'Well,' said Terence, 'that's not doing him much good now, the way things are.'

'He puts his money to good use; that's somethin',' Mrs Macbane chirped.

'Do you call pamperin' half-daft kids a good use? Why don't he spend it on ones that'll be some good? Hours every day he and them nurses spend, just tryin' to get a bit lad around seven to play ball. And there the bairn stands, for all the world as if he was in a trance.'

'So you watch them every day?' said Terence, with a sly smile.

'Me? No. I just happen to be passin'.'

His wife burst out laughing. 'Watch them? Why, he's always watchin' them . . . They got three of the bairns to walk last year, didn't they?' She leant towards her husband. 'And cured nearly ten from stammerin', didn't they?'

'I'll give yer a skelp round yer lug in a minute,' he growled.

She got up, still laughing. 'Aye, he doesn't know anything that goes on down there. Yer da minds his own business, he does that. Well, I'll get washed up,' she added.

Terence rose, saying, 'I'll give you a hand.'

43

'No, lad,' his mother said. 'Sit down.'

'Aye, sit down,' added his father. 'What next! Washing the dishes!'

Terence took no heed of them, but began to gather the things from the table.

'Listen!' cried Mr Macbane suddenly. 'D'yer hear that?' They all remained quiet, listening. Faint squeals and laughter came to them from outside. 'They're at it again! Snowball fights! They want their heads lukkin' at; the whole job-lot of them's barmy, from him downwards!'

In the tiny scullery, mother and son laughed quietly together. 'It's funny,' she said, 'yer can't get a word out of him for weeks on end, but come Christmas or any time he has a glass, then it all comes out. But,' she added, 'it's only his way. And he really thinks a lot of the doctor, for all his talk.' She glanced up from the sink to her son: 'You mustn't mind how he talks about yer, lad, he's rare and proud of yer.'

'I don't mind,' Terence said.

'Yer seem sad, lad. What is it?'

'Nothing.'

'Oh, there's something . . . I know.'

'Well,' he said, after a while, 'it's the different lives people have to live. When he talks it sort of hurts; I get all churned up inside. And I want to smash all the things up at Oxford, the things I have grown to love. And hit out at the people that take them all for granted . . . It's so different, Mother; you don't know, you can't imagine.'

'I often try, lad . . . But don't feel bad about it. Why, yer being up there has brought something into our lives . . . colour and excitement . . . And him. Why, he just lives in a sort of glory about yer. Come on, cheer up. Come on an' tell me what's happened lately. Do yer still have talks with that lord chap, and the Chinaman with the limp? And have yer had any more invitations from those women? Come on, tell me. We haven't had the chance of a crack since ye came home, me out nearly every day and ye away trampin' the roads.'

So he told her, as he dried the dishes, of Lord John Dane Dee, who had money to burn, and burnt it; of the Chinese called Larry; of the feats of Dane Dee as a cross-country runner; and of Larry's love of books and the quiet simplicity of the very learned. When he spoke of the ladies who sent pressing invitations to members of the university cricket team, he laughed.

'Do any of the lads go?' asked his mother.

'Oh yes; they give them rattling times.'

'It's bare-faced, trying to get the lads for their lasses.'

'Oh, you needn't worry about those fellows, they know their way about.'

'Did you ever want to go to them swell parties?'

'Sometimes, just to see what they were like. Mere curiosity.' He didn't say that he had been afraid to go; afraid of the difference in himself showing. Men, on the whole, accepted you; but women, they knew by just looking at you. They had no need to check up. They knew whether it had been a prep or an elementary school; they knew whether there was the supporting wall of an allowance at the back of you, or an uninterested world in which to job-hunt in the future. And what they didn't know, you, with your self-consciousness, thought they did. You imagined they had but to look at you to see the three-roomed cottage; and your father, washing himself in the tin bath before the fire and taking his clothes out of the oven where they had been put to air; they saw your mother, an old woman at forty-five, who sat down only when she had something to mend, who got up in the flesh-chilling blackness of a winter morning and did a load of washing before going out to work; and often it was your washing, to be sent back to Oxford in a parcel, c/o a newsagent's shop.

45

You jibbed at this necessity, but college scouts had sharp eyes for seeing through parcels.

His scout was called Benny and addressed him as 'sir'. It had taken some time to get used to the 'sir'. He thought of the things of which he had deprived himself in order to tip Benny and the porter at the end of term. And, on the day he took his degree, when according to custom Benny helped him on with his hood, the thought of the pound note he gave Benny helped him to keep his head up and eyes level as he walked to the platform. There had been no relations with glowing eyes to see him – his father was down the pit and his mother was out charing – but their images were clearer in his mind at that moment than at any other time in his life.

His mother said, 'We're right glad you're staying up there another year for the teaching course.'

His mouth drew into a thin line. 'I've stayed up there too long already . . . I shouldn't have taken it on. I could have got a job without it. Oh, I wish I was finished!'

'But why, lad?' she asked in surprise. 'What are you all fratched about? What is it? I thought you liked being up there.'

'I should be working!' he said. 'God! it's about time. Nearly five years and not a penny earned.'

'Oh lad, don't be silly.'

'Will you give up this job of yours if I get a post near home?' he asked her earnestly.

'Why, lad, there's plenty of time to talk about that,' she parried. 'Anyway, you'll want a bit of money for yourself. You've had to scrape and scratch for years . . .'

'I have?' he exclaimed.

'Well, it's different for us, lad; we don't want much.'

'And you don't get much! You're stopping work as soon as I get home.' He banged the plates into the rack.

'Ah! we'll see. Anyway, lad,' she laughed, 'ye'll be getting yerself married.'

He sprang round. 'What!'

'Why, lad, don't knock me over. Married, I said . . . People do, yer know.'

'What do you take me for?' he asked. 'That's the last thought in my head.'

'Well, it shouldn't be. 'Tisn't natural. Ye're twenty-two, and you've never had a bit of a lass . . . Not that I want you to get married straight away. But oh, lad,' she smiled at him softly, 'I want to see you happy and enjoying yourself; ye've done nothing but work. I wonder sometimes it hasn't driven yer daft – it's not natural not to have a bit of fun.'

He stared at her. Her utter selflessness hurt him; he felt mean and small before the greatness of it. He pulled her towards him and enfolded her gently in his arms.

'Eeh! lad. Look, I've the dishcloth in me hand, I'll wet you all.' She gave a shaky, embarrassed laugh, then laid her cheek against his. 'Oh, my Terence . . . Oh, my lad,' she whispered.

The light was fading as Mrs Macbane trudged down the lane some twenty yards behind her husband. She had stopped for a last word with Terence, and Mr Macbane had walked on through the snow, leaving her to make her way as best she could. Shouts and laughter were still coming from around the house, and as she neared the gate a small boy dashed out, yelling, 'No! No! Not yet. No, Annie!'

'Ah, Master David, what are you up to now?' asked Mrs Macbane.

'I've got to go in and have my bath, and I'm not going! Oh, Mrs Macbane!' he squealed, and dodged behind her long skirt as Annie came running through the gate.

'Why, hello, Mrs Macbane!' cried Annie. 'Have you had a nice Christmas?'

'Yes, Miss Annie. Fine thanks. And you?'

'Oh, lovely!'

47

Mrs Macbane put her hand behind her and tenderly patted David's head as he pressed against her legs, and Annie asked, haltingly, 'Is . . . is Terence coming to my party?'

'Well, lass . . . Miss Annie, he's not one for parties, you know.'

'Oh!' The bright, laughing face dimmed for a moment. 'He never comes down, he's never come once,' she said frankly. 'Why doesn't he?'

'He's shy.'

'Is he?'

Mrs Macbane looked at Annie steadily. Then, taking a deep breath as if before a plunge, she said, 'Why not go up, lass, and ask him? He only wants a bit of coaxing . . . You go up and ask him.' She hurried away with a backward glance and a smile, saying, 'Good-night, Master David,' and adding, 'He'd come if you could bring yourself to go and ask him.'

Annie called after her, 'Would he?'

Mrs Macbane didn't turn round, but nodded and quickened her pace almost to a run, frightened now at her own daring. And Annie, making an unexpected swoop on her small half-brother, gathered him, kicking and struggling, into her arms and ran up the path, thinking: I will go, I will! I'll go and ask him. Why not?

The house seemed packed with happy, laughing people. Kate and Peggy Davidson were in the bathroom with an over-excited David; Rodney and Peter had retired to the study for a breather before tea; and in the drawing-room, playing a complicated game of cards that took up most of the available floor space, were Michael and Cathleen Davidson, Rosie Mullen, Brian Stannard and his two girl-cousins, and a cherub-faced youth who was receiving everyone's censure in silence, returning only angelic smiles to accusations of being a card-sharp, a sneaking thief and a dirty, cheating hound.

'Get Annie!' cried Michael Davidson. 'She'll play him off

the face of the earth. Tim Bailey, you're a twister! You must be. No-one is that lucky.'

'Annie! Annie!' they all yelled.

'I won't be a minute,' she called from the hall. She dashed into the kitchen. 'Oh Summy, the table's marvellous. Thanks a lot. And you too, Alice.'

Alice smiled, and Mrs Summers said, 'Well, you're not eighteen every day, hinny.'

'Eighteen and two days, Summy . . . Oh, there's the phone!' She ran back into the hall. 'Yes. Yes, this is Annie. Oh, I'm very sorry, Mrs Beaney. What a shame! Tell him I hope he'll soon be better. Yes, we've had a lovely Christmas. Goodbye. Goodbye.'

She went into the drawing-room, saying, 'Poor John Beaney's got a cold and can't come; his mother has just phoned up.'

They all stopped playing and looked up at her.

'Oh, that cissy *would* take to his bed with the sniffles,' said Brian.

'That makes us one man short,' Cathleen exclaimed.

'Two, if the Oxford don doesn't turn up,' put in Brian.

'I say, Annie,' said Cathleen, 'why not ask Steve?'

Annie looked down on Cathleen in surprise. 'Steve? Oh, I don't think he would come – not to a party, anyway.'

'Why not? He's all right! Let's ask him . . .' She got on to her knees, her black eyes sparkling with excitement. 'Let me go and ask him.'

'Well . . .' Annie hesitated. 'All right. I should like him to come, but you'd better ask Mam first.'

'Where is she? Upstairs?'

'Yes, bathing David.' Annie watched Cathleen dart out of the room. What had come over Cathleen lately? She was quite changed. She had stopped picking quarrels on every occasion, and these last few months she had been . . . well, 'charming' was the word. They were all saying how nice she was now, and Aunt Peggy and Uncle Peter looked happier than they had done since Cathleen left the convent and went to the art school. And even Annie didn't mind her staying for weekends now. It was thoughtful of her to think of Steve. But would he come? He had been a bit odd lately. Well, if she got him to come it would make the numbers right. Of course, that was if Terence came too. Should she go down and ask him, and make sure?

With an excuse to the rest of the company, she went into the hall again and stood for a moment undecided, staring at the Chinese lanterns hanging from the ceiling. Should she? She didn't really know what to do. Then one thing became certain in her mind. If she didn't go for him, he wouldn't come. With the thought, the party took on a dullness; she had somehow been banking on him coming in order to break down the barrier that was purely of his making. Why was he so silly? He must come. His mother wanted him to come. Then should she go? Oh, I'll ask Mam too; she always knows what one should do.

When she dashed into the bathroom, Kate exclaimed, 'Oh, go away, Annie! You know what he's like when you're about . . . Now, David,' she said to her struggling son, 'it's no use, you've got to be washed. Oh . . . and Cathleen,' she added apologetically, 'I'm sorry I didn't answer you . . . Yes, of course, go and ask Steve.'

When the two girls had left the bathroom, Kate said to Peggy, 'I hope Steve comes; he's hardly been in the house this Christmas, and he usually spends most of it with us. Rodney's been a bit worried about him lately. He's changed somehow . . . I can't understand it myself. He was like one of the family, and we thought the world of him – we still do, but all of a sudden he seemed to close up and withdraw from us.'

'Perhaps there's a woman in the case,' laughed Peggy.

'Well, you know, I thought of that, but I've never seen any sign of one. I wish it was a woman; I'd like to see him married. He's too nice to be alone, and he's getting on.'

'How old is he?'

'Forty-one or so, I think.'

'Steve is teaching me to twittle, Auntie. Isn't he, Mammy?'

'Whittle, darling.'

'And he's not old, he plays with me. Will he play with me if he gets married, Mammy?'

'Oh dear!' said Kate, wriggling him into his dressing-gown. 'I never seem to learn . . . Come along, darling,' she added; 'Alice has got your tea ready. And when you've had it you may come downstairs and say night-night to everyone.'

When David was settled in the nursery with Alice and they were on their way downstairs, Peggy said quietly, 'You know, Kate, this is the nicest Christmas I've had for years.'

'Me too,' said Kate. 'There seems to be something extra special about it.'

'It's been lovely staying with you these past three days. I feel as if I've been on a holiday for months.'

'I'm glad,' said Kate. 'You certainly needed a change.'

'Yes, I did.' Peggy's face lost its happy look and became grave. 'You know, I thought when the children grew up life would become easy and mellow. But it seems to be just the reverse . . . Oh,' she turned to Kate, 'if only they would stay small like David. I get worried sick sometimes about what's going to happen to them. Not so much Michael, but Cathleen.'

Kate did not immediately reply. But when she said, 'Yes, you do have a constant fear for them,' it was more to comfort Peggy than to make a statement of her own feelings, for she had no qualms about Annie.

As they reached the bottom of the stairs, Annie called from the dining-room, 'Mam! Just a minute.'

51

Peggy went on into the drawing-room, and Annie, pulling Kate behind the dining-room door, whispered, 'Mam, Mrs Macbane says Terence is shy and might not come. But she said if I went and asked him she thought he might . . . Do you think I should? It's funny a girl asking a boy, isn't it? And,' she laughed, 'he isn't a boy, he's a man . . . Do you think I dare? Somehow I think he's shy. But I'm a bit afraid to go,' she ended breathlessly.

'Mrs Macbane told you to go?' said Kate, in surprise. 'When?'

'Just now, when she was passing the gate; she was going out with Mr Macbane.'

Kate pondered a moment. 'Well . . . Yes . . . Yes, I should think it would be all right if you went and asked him. He does seem shy. Perhaps the party will do him good. Yes, go along.'

They smiled at each other, and Kate put out her hand and touched Annie's cheek, a gesture that had more in it than the mere action. 'Wrap up well,' she said as she followed her into the hall.

She helped Annie on with a hooded coat of dark green blanket cloth, and watched her pull on her top-boots, then let her out into the snow, saying, 'Is your torch all right?' As she stood for a while watching the torch's gleam bobbing in the lane, she wondered why Terence had kept so apart; they had done their best. Perhaps he felt the uncertainty of being in between two worlds, sure of his place in neither of them. She knew what that felt like.

She closed the door and turned into the shining warmth of the house again, and the thought came to her that Annie had always liked Terence Macbane. She hoped he was as nice as she imagined him to be. If they became friends it might cool Brian off. For surely Annie couldn't like Brian. Oh, she couldn't! Yet he was always here. Why hadn't he stayed in London? His two years there might have improved his business acumen in buying and selling iron and steel, but it hadn't improved him. He was, as Rodney said, all boast and brawn, and he seemed to keep everyone away from Annie. Yes, it would be nice if she became friendly with Terence. The possibility gave her a warm feeling and she returned to the drawing-room smiling.

When Cathleen left the house by the side door she stood for a while looking up into the night sky. Venus stared down at her, unblinking, and Cathleen whispered into the night, 'I could reach you if I wanted to. Yes, I could. I can do anything I want . . . Oh, it's all so easy. Why are they such fools, gullible fools?'

She ran swiftly down the garden towards the summer-house, which looked like a huge, dark blob in the white garden. As she ran she kicked the dry snow into high sprays before her and hummed to herself. On reaching the door, she paused. Then with an abrupt movement she thrust it open without knocking, and went in.

'What the . . .!' Steve, in the act of pulling his shirt over his head, glared at her across the narrow space of the room. 'What do you want?' he demanded. 'Why can't you knock?' He pulled the sleeves over his wrists and picked up another shirt from the chair before adding, 'I thought I told you not to come here again.'

She walked close up to him without speaking, and stood watching him as he put the shirt on and tucked the tails into his trousers. Then with a swift movement she reached up and, thrusting her face into the opening of the shirt, caught some of the black hairs on his chest between her teeth.

'God!' he exclaimed. 'You little . . .!' He gripped her by the shoulders, holding her from him. They stared at each other. Then both began to laugh. 'One of these days,' he said, 'you'll get what you're asking for.'

She chuckled, a deep, throaty chuckle, then waltzed away,

whirling in the narrow space between Steve's bed and the small couch by the side of the fire before coming to a stop again in front of him. He was buttoning his shirt, his fingers fumbling; his face was stiff again, and he moved his big body restlessly.

'Look,' he said, 'we've had all this out. I told you not to come down here again. Don't you see? If they got to know . . .'

'Oh, wouldn't the holy family be shocked!' she laughed.

'Don't blaspheme,' he said. 'And I've told you this can't go on. If they found out, I'd never hold up my head again . . . I can barely do it now. Look, Cathy,' he pleaded as to one with superior strength. 'Be sensible. Nothing can come of this; I'm old enough to be your father. Look at all the young fellows there are about . . .'

'I do. Young fellows bore me, I've told you. I like them old – but not too old; and round about six foot one, and broad, with hairs on their chests, and doggy eyes . . .'

'Look—' he said.

'Don't keep saying "Look", darling.'

'Well, it's just this way.' His tone became grim. 'I like this job; I don't want to leave it. But if you keep this up I will . . . I'll have to.'

'Why do you like this job?' she asked quietly. 'A servant and a nursemaid to the lot of them! You're clever with your hands; you could get something better than this tomorrow.'

'Perhaps. But I like it here. Besides, jobs aren't so easy to pick up as you imagine; there are thousands unemployed.'

'There wouldn't be any special attraction that keeps you here, would there?'

'Now stop that! We don't want all that again,' he said sharply. 'I like the job; the doctor's fine to work for.'

'Ah! yes. The doctor's wonderful to work for,' she mimicked. 'And Kate?'

He said helplessly, 'She's a fine mistress, I've told you.'

'Ho-ho! That's funny. A "fine mistress"!'

His face darkened with anger. 'Cathy! Stop it! I've explained there are different ways of liking a woman. Your mind is like a cesspool.'

'Really?' She looked at him coldly.

'I'm sorry . . . but you turn things so. Look. What have you come for? If they get to know you're here . . .'

'My pet, they sent me. What do you think of that? They want to know if you'll come and join the party. A youth has not turned up, so I guilelessly put your name forward to Virgin Annie.'

He frowned at her allusion to Annie, and said, 'I'm going out.'

'But, darling, it's a command . . . And besides, I want you to come.' She put out her hand and touched the grey hair at his temple. 'I want to play Postman's Knock and kiss you in the hall. I want to watch you and think: I know things about him that would make their hair stand on end.'

'You little devil!'

She came nearer to him. 'Do you love me?'

He shook his head with the same helpless movement as before. 'I've told you.'

'It's funny,' she laughed softly, 'how that satisfies me much more than "yes". You're not clever, Steve. Do you know the way to get rid of me, darling? Go wild about me. The only things that attract me are the things that elude me.'

She leant against him, her arms round his waist, her head under his chin. 'Be nice to me, sweet, I'm having such a beastly time. I've been charming to everybody for weeks just so I can be up here near you. I've got Mummy and Daddy sitting back and purring; my brother smiles at me and calls me Sis; I'm even nice to the Virgin; and they're all saying, "Oh, she is improving. Getting over the adolescent phase. Perhaps we've misjudged her . . ." Even the Countess Kate has dropped her defences. The only one who doesn't unbend is that haybag contralto, Miss Rosie Mullen; she's more clever than I imagined . . . But oh, Steve, I can't keep it up. I hate even the pretence of being good. I was tempted to flirt with Tim Bailey, when the idea about you came into my head. Oh, Steve!' she chuckled, 'imagine their reactions to me setting my cap at Tim – he's an embryo priest, you know. My mother would have his uncle up to exorcise the Devil out of me.'

Steve tilted her small pointed face back and gazed down into her bright, dark eyes, half hidden by the thick, curling lashes. He shook his head slowly. What was it about her that got into your blood? Why had he let himself in for this? Life had been easy and pleasant before. What gave her the idea about him and the mistress? God! The things she said put him in a panic. Some of them were true, too. How did she know? But it wasn't true he was in love with Ka . . . the mistress. Well, not as she implied. He thought of Kate as a being apart. She was the doctor's, very much the doctor's. But Cathleen had unearthed this feeling and brought it startlingly into the light, terrifying him. She was uncanny. He said aloud, 'You're uncanny, you know too much. How do you know so much?'

Her lids hid the expression of her eyes; she pressed closer, wriggling against him.

'You're a witch,' he said. 'I shouldn't wonder but you've been burnt already.'

She laughed, and the sound had the tone of a bell, wide and deep and in strange contrast to the slightness of her body. 'Do you think so? That's interesting, for I've already come to that conclusion about myself. You're the only one that's troubled to think what I'm like. The others are like children, and they're afraid of me . . . Yes, they are. Sometimes I feel old, old, old. Do you know, I can tell what the reactions of others will be to any situation. I love creating situations just to prove myself right.' She drew her finger lightly round the outline of his lips. 'I knew I could make you want me; I knew exactly what would happen when I started. Remember the first time I came in here? You nearly had a fit.'

He pushed her roughly away. 'I know what I should have done that first time,' he said. He began putting on his collar, tugging the ends to meet the stud. 'I can tell you something I do know,' he said, turning his back on her: 'this is going to mean disaster to both of us if you don't stop it. You started it thinking you would hurt someone else. But you were mistaken; you'll be the one who gets hurt in the end, cock-sure as you are . . . and me too, more than hurt. Something will happen if this doesn't stop.'

When she made no reply, he turned round. She was standing with her hand on the latch of the door. She looked tiny, like a wisp of dark gossamer. Her voice sounded very small and pathetic when she said, 'Will you come up then?'

He took two strides towards her and lifted her hand off the latch. 'Cathy, you do see, don't you?'

Her fingers curled round his and his flesh leapt under her touch. 'Cathy, I don't want to hurt you . . . I'm afraid of . . . of this going further . . . of anything happening. Don't you see?'

She lifted her hand, and without taking her eyes from his switched off the light. They stood apart. She saw him as a great, black shape outlined in the glow from the fire. She made no further move, but waited. Then her feet left the ground, and his mouth came searching blindly for hers; his hands moved over her, pressing her into the curves of his body; she felt the hardness of the door against her shoulder-blades and the hardness of his muscles against her thighs, and out of the caverns of her being rose a deep laugh.

*   *   *

57

Terence was leaning back in the chair, his feet perched on the hob, his eyes on the low ceiling.

River reed pipes, soft-lined for water notes,
Play the tune of ripplets lapping the stalks . . .

Now what? He saw floating in the ceiling that river in Norfolk, with the tall rushes swaying gently in the breeze, and the dying sun taking with it the red from the river; he could see again the moon stealing up from a corner of the sky, and feel the sense of quietude and peace that comes on a river unawares, and touches you if you remain still. He wrote on:

Sent from the moorhen as she swiftly floats,
And the night moths as they alight and walk.
River reeds, play gently to the wind's time
And sway your slender forms into the dance,
Nodding your heads gracefully to the moon
And stilling all the river things in trance.

It didn't really express what he had felt that night sitting alone by the river. Could one ever express what one actually felt? No: only the shadow of what is in one's mind can be transmitted on to paper, for the thought loses most of its substance in the actual transmission.

From the stark facts of mathematics, from Eddington's interpretation of Einstein's theory of relativity, his mind would revert, and there would well up a desire to express something that needed no proving, that could be made concrete by feeling alone, to express a thought by a word, however inadequate, and add another, and another; and there you had a picture; and the picture was real, holding for all time the shadow of the thought that would have been lost. Where did thought go when it was allowed to slide away? Did it float in the ether of your own particular aura, round and round, waiting for you to pluck it out? That was something like Larry's idea: your thoughts built themselves into a mattress on which your body was transferred after death to the next stage of its journey. If the thoughts during your life were mostly good, the mattress would hold together; if they were bad, your body would fall through, and you were born again into this world, and renewed your apprenticeship.

John Dane Dee and Larry; strong tea and anchovy toast; and debates going on and on into the night, ranging from the mentality of a worm to the illusion of the sovereignty of princes. Soon they would be gone for ever, merely another memory floating in the ether.

He started when he heard the knock; it was unusual for anyone to come to the cottage after dark. He slipped the book in which he had been writing under the cushion of the chair, and went to the door.

'Hello, Terence,' said Annie shyly.

He didn't answer, but stared at her. Although she had been but a matter of yards from him for the past few days he was as surprised as if she had come from another world. She stood below him in the snow, a green thing with a golden head. The hood had fallen back on to her shoulders and her hair of pale liquid gold framed her face; her eyes, like the clear green of the river, looked up at him. And he thought, as he had thought years ago, why has she to look like that? He said haltingly, 'Hello. Won't you come in?'

She walked up the two steps and into the full light of the room. Still he stared at her. Now that they were on a level he saw that she had grown considerably during the past year. She was tall like the river reeds about which he had been writing, and as graceful. But she hadn't much shape; she was rather flat, like a boy, immature still. She must be – what? Seventeen? Eighteen? Yet her expression remained that of the child he had known, trusting, open, unable to hide what it felt.

'Won't you sit down?' he said at last. 'My mother and father are out.'

'Yes, I know,' she replied. 'I saw them going.'

'Oh!' His eyebrows were slightly raised.

'Terence . . . Are you coming to my party?'

He turned from her and took a cigarette from a green packet on the mantelpiece, and tapped it quickly on the back of his hand. 'It was very good of you to send me an invitation, and I suppose it was very bad of me not to reply; but . . . well, I'm not much use at parties; I'm the kind of fellow who gets stuck in a corner and remains there.' Lighting the cigarette, he took two quick draws, his back still towards her. He seemed to be waiting for her to say something. When she didn't speak, he turned towards her again: 'I'd most likely put a damper on the whole thing. I can never find anything to say; I'm not what you'd call a party man.'

'It doesn't matter; we'd love to have you. Won't you come?' Her eyes were soft now, misty, and he found himself fascinated by the movements of her lips as they shaped the words. Laughter, young and free, glinted on their full redness. His mother said she'd grown into a 'nice lass'. Lord! what an adjective to describe her . . . 'nice'! Dane Dee could put her into words, he'd never be able . . . But he was not going to that party . . . he wasn't starting anything. Oh no!

'Your mother told me to come along for you,' Annie said, her smile widening.

'My mother!' he exclaimed in surprise.

'Yes. She said you might come if I asked you.'

'Well well!' he laughed.

'Oh Terence, do come!' She made a small, pleading motion with her hands. 'You'd only be sitting here alone . . . That is, if you're not going anywhere else.'

60

He was on the point of saying that he was sorry but he was going out, when she put out her hand impulsively and caught his: 'Come on, Terence. Please. It's my birthday party, I'm eighteen – and two days,' she added, laughing.

He looked down at her hand on his as she went on talking. She still retained the spontaneity of the child who had buried her head on his chest and cried. Lord, he had been scared that day! And hadn't it been a job keeping out of her way? It had been like fighting two people, himself and her. Odd, but it was through her he had acquired the walking habit . . . The miles he had tramped during the vacs; the places he had seen. Really he owed her quite a lot . . . He had never been as close to her again since that day on the Jarrow road . . .

She was saying, 'I never used to have birthday parties at all; no-one seemed to think about it, because it falls on Christmas Eve. I forgot I had a birthday myself. But now Mam always gives me a party on Boxing Day . . . Won't you come?' Her face became grave. 'I . . . I promise not to cry all over you.'

The room filled with laughter. She watched his head go back. How different he looked when he laughed, and she hadn't thought he was so tall. Oh, he was nice. She had always known he was nice.

'I was just thinking of that day,' he said.

'So was I. *Have* you an aunt who drinks?'

'No. I'm afraid my only aunt is a staunch Wesleyan.'

'Oh, how funny. You lied beautifully,' she said. 'I did use to howl, didn't I? When I look back I see myself in stages: there was the period when I was always falling down and tearing great holes in the knees of my stockings; then the crying period. Somehow you seemed to figure largely in that.'

'Well, you know, you seemed always to be at it whenever we did meet.'

You didn't stay long enough to get to know me when I wasn't crying, she thought to herself as she continued to smile at him. You avoided me . . . Why? Was it because we have money and things? Oh, that would be stupid. Well, what was it then? . . . Oh, what does it matter, she chided herself, so long as he comes now? Oh, he must come, he must come. Her eyes all appeal, she said, 'You'll come?'

He heard himself saying, 'All right then, I'll come. But be it on your own head if your party goes flat . . . I'll be down in about a quarter of an hour.'

'Oh, I'll wait for you,' she said eagerly. His eyes twinkled, and again they laughed together. 'Well, you see, I'm afraid you'll change your mind.'

What a child she was! Were all girls so frank and open? He guessed not. But of course he didn't know much about them. Yet he felt sure she was entirely different. Girls of eighteen generally assumed that grown-up air, they tended to fly to sophistication, but there was something so utterly . . . utterly . . . what was it? He smiled at her. 'All right,' he said, 'sit down. I won't be a few minutes.'

She watched him mount the steep stairs, with the rope banisters, that ran up by the wall in the corner of the room, and disappear through a hole in the ceiling. She glanced about her. Everything was very clean and neat. The small room had a comfortable, homely look. There were bunches of herbs hanging from a beam and holly trailed over the pictures and mantelpiece. She looked into the bright fire. She was sitting in Terence's kitchen, and he was coming to her party. She gave herself a hug. Everything would be marvellous from now on . . . the ice was broken. Why didn't she do this last year, or the year before? She told herself laughingly she would never have dreamt of doing it but for Mrs Macbane.

When he came downstairs again, he had changed into a dark, pinstriped suit that made him taller and thinner than ever. The only part of him that seemed to have expanded during the years was his shoulders.

He stood before her, buttoning his jacket. 'Shall we go?' he asked.

'Aren't you putting on a coat?' she said, standing up.

'No. I very rarely wear one.'

'But the snow . . . It's so cold.'

'I don't mind the cold.'

Her face showed concern. 'But you're so—' She stopped.

He smiled, a little twisted amused smile. 'Yes, I'm so thin . . . Look!' He went to the back of the door and took a top coat from a peg. 'I do have a coat . . . but I really don't feel the cold; it's just what you're used to. Now do you believe me?'

'Oh, I'm so sorry.'

He laughed at her downcast face. 'I remember,' he said with mock-seriousness, 'you once tried to feed me because you thought I was hungry . . . Now you must get it into your head that I am neither cold nor hungry.'

The hot blood rushed over her face and neck, and she hung her head before him, as she did years ago. 'I'm quite tactless,' she murmured.

'Of course you're not,' he laughed. 'I was only meaning to be funny. You see what you've let yourself in for? I'll most surely say all the wrong things at the party . . . Shall I come?'

Her head came up with a jerk. 'Oh, of course!'

'All right then. Let's go.'

Outside, waiting for him while he locked the door and put the key under a loose brick of the step, she experienced a whirling spring of joy. It trembled through her, making her draw in great draughts of air to feed it. There were times before when she had felt this light, quivering joy, but not so intense as now. It was the signal for movement, for flying feet, for her arms to be flung wide, for her to race over the earth, for her exuberance to lift her into the very sky itself. Terence was amazed to see her fly from him into the lane, her dark shape leaping against the snow. When he reached the gate she was running back to him, and a soft snowball hit him on the shoulder. She let out a little yelp of joy, and was off again.

He hesitated a second. Then the reticence of years was flung off, like chains from a prisoner, and he was after her. No time now to say, 'This must not start,' but let the feeling have rein at last . . . on, on, to catch her, and touch her, to explore that radiated joy, to hold the youth that emanated from her.

He caught her before she had gone very far. Gripping her with one hand, he gathered up snow with the other. She struggled, and cried, 'No, no! Don't scrub me!' She bent down, hiding her face, and he bent over her, saying nothing, just struggling with her gently, playfully. The snow-banked lane hemmed them in, and they swayed together in the dark. Then quickly they both straightened. She was in the circle of his arms; her face was hidden in her hands. They were still now, standing close. One minute his arms were about her, and she was surprised at the strength and hardness of them; the next she was standing alone, and he was saying in a low voice, 'All right, I'll let you off this time.'

Somewhat self-consciously, they walked a little way down the lane in silence. When they bumped against each other in the rutted snow they made small laughing noises and put some distance between themselves.

Annie's voice sounded high-pitched even to herself when she said, 'We had a marvellous snowball fight today. Will you come out tomorrow?'

'There'll be a heavy thaw during the night, there won't be any snow left.'

'Oh, don't say that.' She sounded forlorn.

They walked nearer to each other again, and she said suddenly, 'I've left school, Terence; I'm at college. I'm going to be a teacher too.'

'You've left the convent then?'

'Oh yes,' – she sounded as if the convent were a thing of bygone ages – 'I'm eighteen, you know.'

When he laughed out loud, she said, 'Oh, you make me feel as though I am only eight.'

'You are.'

'Oh, Terence! That isn't fair. I'm very grown-up . . . I'm putting my hair up next term.'

'Oh no, don't do that.' He drew up for a moment and peered at her in the darkness. 'Once it's up . . .'

He hesitated, and she put in, 'Yes. That's what Mam says: once it's up, it's up for good.'

His voice was deep as he said hesitantly, 'Keep it . . . keep it down.'

They walked on again in a strange, rapt quiet. It was as if her hair had drawn them tightly together.

5

As they neared the gate, a sound of singing came from the house and Terence said, 'What a fine voice! Is it a gramophone record?'

'No,' laughed Annie; 'that's Rosie. She's a friend of mine. She's so nice,' she added. 'You've seen her, you know, down in the wood.'

He shook his head. But as he walked up the path he saw the short figure standing near the piano in the drawing-room. 'Oh yes,' he said. 'I remember her. She has an amazing voice.'

'She's going to be a great singer.'

'I should imagine she's one already.'

'Yes. But I mean she's going to be famous. I'm sure she is. She's sung in some big concerts already this winter, and she's going up to London for an audition shortly.'

'Really? It all sounds very romantic. Who's that accompanying her?'

'Oh, that's Michael. Michael Davidson. He plays beautifully. He wants to be a concert pianist, but Uncle Peter, his father, won't let him take it up . . . Michael's nice,' she added.

Everyone was 'nice'. She was so very naïve. 'Who's the giant?' he asked as they still stood on the path, listening.

'That's Brian. He's just recently returned from London. We travelled to school together at one time.'

'Oh! I remember him. He was the fellow who used to hang around in the wood for you. I always felt like a worm beside him.'

'Oh, Terence! You couldn't feel like a worm.'

'There you go again,' he laughed. 'You won't even let me feel like a worm . . . Now, if I want to be a worm I'll be a—'

'Oh, come on, you silly billy!' It was as if they had been close friends for years. She gripped his hand and ran, pulling him after her. As he entered the house his mind was lifted from her to her everyday surroundings. It was the first time he had been inside, and at once the air of comfort struck him. Here no clippy mats covered the floor, but thick, red Turkish carpet fitted into the corners of the hall and covered the broad, shallow stairs. An Adam mirror hung above an antique hall-table, and huge bronze and white chrysanthemums stood in tall vases in the corners of the hall and on top of a carved oak chest. The old mixed feeling returned; antipathy and reticence fought the desire to accept all that was being offered. But the old feelings were of long duration and would not be ousted.

Awkwardly, not wanting to touch her now, he helped her off with her coat. Why the Devil had he come? he asked himself. The girl was still singing: 'One love for ever, one love alone.' Annie whispered, 'We'll wait until she's finished.' She stood looking towards the drawing-room door, and he looked at her. The dove-grey woollen dress made her hair appear fairer than ever; it hung down her back in two long twists that were drawn together by a green watered-silk bow at the nape of her neck. She still wore a fringe, as she had done when she was a child.

She felt his gaze on her, and turned towards him, smiling frankly into his eyes. In spite of himself, he smiled back . . .

You couldn't help smiling at her, she was so lovely. Had she always been as lovely as this?

The side door leading from the garden opened abruptly and Cathleen and Steve entered. Annie whispered, 'Hello, Steve.'

Steve nodded to her and stood still, just within the door, wearing a strained, rather hangdog expression.

He seems as out of place as I do, Terence thought. Then he noticed the girl. She had walked towards Annie but was looking at him. His first impression of a slight, dark child of fourteen was immediately replaced by that of a woman of twenty, or twenty-five. In fact, of any age; he could not place her at all. How odd, he thought. These girls! Why can't they look what they are?

He returned her glance for a second, and felt himself grow hot, for she was looking not only at his face, but at his body. Over his shoulders, down his thighs to his feet, her eyes quickly travelled, then up again. He shivered as if he were naked. She stood sideways to him whispering to Annie, and he was conscious of the curves of her small body in contrast with Annie's boyish flatness.

The singing stopped and the drawing-room door opened. There was the sound of clapping, and Kate came into the hall, followed by Rodney. 'Hello, Steve. I'm so glad Cathleen persuaded you to come.'

Steve smiled at Kate and nodded, but made no reply. And she turned to Terence, who was shaking hands with Rodney. 'Well, Terence, here you are at last! This visit's long overdue. How are you?'

Terence made a suitable reply. For the first time he found himself looking closely into the face of this woman who was Annie's mother. There was no resemblance between them, but she too was beautiful, with a happy, serene look in her eyes. He felt he could like her. He noticed she was pregnant, and thought it added strangely to her beauty.

'When we can we'll have to have a talk,' Rodney said; 'there's heaps of things I want to ask you. Do you know, I've never been back to Oxford since I came down. Year after year I intended going, but something always came up.'

It was all so easy, and the feeling of strain lifted. It was as if he had been here many times before. Terence found himself in the drawing-room, shaking hands with one after another. And he laughed when he realised he was using Annie's expression to himself: They're nice. With one exception he used it, and that was when he shook hands with Brian, and found his fingers crushed in an unnatural grip. He noticed that Brian drew himself up to his fullest height, and when it did not exceed his own he knew a momentary satisfaction, in spite of the fact that Brian's breadth must have made him look like a pole beside a giant tree trunk.

Brian's broad, fresh-coloured face grinned good-naturedly, but his round, sharp eyes were weighing Terence up; and Terence made up his mind, there and then, that he couldn't stand the fellow.

At tea, Terence was placed between Rosie and Annie, with Brian on Annie's other side. With Rosie talking to Michael on her other side and Brian monopolising Annie, Terence found himself, now and again, looking straight across the table into the eyes of the girl called Cathleen. They had not been introduced, and he supposed Mrs Prince had taken it for granted that Annie had performed this duty in the hall. He wondered vaguely who the girl was. Certainly she was nothing to do with any of those present; she seemed alien, belonging to another social world altogether, though to what particular one he could not say. Her hair was cut in an Eton crop, and although he disliked girls with short hair, he admitted that the style suited her. Its glossy sheen was like a starling's back.

*   *   *

The party, which at first filled Annie with such ecstatic joy, slowly began to lose its sparkle. At what point she began to notice it, she couldn't say. Was it when she saw Cathleen sitting next to Terence and making him laugh? But then she was making everyone laugh by teasing Steve so. Or was it when she realised that Terence hadn't chosen her for a partner in any game in which he would be expected to kiss her? Yes, she thought frankly, it was then that the party began to lose its zest. She watched him kissing the other girls with quick pecks, and wondered if he was avoiding kissing her on purpose. After a while, she felt convinced that was what he was doing, and she was filled with a wild, crazy desire for him to kiss her. It burned in her and became a pain, which showed in her eyes when she looked at him. Sometimes he would smile across the room at her, and she thought he had the nicest grey eyes in the world; they could look so kind. Then why wasn't he kind to her?

It was her duty to see that they were all enjoying themselves, and she did this conscientiously. It helped to hide her diminishing spirits, but not to stop her thinking: Why is he being like this to me? He was so nice at first. It isn't really because he's shy. Then why is it? He's treating me now as he has done all these years, he's avoiding me . . . But why? Why? The question became an ache. His attitude was so contrary to what she expected from his friendliness in the cottage and then in the lane . . . Yes, in the lane. If there hadn't been that . . .

During the game of Postman's Knock, she did not expect that either by design or by chance he would call her number. When he did she was too surprised to move. It was Rosie who, laughingly, pushed her through the door and into the hall amid cries of 'Dreamer!' And there Terence was waiting in the dimmed light. Once the door was closed and they were alone she found that she was trembling and could not move the few feet towards him. Irrationally now she wanted to run from him. They stood gazing at each other. It was as if they had been parted for a long time. Their eyes searched each other's face, until Annie's dropped away from his. He put out his hand and drew her to him. 'Hello, Annie Hannigan,' he said softly, banteringly.

She gave a little gasp, and whispered, 'Hello, Terence Macbane.' She waited breathlessly, gazing up at him. But he didn't kiss her; he lifted her hand and, bending his head, placed his lips on her palm.

For a moment she was tempted to kiss the straight, black hair so near to her, but he raised his head and was looking at her again. He still held her hand, and without taking his eyes from hers, he lifted it and pressed it against his face.

As he moved away, she could not believe she was hearing aright. Did he whisper, 'You're very lovely, Annie'? The murmur had been so low. She closed her eyes. Oh, it was better than just being kissed; he had made it all so wonderful. They seemed to be close, like . . . Well, she couldn't explain what it was like, for she had never experienced anything touching it before.

She was dizzy with joy, and gave a number at random, hoping vaguely it would not be Brian's. It was.

He came striding into the hall, buttoning his jacket as if ready to do battle. He gave a deep chuckle and said, 'Ah, you're good at counting!' As he took her into his arms she pressed her hands tightly against his chest and turned her cheek to him. 'Oh no! We're not having any of that. Come on, play the game properly.' She felt his chest vibrate with the rumble of his laugh.

'Stop it, Brian!' she whispered fiercely. 'Don't be silly.'

'Don't be silly,' he mimicked. 'We're not at school now, you know. Look here, Annihan . . .'

'Don't call me that, Brian.'

71

'Well, all right, I won't. But see here, Annie, you've been keeping away from old Brian all day. Oh, come on!' His mouth sought hers; soft and warm, his lips moved over her face as she twisted and turned. Then, lowering herself suddenly, she gave a wrench and dropped from under his arms. Her hair dishevelled, her face ablaze, she ran from him and up the stairs. He shrugged his great shoulders and pursed his lips as he looked after her. For a moment his face took on an ugly look and he nodded his head as if assuring himself of something, but when he shouted into the drawing-room, 'I've exhausted the last delivery, and I've a parcel here for number eight!' he was the old laughing Brian again.

Annie sat on the deep windowsill, hidden behind the thick curtains. The last game of the party was in progress; it was Hide and Seek, and she had picked on this spare room as being the place least likely to be detected. It was next to David's nursery, and most of the games had been kept from this part of the house in case of waking him. She thought it gave her an unfair advantage to hide in here, but she knew Tim could cope with any disadvantage, fair or otherwise.

She sat waiting, feeling safe, and listening to the distant cries of 'Come out of that!', 'I can see you, Rosie', 'And you too, doctor.' She wondered where Terence was.

Before running upstairs she had looked at him, hoping that perhaps he would come with her. But Cathleen was talking to him. Since Steve had left, Cathleen had kept near Terence, but oddly enough it did not disturb Annie, for she felt Terence belonged to her now. The little scene in the hall had in some way taken the form of a vow, more sealing because nothing was said, only that whisper. She pressed the palm of her hand to her mouth . . . Oh, there was no-one like him! The boys she knew seemed immature and silly beside him. They always had. Terence had an air of polish about him that made them seem very young in comparison. She supposed that all these years she had been waiting for him . . . And now there was tomorrow and the next day, and the next . . . nearly a fortnight of the holiday still left. Now he would no longer pass the gate with merely a nod, or cut through the top field, as she knew he sometimes did, to reach the main road. Oh, Terence, Terence.

She heard the door squeak and a soft padding on the carpet. Someone was coming in. Thinking it was Tim on his search, she remained still, her fingers held against her lips. Then a whisper, low and unintelligible, came to her, telling her there were two people in the room. She was about to part the curtains and give a warning hiss when she heard the springs of the bed creak. The sound created a quick feeling of fear mixed with embarrassment. It stilled her hand and she sat stiff, waiting. There was a laugh, soft and deep, which she recognised. Then the bed creaked again, as if someone else had sat down. There came low, murmuring, intimate sounds, a different laugh, smothered quiet, followed by more creaks. And Cathleen's voice came to her, very low but clear, 'Now we're introduced properly, Terence.'

And Terence's voice answered, equally low, 'Rather late in the evening, isn't it?'

What Cathleen's rejoinder was Annie didn't hear. She was staring, unseeing, into the palm of her hand, and her teeth were biting into her lower lip. The murmuring sounds began again, their implications making her sick. She thrust her fingers into her ears, and feelings of shame and humiliation flowed over her in giant waves, the feelings she thought she had vanquished for ever, so deeply buried in her childhood that nothing could resurrect them into this life. But this feeling of shame seemed also a betrayal, and had a tearing, lacerating power which made those bygone agonies puny in comparison. Prayer words galloped through her mind, petitioning

73

strength: 'Sweet Lady, don't let me cry until I am in bed . . . Oh, dear Lord, teach me to hide from him what I feel. And don't let Cathleen Davidson see what she's done.'

She stopped praying, and cried to herself, She hasn't changed! She's wicked, and I hate her! . . . And him? Oh, and him! she added.

6

The wind was living up to its March reputation. The trees, which yesterday had promised sprinklings of delicate green, were waving so wildly that nothing but their bare, contorted arms was evident. The car was at the door, and Kate, dressed for outdoors, stood in the hall with Rodney and Mrs Summers. She looked from one to the other with patient exasperation: 'You know I never go right up to the fifteen streets in the car. And the case isn't too heavy. You are both being ridiculous.'

'You can say what you like,' said Rodney, 'you are not taking it unless you let Steve drive you right to the door. Anyway, why take it yourself? Let Steve drop it in some other time.'

Kate sighed. 'You know, dear, I couldn't do that. It would look too . . . so . . . Oh, all right. Let Steve drive there.' She pulled on her gloves.

''Bout time, too, doctor,' said Mrs Summers. ''Bout time you did put your foot down. She looks like a chalk doll. And going out a day like this! And proposing to carry that thing from the docks!' With an offended look at the case, she stalked from the hall.

'She's right,' said Rodney. 'It seems madness going out in

this weather. And you're not looking too good at all . . . Darling, don't go. Or wait until I've done my afternoon round and I'll come with you.'

She came and stood close to him. 'Don't keep worrying, my dear; I'm perfectly all right. Please trust me not to do anything silly.' She kissed him swiftly on the lips. 'You know, it isn't only taking the case; I'd want to be there when Rosie gets in, to hear her news.'

'She should have phoned,' said Rodney a little stiffly; 'she would have known the result yesterday evening – I think it's very bad of her not to have done so.'

'Something must have prevented her, my dear; I know Rosie would have phoned if she possibly could.'

'Yes, yes, I suppose she would,' he said, and added, 'Annie's meeting you up there, is she?'

'Yes, she's coming straight through. She may meet Rosie in Newcastle if the train's on time. It will be lovely having her for the weekend, won't it? I can never get used to her not coming home every night.'

Steve came into the hall, and Rodney said, 'No matter what Mrs Prince says, you drive right to the Mullens' door, Steve. You understand?'

Steve nodded and said quietly, 'Yes, sir.'

Rodney closed the car door on Kate and she waved to him as the car moved away.

Leaning back against the soft upholstery, she relaxed and admitted to herself that she was a little tired; the child, now at seven months, was beginning to drag. But oh how she hated the thought of driving in this luxurious car into the meanness and poverty of the fifteen streets. She always made a point of wearing her plainest clothes when going up there, but even those spoke of money. Years ago, when she had lived there, she wore the clothes Miss Tolmache bought her with pride, but now, with all the money she wanted at her command, she did everything to hide her affluence from the people of those streets to whom her good fortune was in the nature of a miracle.

In the face of the conditions prevailing generally in the fifteen streets these days, it was understandable that Kate did not want to drive there, and she knew Rodney's insistence was merely because of his fear for her health. The case of groceries would be, she knew, a godsend to Mrs Mullen, with Mr Mullen on short time and the only wage-earning boy left at home out of work, and three young children. Money, as in most houses on the Tyne, was short.

During the last three years that Rosie had been training, Mrs Mullen had accepted eight shillings a week from Kate in lieu of the amount she would have received if Rosie had still been in service. It had taken quite a lot of persuasion for her to fall in with the idea of receiving Rosie's money as if she were still at work, for, as she said, it was like expecting your bread to be buttered on both sides.

As if reading Kate's thoughts, Steve said, without turning his head, 'How would it be, ma'am, if we left the car a little way down the main road, and I carried the case up?'

Kate did not reply for a moment; she was still sensitive to the remarks of the women and she could hear them saying, 'Aye, brings her servant t'carry her bag for her.' But it was the lesser of two evils, so she said, 'Thanks, Steve. I do think that would be better than driving up. Yes, we'll do that. Thank you for suggesting it. And it won't be entirely disobeying the doctor's orders.' She gave a little laugh.

But he did not turn his head and smile his quiet smile as he would have done some months ago. And she thought: What is it? What has come over him? It's as Rodney says, he seems to have something on his mind.

When they were within a few minutes' walk of the fifteen streets, Steve helped her out of the car. They walked along

77

side by side in a rather strained silence. As it was just after three in the afternoon the road was practically deserted. It ran straight for about a quarter of a mile, with the fifteen streets branching off it to the left ahead of them, and a blank stone wall edging the pavement to their right. The only other people to be seen on the road were a young couple, who were sauntering towards them, bending close together against the wind. Kate thought they seemed familiar, but her eyes passed over them to a tram that was approaching. Then her mind was distracted by the case jolting violently in Steve's hand. He changed it to his other hand, and she asked if it was heavy.

'No,' he mumbled. And she looked to where his eyes were fixed ahead and saw, with a start of surprise, that the couple were Cathleen and Terence.

Why, she thought, I didn't know he was home. And she – she should be at the art school.

As the distance between them lessened, she felt that the surprise was mutual. Terence looked rather sheepish, but Cathleen was using her surprise, and Kate, under the unblinking stare of Cathleen's eyes, found herself feeling, for no reason whatever, at a disadvantage.

Cathleen spoke first, and her tone managed to convey the expression of her eyes: 'Well, well!' she drawled. 'We never know, do we?' Her eyes darted to Steve, then back again to Kate. 'Walking it are you? Giving the car a rest?'

Kate grew hot, and thought: What made me think she had improved? What does she mean? . . . And this is what has been upsetting Annie, ever since the night of the party: she couldn't bear Cathleen to be friends with Terence.

As she found herself explaining her presence with Steve, she felt furious, but went helplessly on, 'I didn't want Steve to drive right up to the fifteen streets, and the case is rather heavy.'

She was still further dismayed when she realised that Steve, without a word or a glance, had stalked straight ahead. Now why had he done that? 'I didn't know you were home, Terence,' she said.

He was standing stiffly, ill at ease, and seemed to have lost the calm sureness of manner that she remembered admiring at Christmas. 'I came last night,' he replied.

'And tempted me to stay away from school today. What do you think of that?'

Terence turned quickly towards Cathleen, his brows drawn together. He seemed to be on the point of speaking, but, instead, gave a bewildered shake of his head.

And she went on, 'You won't split, will you, Kate? You won't tell Mummy or Daddy?' She gave a little wink. 'And I won't tell Uncle Rodney.'

Kate could hardly believe her ears. The implication was so bald, so direct, and in front of Terence Macbane, too. 'Cathleen! How dare you!' she cried, her eyes wide and angry. 'How *dare* you say such a thing!'

'Oh, I was only joking. You know I was only funning.' Cathleen was all contrition. 'Don't be vexed. I'm sorry.' She smiled at Kate appealingly.

The girl was impossible. She could say or do the most outrageous things and smile and coax her way out of them. What on earth had made Kate think she was improving? She was worse than ever!

'Well, in future please don't joke about such things to me, Cathleen. Goodbye. Goodbye, Terence.'

Kate walked swiftly away, filled with indignation. How dare she! Implications like that weren't made on the spur of the moment. Why did she say that? What was she trying to do? How dare she insinuate! Oh, it was unpardonable. Just supposing she said some such thing in front of Rodney. Kate shivered. Rodney had no reason to be jealous of her, God knew, but his love for her was possessive and threaded with jealousy. She had to show him in countless little ways that he was her life, for his physical handicap had taken away his natural arrogance and deprived him, not a little, of his self-confidence. So just suppose he should think . . . Oh, that girl! This wasn't the first time she had coupled Kate's name with that of Steve, but there had seemed to be no ulterior meaning in it before, no threat. And then there was this business of Terence Macbane – she had certainly made headway there. Why didn't Annie fight her? She had all the weapons to her hand . . . But no, Kate admitted somewhat sadly to herself, Annie wasn't a fighter.

Kate was so disturbed she almost walked past Father Bailey, who was standing at the corner of Whitley Street. He was talking earnestly to a man in working clothes, but at the sight of her he turned and cried, 'Ah, it's you, Kate. Are you on your way to Mrs Mullen's? . . . You are? Then I'll be up after you. I've been meaning to come and see you for ages.' He turned quickly back to the man again, who was showing signs of trying to escape, and Kate heard him say, 'You know, Jack, you're a bigger liar than Tom Pepper; you've told me a different story altogether from your missis.'

Kate had to smile, in spite of the intense feeling of irritation that possessed her. Dear Father Bailey. Still at the job of trying to straighten out lives, whether they wished to be straightened or not.

Steve was standing by the Mullens' door, and she said without looking at him, 'Will you meet me at five o'clock, Steve, at the same place?'

He made a motion with his head, touched his cap and walked away. There was a droop of dejection about his shoulders that filled Kate with sudden pity and uneasiness . . . Could Cathleen have said something to him? Could she have hinted? Of course not, that was nonsense.

Mrs Mullen opened the door, exclaiming, 'Oh Kate, lass, what a day to come!'

'What a day to wash,' said Kate, following her into the kitchen, which was strewn with wet clothes. 'And you expecting Rosie too!'

'That's the reason, lass. I just couldn't sit still, I had to do something. And it would have been all right,' she exploded, 'if that bitch of a Mary Overton hadn't started to shovel her coal in. She just did it to nark me. Funny what people'll do when they think your bairns are getting on. We're not speaking, you see.' She suddenly laughed, her small eyes twinkling behind their wrinkled lids. 'What a life! When you're expecting something good to happen, you can't sit still and enjoy the waiting. Anyway, how are you, lass? And I say!' she cried, looking at the case, 'you didn't carry that up yourself?'

'No,' said Kate. 'Steve brought it.'

'That's all right then. But, lass, I keep telling you, you shouldn't do it. It's no use talking.'

'No,' said Kate, 'it isn't. I'm about as stubborn as you are.'

Mrs Mullen bundled the wet clothes into a zinc bath and pushed them under the table, saying, 'I'll put them up tonight when I get them off to bed. Now for a cup of tea, eh?'

'You'd better put out three cups,' said Kate. 'Father Bailey's on his way.'

'Is he?' exclaimed Mrs Mullen. 'Well, it never rains but it pours. Still, we see him pretty often now. But I don't mind Father Bailey . . . Remember Father O'Malley, Kate? By, he was an old devil, wasn't he? You know he's givin' up?'

'No,' said Kate, 'I didn't.'

'Yes. He's retiring on his rheumatism. By, there won't half be some sighs of relief when he goes. I should think Father Bailey'll get the parish, won't he?'

'I should think so.'

'I'd better tell you,' went on Mrs Mullen as she mashed the tea, 'we've got somebody you know in your old house next door. She's been there some weeks now. I didn't like to put it to you before, but seeing as how Father Bailey's coming, he may mention her to you, for he's always dropping in there . . . It's your cousin Connie, Kate.'

'What! Connie Fawcett, living here?'

'Aye, I thought you'd get a gliff. It was funny her coming next door. And she's going from bad to worse, never sober if she can get it . . . That Jake Riley's there, when his boat's in. And there's high-jinks as long as the money lasts, and then they're borrowing and pawning for the rest of the time, for she won't work. I doubt if she could if she wanted to, with that fat. I think there must be something wrong with her.'

'How is her boy?'

'Oh, it'd break your heart to see him! He looks after her like a mother; he waits for hours round the docks and brings her home, staggering drunk, and very often puts her to bed. Poor bairn, and him not nine yet. Oh, it'd break your heart. It would be bad enough if he was a bit of a lass . . . You don't mind me telling you, Kate?' she added.

'Not at all,' said Kate. She was sorry that Connie was next door, for she didn't want to meet her. But after all, what did it matter? She couldn't explain to Mrs Mullen that Connie Fawcett was no relation of hers whatever without giving away the secret her mother had imparted to her as she lay dying, and explaining that Tim Hannigan had not been her father.

'Oh dear!' exclaimed Mrs Mullen. 'Here comes Father Bailey, and I wanted to have a talk with you about Rosie.'

'Ah, there you are. A cup of tea too!' cried the priest, putting his weight against the kitchen door in an effort to close it. 'What could be better, eh, Kate, on a day like this? It's enough to blow the whiskers off Michael Finnegan's chin again.' He threw back his head and laughed at his own sally, and both Kate and Mrs Mullen laughed with him.

'And how is that heathen of yours getting on?' he asked as he drank his tea.

'He's very well, father,' smiled Kate.

'Oh, father! Fancy calling the doctor that! And him one of the finest men living,' said Mrs Mullen.

'That's as it may be, but there's room for improvement . . . You don't agree with me, Kate?' He leant across the table and looked at her through half-closed lids.

'I never agree with you, father. You know that by now.'

'Sure. Sure. But time will tell . . . Ah, yes.' He turned to Mrs Mullen and smiled benignly. 'It looks like a big wash you've got today.' He indicated the bath under the table.

'Oh, just about the usual, father.'

No-one spoke for a moment. Then, with a well-feigned start, Mrs Mullen got up, exclaiming, 'Goodness! I've left some things in the pot, they'll be boiled to bits!' A wink's as good as a nod to a blind horse, she thought as she dashed out; he wants to get at her again . . . Poor Kate.

Kate sat smiling at the priest, and waited. With the finesse of an elephant, Father Bailey led up to the subject he considered it his duty to discuss whenever they met.

'And how are you feeling, Kate?'

'Oh, quite well, father.'

'And are you hoping for a boy or a girl?'

'I think I'd like another girl, father.'

'Ah yes. Another Annie. There's a girl for you. They thought the world of her up at the convent. The Mother Superior has every praise for her, and she was the light of Sister Ann's life. Sister Ann really loves that girl. Did you know that, Kate?'

'Yes, father. And Annie's very fond of her.'

'Yes, another girl like Annie.' Father Bailey rested his

hands on his round stomach and tapped his fingers gently together. He seemed to be addressing the huge black kettle that stood on the hob when he said, 'Do you think Annie's nature would have been as sweet as it is if she hadn't been brought up in the faith?'

'She would have still been herself, father.'

'No, Kate. No. Annie is more soul than body. I know. And the glory of her faith has brought it out.'

Kate moved restlessly, and Father Bailey turned swiftly towards her, his hands no longer in repose but stretched out to her across the table, the palms upturned, expressive with pleading. 'Kate, don't you see what a sin you're committing by not having the boy christened? Don't add to it with another.'

'Oh father, don't go into it all again. You know David was christened in the Church of England.'

'But that's not your church, Kate.'

'I have no church, father.'

'Nonsense! Nonsense! Far better not have him christened at all than you should have him done outside the true church.'

'Well, all right,' said Kate, tartly. 'I'll follow your advice with this one.'

'God forgive you for even saying such a thing, Kate!' The priest was becoming red in the face. 'You know you are responsible for the lives you bring into the world. You know that, don't you?'

'Only up to a certain point; I believe that a child is an individual from the moment it is born.'

'Ho ho! Here we go again. Doctor Rodney Prince's ideas,' scoffed Father Bailey, 'not yours, Kate.'

'Yes, mine, father.' Kate's voice was angry now. 'That's the trouble with you all, you don't give people credit for thinking things out for themselves. You don't want them to think at all, just follow blindly on.'

'Hell, no doubt, is full of people who have thought things out for themselves, Kate. In your thinking, have you ever thought about that point?' The priest's voice was quiet.

'Yes, I have thought about it – and dismissed it; for hell is absolutely alien to the real meaning of Christianity.'

'Oh is it?' said Father Bailey with an air of having just learnt something. He nodded at her. 'How nice and comforting for you to have gone a step further and dismissed hell.'

'I just cannot accept the idea of hell, father. In my mind, it's the contradiction of the very idea of a god who is Love . . . Oh, it's all so childish, pandering to the superstitions of the ignorant.'

'Away with you, Kate. Simple justice points to it!' Father Bailey stood up and confronted her. He leant towards her, his hands on his knees, his face level with hers: 'Would you like to see Tim Hannigan being received by God on equal terms with your poor mother?'

Kate stared at him. 'It's a question whether God receives anyone. To me hell and heaven are right here.'

'Kate . . . Ah well!' He straightened himself and smiled. 'God has mysterious ways of working. Kate, you are a queer woman.' He sat down again and mopped his face with his handkerchief. From the wash-house across the yard the squeaking, clanking, jangling sounds of the mangle could be heard in the quiet of the kitchen, terminated every now and again with a sharp groan which ended in a thump as some garment was released from the rollers. The ragman's voice came from the back lane.

Father Bailey broke the silence: 'I shouldn't be worrying you at this time. I'm sorry, Kate.'

She smiled at him gently: 'I understand, father. I think I'd miss it if you stopped.'

'I pray for you often, Kate,' he went on, mopping his face, and the words came, muffled and embarrassed, through the handkerchief: 'I cannot explain it, but I've always had the idea that some time you are going to need me, that our lives are definitely crossed for all time. Oh, I cannot explain it.'

Kate looked tenderly at the priest, at this good priest, and thought, as she had often done before: Had I come under him instead of men like Father O'Malley, I wonder if I would have rebelled so much? She said gently, 'You have always been good and patient with me, father, and it grieves me when I have to disappoint you.'

He rose and took up his hat from the table. His face showed his broad smile again, and he said, 'Don't worry. God's good. And you know what they say: the Devil's not bad, for he looks after his own.' He laughed, and patted her shoulder: 'Well, I'm off. Now take care of yourself, Kate, and remember me to that heathen of yours . . . God bless you. I'll look in on Mrs Mullen down in the wash-house. Goodbye, Kate. Goodbye.'

He was gone, and he hadn't mentioned Connie. For that at least Kate was glad. She sat as she always did after an argument with him, filled with sadness and regret, and she realised, not for the first time, that the spirit passed through valleys of loneliness in its search for freedom. And somehow Father Bailey always emphasised that loneliness, and made her look back with regret on the sense of security the Church offered to the faithful . . .

It was nearly half an hour later when the back door opened and Rosie came in, and the look on her face told Kate and her mother what her news would be. In appearance, Rosie had altered little during the past four years; she still remained stocky, and her face maintained the round, buttony look of her childhood. It wasn't until she spoke that the difference in her became evident. Although she addressed her mother as 'Ma', and the inflexion of her voice was still that of the Tyneside, there was a quality about it that definitely stamped her with personality. She put her case down, looked from one to the other, and said, simply, 'It's the Albert Hall, the first week in October, in Verdi's Requiem.'

Mrs Mullen, drying her hands on her apron, shook her head from side to side, but said nothing. Kate, too, was silent for a time. Then she burst out, 'Oh, Rosie, how wonderful! Oh how wonderful! The doctor will be delighted . . . And at the Albert Hall!'

'I tried to get through twice last night, but they said the line was engaged; I wanted him to know first. I was going to try again this morning, but there wasn't time, as I caught the first train. Oh, I was glad to get out of London!' she added. 'I didn't like the little I saw.'

Mrs Mullen still stood shaking her head and gaping at her daughter. The shake became a jerk, and she blinked her eyes rapidly. Rosie said banteringly, 'You'll have to make a fur coat with those rabbit skins you're curing, Ma, and get going on a dress suit for me da; he won't be able to sit in a box with his old mac on.'

'Eeh, lass! I just can't take it in . . . And what the father'll say, God knows. You won't be able to hold him down now . . . Eeh, Kate! And all through the doctor's kindness.' The tears let loose, she put her apron to her face.

'Oh, come on, Ma,' said Rosie; her mother's rare tears always caused her deep embarrassment. 'Come on. Here am I dying for a cup of tea and all you do is howl.'

'Oh yes, lass, you'll be parched. Eeh, but it's knocked me into the middle of next week . . . Yes, let's have a cup o' tea.' But instead of moving, she looked at Kate, and asked, 'Oh Kate, lass, what do you think of it?'

As Mrs Mullen bustled about the kitchen Rosie described her audition to Kate, telling her what the great Caroli had said about her voice. She was still dazed with her stupendous good fortune, for she was the only newcomer to be given one of the four solo parts of the Mass.

'I'm so happy for you,' said Kate. 'It's going to mean a new life for you in many ways. You'll have to get to like London, you know, Rosie – and other big cities. You won't see the old Tyne very often now.'

This remark of Kate's uncovered a dread in Rosie's mind; she knew the new life which was opening for her would separate her from her people, and the thought of leaving her father, in particular, was an actual pain. But the pain was intensified when she realised that the career before her would lift her out of Michael Davidson's life even before he became aware that she was in it. She was twenty, and Michael was eighteen. The two years' difference in their ages seemed a wide gulf now, but once he reached twenty it would narrow. She had found a strange contentment in waiting; he was always nice to her, and in spite of his youthful love for Annie, deep within herself she dared to hope that through her singing and his playing something would emerge. Neither by look nor sign had she indicated her real interest in him. At that party at Christmas she was tempted to sit near him all the time and to choose only him as a partner, but her native caution warned her that Cathleen's caustic remarks, should she sense any bond of interest between them, would come raining down on them; she was wise enough to know that ridicule is like a black frost to budding love. No boy had ever asked to take her out; even the lads round the doors had passed her over. But it hadn't mattered; there was always hope. But now, if she were to leave the north she would leave Michael. But perhaps before that time something might happen. Yes, something might happen.

When Kate left them, Cathleen and Terence had stood for a while looking after her. Then Cathleen flounced round, the smile gone from her face and her lips moving over each other in an odd, rolling motion: 'Who does she think she is? "How dare you! How dare you say such a thing!"' she mimicked. 'She's got a nerve when you come to think of it. She maddens me with that virtuous front of hers. She must forget she had a kid when she was seventeen, and was the doctor's fancy piece for years.'

Terence closed his eyes for a second. It always astounded him, and grated on some finer sensibility, when this girl with her convent education took on the vernacular of some dock woman. She seemed to slip from one character to another so swiftly that he was at a loss to know which was her, and it especially grated that she should speak of Kate so. He was about to make a remark on the inadvisability of misusing rumour when Cathleen's next words arrested him. 'She's as sly as a box of monkeys, and winds Uncle Rodney round her finger. Her latest move is, she has got Miss Annie an allowance. Since the Virgin has decided to go in for teaching, Rodney is allowing her two pounds a week . . . Two pounds a week, mind! But of course, she has the dreadful hardship of buying her own clothes out of it!'

In the ramble of abuse, Terence's thoughts hung round the phrase 'Two pounds a week'. Good Lord, two pounds a week . . . and nothing to do with it! Sometimes he hadn't as much as that to last him a term. He had to count each farthing; if he bought a book, he had to cut down on everything for weeks, even the twopenny packet of Woodbines, bought sheepishly from a little shop in a side street, became a luxury . . . And she had £2 a week!

Cathleen's next remark seemed to precede by a fraction his own train of thought. 'Who do they expect her to marry?' she asked. 'Some wealthy lord? No ordinary fellow will be able to keep her in the way she's being brought up, like some damned princess!'

She was right, Terence thought. Yes, she was right. Cathleen had her feet on the earth; she made you see things in their right perspective. He would neither think nor worry any more about the change in Annie.

Up till that evening at the party he had deliberately thought of her as a child – it was a protection against her – but the next day when they had met the change in her was evident. Her childishness had been replaced by a poise which was far beyond her years; she had not played snowballs with him. He went to the house, on Rodney's invitation, to have a talk, and stayed to tea, wondering all the while at her coolness, which was so foreign to her.

It was the expression on her face when Cathleen put in an unexpected appearance that gave him the explanation. His mind clicked back to the game, and the kisses in the bedroom, and he went hot under the collar at the realisation that some-where in that room Annie must have been hiding. After spending some miserable days wondering how he could explain it to her, but knowing he couldn't, he finally came to the conclusion that it was the very best thing that could have happened. It made him see what he had known all along, that she was the kind of girl who thought a kiss sealed one to her for life; and, as he had already told himself, he wasn't starting anything . . .

Yet he had started something with Cathleen, hadn't he? Yes, but she was different – she didn't take things seriously. And he didn't mean to keep it up . . . But somehow he couldn't get away. He often asked himself what he thought about Cathleen, but got no coherent answer. When she had kissed him in the bedroom that night she had released something that craved constant feeding. He kept himself from her embraces as long as he could, but once he allowed himself to kiss her a power suffused him and tore at him for expression, so that towards the end of the Christmas vac he felt he was becoming drunk with her. He wondered if the intensity of his feeling was due to his lack of association with other girls.

Cathleen broke into his thoughts again: 'Why should she worry about who she marries? She knows Rodney will back a husband, as he does one of his pet projects, like the clinic or Rosie Mullen.' She cast a sidelong glance at him, and suddenly changed character again. 'Come on, pet,' she laughed. 'Why should we care? Let's go up Simonside, where it's quiet. I was a fool to ask you to meet me in the town anyway, but I thought I knew exactly where my respected parents were and that it would be quite safe. I didn't bank on meeting the Countess.'

She tucked her arm in his, and danced along beside him, happy with herself again. She had managed to get quite a lot over. Her gaiety was momentarily chilled by the thought of Steve. He had looked furious. Well, let him. He was always telling her to get a young fellow – and he was right, too. She was becoming just a little bit tired of Steve; he no longer had to be coaxed to make love. Once she got Terence crazy about her, she would drop Steve altogether.

Terence was a bit of a stick-in-the-mud: he never seemed to get past the kissing stage, he needed coaching. For no reason that was apparent to Terence she gave her deep, throaty laugh. Oh, it was going to be fun, especially since the Virgin was goggle-eyed about him . . . That night at the party, she had looked like a sick cow!

They stood kissing behind a hedge in a deserted lane. But today there was a difference. The force of the wind was not stronger than Cathleen: she carried Terence to the brink of a gulf that promised peace to his torn nerves once he jumped. Time and again he said to himself, What odds! but always he hesitated, until at last he drew away, saying, 'It's getting on; I said I'd be home for tea.'

There was a bleakness about Cathleen's face, but she laughed and said, 'All right, pet. We'll go together. I was supposed to be going to look up Uncle Rodney, anyway.'

As they walked back into the town a strange flatness descended on Terence. He was half filled with regret for not taking advantage of the opportunity that had been offered to him with such abandon, and at the same time there was a feeling of repulsion towards Cathleen.

During the half-hour it took them to reach the station he hardly spoke. And she too was strangely silent. But her silence was heavy with power . . . her whole being was in revolt. She had been spurned! The fool! He was afraid. Well, she'd make him forget he was even civilised. With a sudden fierceness she tucked her arm in his and, gripping his hand, twined her fingers about it.

It was like this that Annie came face to face with them in the narrow, walled incline that led to the station. She was coming down in a surge of workmen, faces begrimed with dirt and sweat under their greasy caps, bait tins swinging and clashing. It was in an endeavour to sidestep some people coming up that she found herself wedged for a moment face to face with Terence. Their faces a few inches from each other, their bodies touching, they stood in the surge, isolated. Their eyes, taken unawares, stared their thoughts for one brief second; then Cathleen's arm jerked them apart, and as they were moved on her voice cried back to Annie, 'See you later, darling . . . going to look in on Uncle Rodney.'

Annie walked to the dock gates. The Jarrow tram was in, but she went past it; she would walk to the fifteen streets, she must think. If a thing worries you it must not be buried, Rodney had said, it must be brought to the surface, right out into the open, and dissected; it was the only way to cure a worry. Oh, if she could only cure herself of this feeling. She thought she had, but now it was back, as bad as ever . . . worse, because of the arm that had been tucked in his. Oh God, forgive me. Oh sweet Lady, forgive me. Stop me from hating her . . . How did she know he was back? They must have been writing to each other. Oh Mother of God, take all jealousy from me. He must like her or he wouldn't be with her, would he? she asked herself. No. And he could never have really liked me, because he's always avoided me; he's avoided me for years. But that night in the hall when he kissed my hand . . . he liked me then. I know he liked me then. And in the lane in the snow . . . Oh , I can't bear it! I wish I were dead and at peace. There's no peace anywhere . . .

That wasn't really true, it was peaceful at home and in the convent. But Sister Ann said peace must be born inside of one; there was no lasting peace to be got from outside. Annie felt that was only partly true, for she had only to enter the convent gates to feel a certain peace flow through her. She loved the convent and everyone in it. That kind of love brought peace. Not the kind of love she felt for Terence, or Brian felt for her. And that was another worry . . . Brian. She had come to be a little afraid of Brian since that night, some weeks ago, when he asked her if she would become engaged to him when she was nineteen. She had said hurriedly, 'No! No! I don't want to become engaged to anyone, now or ever.' The facile good humour had left his face, and she saw what she had often suspected, a Brian strong in his own conceit, unable to accept defeat on his personal merits.

'I won't stop trying,' he said. 'You've been my girl for years, you know you have. One thing I do know: there's no-one else going to have a look-in while I'm around.'

He still visited the house whenever she was home on holiday. Although she had told him plainly that his visits must stop, he would laugh and joke, saying he hadn't come to see her, that there were other members of her family. But under his laughing good humour there was an iron determination which frightened her.

What would it be like, she thought, not to feel frightened, not to worry, and not to have this sickly pain filling her being whenever she thought of Terence Macbane? Would she ever again be the same person she was before Christmas?

She lifted her eyes from the greyness of the road to the sky. There was turmoil even there. Dirty white clouds were scudding frantically across a grey expanse. Nothing but grey, below and above her. The cloud formation at one point seemed to boil, churning round and round. As she watched there came a break; a patch of delicate green showed. It grew bigger, changing tone, colour after colour added to it, now pink, now pearl, now blue . . . Our Lady's blue, she thought. There was a sudden brightness overhead and around her. The greasy street shone; the grey walls became pink-toned and warm; the sun was out. She caught her breath. It seemed like an omen, as if God were telling her not to worry; and a picture of the convent loomed before her eyes. She stopped dead on the road and stared up into the sky. The peace within the convent walls, the gentleness there . . . Sister Ann. Could it be? Could it be that God was telling her what to do? That this was the way? She walked on again slowly, dazed with the thoughts that were crowding into her mind.

Unseeing, she almost ran into a group of four little girls. They stood, shabby and dirty, clapping each other's hands in turn and chanting:

'Okey-pokey, wunfy-fum,
Putty Bo-peep and Calabar-cum,
Chingery-wongery, wingery-woe,
King of the Cannibal Islands.'

They grinned at her, chanting all the while, their noses tilted, one very dirty and ringed with a yellow crust. Annie paused for a while and smiled down on them . . . children. She was going to teach children. She would never have children of her own, but she would be among children always, in the convent. These were from the fifteen streets. They were playing on this very road where she once played. And she thought, with what she imagined was a revelation, that God knew on that far-gone day what he wanted of her. He had let her experience misery and fear; He had shown her wealth and comfort, and let her fall in love . . . For what? To prove to her that they were as nothing, that He wanted her for Himself, that in Him she would find that divine peace . . . once she became a nun.

7

During the Easter holidays the revelation of her true vocation, as Annie had come to think of it, was strengthened day by day. Cathleen's almost nightly popping in, her gaiety, her constant reference to 'my Terence', turned Annie's decision to enter the convent into an intense desire, more intense because her thoughts found no outlet. She must wait until the baby was born, though, before telling Kate. She dreaded her disclosure to Kate and Rodney, but particularly to Kate. She foresaw a struggle, and she wanted no struggle with Kate; she desired only to please her in all things.

It was Saturday morning, and she had been down to the wood to gather primroses for the little altar in her room. She arranged them now in two low, rose-coloured bowls and set one before the statue of Our Lady and the other at the bare feet of the brown-habited St Anthony. In front of the crucifix in the centre of the altar, she laid a red rose from the greenhouse. She stood back and reviewed her handiwork. The altar looked beautiful: surely, surely, if she prayed hard enough, this burning jealousy of Cathleen would go, together with the ache that the very name of Terence Macbane brought up.

Impulsively she knelt down on the little plush hassock and

beseeched God to help her. She was afraid she didn't keep all the good intentions she made; she could only keep them so long as she didn't see Cathleen. But David's voice brought her from her knees, shouting, 'Ooh-ooh! Annie. Where are you?' The bedroom door burst open, and he ran in, crying, 'There's someone downstairs to see you – a man.'

'Oh, David! April Fool's Day is passed . . . Look, darling.' She crouched down on her heels, and faced him, holding his hands. 'It ends, as I told you, at twelve o'clock on the first of April.'

'I like April Fool's Day, but there's a man at the gate. I told him I'd tell you as Mammy and Daddy are at the clinic.'

'Oh, you silly billy!'

'I'm not a silly billy!' He danced away from her and round to the other side of the bed: 'I'm Hannigan Prince.'

'Who?' Annie laughed.

'Hannigan Prince. That's what the postman called me. I like that name . . . Hannigan Prince.' He danced round the room.

'It's a silly name, the postman was just being funny.'

'I like Hannigan Prince.'

'You are David Prince!'

'No. Hannigan. I want to be Hannigan, like you,' David laughed gleefully. Then with a swift change of expression he walked solemnly to the altar and said, 'Annie, why can't I have an altar in my room? I want an altar.'

She took his hand and led him out of the room, saying, 'You have some nice pictures of the baby Jesus.'

'But I want an altar.' They were descending the stairs, and he added, 'Look, there he is, the man at the front door. He's not April Fool, see.'

In the open doorway stood a young man Annie had not seen before. He was tall and well-made, but his face seemed to belie the masculinity of his body, for the delicate bone

97

formation would have given beauty to a woman. He said, 'Good-morning. I didn't ring; the little boy said he would tell you . . . I'm sorry to trouble you, but I'm lost.' He smiled at her.

Annie smiled back at him, thinking what a lovely voice he had. She asked, 'Where do you want to go?'

'Well, I'm looking for the house of a friend of mine, Terence Macbane. I've walked further along the lane, but all I could see were trees and the gleam of water in the distance.'

'That's the stream,' said Annie. 'The Macbanes' cottage is to the right, and their garden runs down to the stream.'

'Thank you.' He stood looking at her for a moment, then stepped back, saying, 'It's rather a lovely old house you have.'

'Yes, isn't it?'

'And a most delightful garden.' He seemed reluctant to take his leave, and smiled at her again. 'Well, I must get along. Goodbye, young sir.' He laughed down on David and, raising his hat, he gave Annie a slight bow. 'Thank you. Goodbye.'

She watched him walk down the path, and when he reached the gate, he turned and gave her a wave. She raised her hand once in return and smiled a farewell, before turning into the house again. He's nice, she thought, and he must be a friend of Terence's, and – the tearing stab came again – Cathleen will get to know him and we'll never hear the last of it. Oh, if only I didn't have to listen to her . . .

For the tenth time in an hour Mrs Macbane went down to the gate and looked along the lane. At last she was rewarded by the sight of her husband. With a backward glance at the cottage, she furtively ran to meet him; and, as in all the twenty-six years of their marriage this had never happened before, Mr Macbane stopped dead and awaited her coming, his first thought being, The lad! Summat's happened to the lad. No, no, nowt must happen to the lad!

98

But when she came close to him and whispered agitatedly, 'It's the lord . . . He's come,' he thought: God Almighty! She's gone barmy. But anyway, that was better than anything happening to the lad. So he said, 'Oh aye . . . Weel, there's plenty of room fer him.' He walked on, glancing at her sideways, and she said, 'You don't understand. You'll have to slip in the back way and get a wash in the scullery.'

'Aye . . . Aye,' he said slowly. 'Weel, yer know, missis, I've never washed in the scullery yet, and I'm not going to start now, not fer anyone, from the bloody Lord downwards.' Nice kettle of fish. And at their time of life, too. But he should've expected it; they all went a bit queer at the change. It'd likely pass. 'The lad in?' he asked.

She answered, 'Yes, of course'; then plucked at his arm in agitation: 'What's the matter with yer? You don't understand. Don't wash in the room, man, the lord has never likely seen anything like that.'

He drew his brows down in a puzzled frown and shook his head. 'Weel, don't fash yerself,' he said soothingly; 'He's seed more than that in His time, if ye're to believe the Book.'

She looked at him, puzzled, and dropped a step behind him. He turned in by the little gate and walked resolutely to the front door. Pushing it open, he marched over the threshold, only to pull up short, his mouth dropping open and his whole demeanour showing surprise. He stood gaping at the tall man rising from the armchair by the fire. God, what a blasted fool he was! It must be Terence's lord. She wasn't barmy. He glanced quickly back at his wife with a look as near to an apology as he would allow himself.

Terence was standing by the hearth. There was an air of defiance about him. He moved forward, saying in a voice that seemed too loud for the room, 'This is my father . . . Da, this is Lord John Dane Dee.'

The young man came forward with outstretched hand, and

Mr Macbane went automatically to place his in it, then with-drew it again, saying, 'I'm reet pleased to meet yer, sir. But see, I'm all muck.'

Dane Dee laughed and gripped the reluctant hand, shaking it heartily. 'Mine will be all the better for it,' he said. 'And I, too, am very glad to meet you, Mr Macbane. I must apolo-gise for coming like this without an invitation, but I really came to renew my efforts to persuade Terry here to join me in a little sailing before we go up to Oxford again. But I must admit I have failed. So,' he laughed, 'I shall spend the rest of the vac making him show me Tyneside.'

'Aye,' said Mr Macbane. 'Weel, there's not much to see round here. Nowt but muck.' He looked at his son.

He knew why Terence wouldn't go with this fellow. It was hard when you couldn't stand your whack. He felt his wife take his bait tin from his hand, and he made a big effort to assert himself as boss of his house and as host: 'Sit doon, sir . . . Sit doon and make yerself at home, for ye're very welcome.'

He sat down, and listened intently to Dane Dee talking easily on. But he wasn't taking in what was being said, for he was thinking: A lord in my house! By, who'd've believed it? And a pal of our Terence's. Eeh, lad, wait till this gets aboot the pit!

Terence brought him to himself by saying, 'You'll want to get washed; we'll have a walk.' There was again the same odd note of defiance in Terence's voice. Mr Macbane hurriedly rose to his feet, and with raised hand exclaimed, 'No, lad. No. Sit yerself still. There's nowt to stop me washing in the scullery, nowt at all.'

Giving an imperceptible shake of her head, Mrs Macbane stared at her husband, then followed him into the scullery.

Dane Dee remarked to Terence: 'He seems a fine man.'

'He's all right,' said Terence non-committally.

'You're very like him, you know.'

'I suppose that's to be expected.'

'Oh, come on!' Dane Dee appealed. 'I know I shouldn't have landed on you like this; but being in the next county, it seemed such a good idea to look you up, and I thought it would be fun if we could have a week on the river. If I'd written you'd only have said no. Do unbend. Be yourself. You know what's the matter with you, Terry, don't you? You're a snob.'

Terence made a sound like a snort, and leant his head back against the chair, saying nothing. How easy it was for people like John to call others snobs! Why the Devil had he come? He belonged in Oxford, to discussions and poetry, to walks by the river. Up there, he himself had contrived for a time to be on the same plane with him, at least mentally. Now he felt he never could be again. Before the vac John had written to him at the school where he was spending the term doing his teaching practice, asking him to go on a motor tour of France and afterwards to stay for a time at his sister's place in Northumberland. He had refused the offer, saying there was a great deal of work he must get through during the vac. He realised now that John must have guessed he was hard-up, for they had spent much of their leisure time together at Oxford during the term preceding his teaching practice, and not once did John suggest they should go anywhere which would cost money. He liked his friend. With the exception of one thing, he thought he was a fine fellow. That one thing was his casual attitude towards women. But he wished he had not come here.

Dane Dee leant forward and put his hand on Terence's knee. 'You put too small a value on yourself . . . Come on. Snap out of it! Whether you like it or not, I'm going to enjoy my stay on Tyneside. I've left the car in the village,' he added; 'she wants a bit of first aid, I've been running her hard . . . We'll get around.'

Terence relaxed. It was impossible to keep on one's guard against such a friendly overture and he was really glad to see John. He gave a half-smile, and was about to say, 'All right, just as you say,' when John went on, 'Extraordinary-looking neighbour you have . . . Never seen such a blonde . . . green and gold goddess.'

Casting a keen, startled glance at him, Terence rose hastily from his chair.

'Ah-ha!' said John.

'No, it isn't ah-ha!' Terence snapped, and suddenly felt ridiculous.

'Then if it isn't ah-ha, why the excitement? All right, all right, I promise you faithfully, no trespassing. Relax, man. Relax.'

'It isn't that. Oh, forget it!' Terence closed his eyes for a moment and turned away. What an utter fool he was! But the idea of John amusing himself with Annie was infuriating. His friend's exploits with women were well known to him, and they never ceased to puzzle him, for he knew Dane Dee to be deeply in love with the girl he was going to marry. She was at present on a visit to America with her parents, which accounted for his being at a loose end. Although the marriage was partly a matter of arrangement between two old families, fortunately both the parties concerned had fallen in love. But that did not stop John from having his affairs, and the thought that he would likely make Annie Hannigan one of them was unthinkable.

'Come on,' said John, getting up. 'Let's walk this mood off.'

In the scullery, Mrs Macbane washed her husband's back as he stood naked in the tin bath. He chuckled as he soaped his arms. 'I thought ye'd gone barmy, lass, I thought yer meant God had come. Fancy our lad with a lord fer a pal, eh, missis? He's gettin' hisself some posh friends: thor's that doctor's lass tacking aroond him . . . Not that I give much to her, somehow . . . And now a lord pops in to see him. Just like that!' He snapped his fingers. 'Eeh, by, lad! Eh?'

Mrs Macbane said nothing. Posh friends or no posh friends, she knew her lad wasn't happy. Her mind couldn't formulate the term 'internal conflict'; she could only think: He's not happy inside.

Kate, Rodney and Annie sat looking at Cathleen, who was standing in the middle of the drawing-room, moving her hands expressively as she talked. 'I think John's a pet . . . And can't he make that car move! Phew! Fancy' – she turned towards Annie – 'my Terence hobnobbing with a lord!'

Annie's expression did not change from its fixed smile, and the pain behind it hurt Kate so much that she felt almost compelled to get up and go to her, to touch her and to give her some comforting word. It was with great difficulty that she continued to sit still and listen.

'John wanted us to go to a play in Newcastle,' went on Cathleen, 'but old Terence wouldn't go.' She made a wry face and pursed up her full red lips. 'Stupidly independent! But as I told him, that fellow has so much money he doesn't know how to get rid of it . . . You know, Uncle Rodney,' she turned to where Rodney sat watching her with unconcealed amusement, 'his family date back to the fifteenth century. I looked it all up today. And he's the only son. And what do you think? He's got his own yacht.'

Rodney let out a burst of laughter. 'Poor Terence! I can see what's going to happen to him. Thrown in the gutter for a lord!'

'Oh, stop teasing me, Uncle Rodney!' Cathleen ran to him and shook him playfully by the shoulders. 'I wouldn't give

Terence up for the world . . . Exchange my Terence?' She turned swiftly from Rodney on a high note of exclamation, and her eyes seemed to send streaks of dark light towards Annie as she continued, 'Terence would have something to say about that . . . No. I was only thinking, what a chance for you, Annie!'

Kate's face stiffened. This was like sticking pins in a fly. Oh, why didn't Annie fight her? Why didn't she say something instead of sitting there with that fixed smile on her face? It was unnatural. She rose, saying, 'I'm a little tired; I think I must say good-night, Cathleen.'

'Oh well, I'm just going,' said Cathleen. 'It's nearly ten, and I've got to go home by myself tonight.' She grimaced. 'It's my own fault; I insisted they should have this evening to themselves. Good-night, pet.' She reached up and kissed Rodney, who had risen and was standing by Kate.

Kate saw the red lips press into Rodney's cheek, and she shivered. What was it about this girl that repulsed her so? She seemed to turn an affectionate kiss into the embodiment of sex. She remained still when Cathleen's hand touched her. 'Good-night, Kate. Take care of yourself.'

Cathleen's voice, softly sympathetic, elicited no reply from Kate, but Rodney answered, 'Good-night, my dear. Be a good girl, mind.'

She laughed and flashed what was meant to be a wicked glance at him. And over her shoulder, as she went out, she called, 'Good-night, Annie.' And her voice, ending on a mocking note of laughter, cried, 'You be a good girl too, mind.'

Rodney followed Cathleen into the hall, and Kate turned to where Annie sat, quite still, the smile fixed on her face. Standing in front of her, she said softly, 'Annie, my dear . . .' They looked at each other, their eyes wide. 'My dear,' said Kate again, 'don't mind.'

'I hate her!' Annie's voice, a mere whisper, was thick with

concentrated feeling. 'I hate her so much I feel I could kill her! . . . It's wrong, I know it's wrong, but I can't help it. Oh, Mam! There' – she relaxed against the chair and inhaled deeply – 'I've said it! Oh, Mam, am I wicked?' She looked up beseechingly.

'No, my dear. No. If it were me I think I should fly at her. Coming in here night after night bragging about that fellow!' Kate put out her hand and stroked Annie's hair.

Annie caught it and held it tightly between her own. 'Rodney likes her. He really likes her!'

Kate shook her head. 'Yes, I know. But it's mostly because he thinks he owes so much that cannot be paid for Peter's and Peggy's kindness to him after he came back from the war. I'm sure his liking is mostly because of that, dear.'

Annie shook her head, unable to understand. 'I'm going to bed. It's dreadful to feel like this, dreadful. It makes you hate yourself for hating.'

They kissed, and Kate held her tightly for a moment, then watched her go out. If only there were some way in which she could help. She heard Rodney call after Annie, 'Good-night, princess.' And when he came in he remarked, 'She seems a bit off-colour. Is anything wrong?'

'No,' said Kate, after a pause, during which she had been tempted to tell him what the trouble was. But she could hear him saying in his tolerant way, 'Well, you know, dear, you can't order love . . . We two should know that.' And he would kiss her and repeat his old formula on Cathleen, 'She's a bit wild, but there's no harm in her.'

Rodney asked, 'Will you go to bed, my dear, while I do a last round at the clinic? I'm not happy about Tony Batey. I could phone Sister, but I'd rather have a look at him . . . Will you be all right?'

'Perfectly, darling.'

'And you'll go to bed?'

'No, not yet. I'm not really tired. I only said I was to speed our parting guest.' They laughed together. 'How long will you be?' she asked.

'Oh, not more than twenty minutes, I should think.'

'Well, I'll come and meet you in a little while . . . Yes, I will,' she insisted as he began to protest. 'It's a beautiful moonlight night and I'll sleep better for a little walk.'

'Mind you see it's only a little one,' he warned her before going out.

Kate thought of going upstairs to Annie, but decided against it. Tomorrow she would talk to her. She waited fifteen minutes after Rodney's departure before setting out to meet him. The moon wasn't as bright as she had imagined. It was sailing along behind drifts of pearl-grey cloud; now and again it would escape, and the path before her would show each blade of grass silver-pointed, and in the brightness the cypress hedge would become one with its shadow and seem to have immense depth.

When she reached the swimming-pool, which lay by the side of the stream, the moon disappeared behind a bank of cloud, and she stood waiting, hoping it would reappear, for she liked to see the reflection of the bridge in the stream and the bushy top of the otherwise naked Scotch fir, which grew on the far bank, cast its shadow across the pool. But the pearl mist about the moon thickened, and she walked slowly on.

The path broadened and met the main drive to the clinic. She turned into the drive, and in the distance she could see the lights of the clinic, like little lanterns hanging on the trees. She decided to walk no further, and made for the rustic seat that stood on the grass verge, where she sat down to wait for Rodney.

The wood around her was alive with soft hushed movement. She wasn't aware of it until she sat quite still. Then the silence became full of scurryings and flutterings.

When she first heard the whisper, it came to her as part of the night sounds, causing her no alarm. But when it was repeated, and followed by a 'Shh!' she stiffened and sat alert. Someone was behind her in the thicket, and he wasn't alone. Tramps, perhaps; the roads were full of them now, a mixture of the workless, the residue of the war, and the idle who would neither work nor want. The wood often bore evidence of their little fires. Should she get up and walk on, or sit still? Evidently they weren't sure of her whereabouts. Rodney should be here at any minute. She wasn't afraid; they wouldn't touch her; very likely they were the couple of young men Summy had fed earlier in the day . . . Still, she wished Rodney would come.

The whisper came again, and this time it brought Kate to her feet, for she recognised the voice and she heard the whispered words, 'Go and see.' Holding herself taut, Kate stepped behind the seat to where the shadows were deepest. She knew if Cathleen found her here she would accuse her of spying on her and Terence.

A few feet away someone was moving. She felt the movement rather than heard it, it was so cautious. Then on the edge of the shadow of the trees appeared a bulky figure. After standing quite still for a time it turned its head, first up, then down the drive. Kate saw the pale blur of the face standing out against the darkness of the clothes. She gripped her coat tightly about her, and drew in her breath. She felt that the great start of surprise she gave must have been audible. For a moment it was impossible to take in the meaning of the situation: Cathleen and Steve. Cathleen and Steve!

Steve moved back into the thicket as noiselessly as he had emerged. There was no sound for a while, until Cathleen's voice, low and biting, said, 'Sneaking around!' Now the voices seemed to Kate to be almost behind her back. Steve was saying, 'He's likely at the clinic, and she's going to meet him, though I've never known them go up there so late as this. You'll have to go out through the wood; you should have done that in the first place. My God!' – there was terror in his voice – 'we nearly walked into her.'

'Whose fault was that?'

'Look,' said Steve, 'get this straight, once and for all: you've done all the ordering and arranging so far, you'd take any risk to suit yourself. Now you're going to take them to suit me.'

'But if I don't want to . . . if I don't want to come? What about that?'

'You'll come nevertheless. You started something that's grown a bit too big for you.'

'You're jealous.'

'Yes, but not in the way you imagine . . . I've told you to leave Macbane alone.'

'But you told me I should get a young fellow.'

'Yes, I did. But not Macbane.'

'Why not him?'

'That's my business.'

'Ho-ho! He's mine too, very much mine.'

Kate closed her eyes tightly as she heard Cathleen say, 'Don't! Don't be the he-man!' and Steve reply, 'He-man! I couldn't be he-man enough for you at one time . . . By God! I could kill you for what you've done, egging me on till I'm half mad.'

'Oh, don't talk like a male virgin.'

There was a sound of a ringing slap, then silence. Cathleen's voice sounded old and thin as it came to Kate's ears, saying, 'That was a mistake which you'll pay for . . . Don't think you can frighten me. How will it sound when I tell them you were in love with Kate, and when you found out that I knew you enticed me to your room and seduced me, a young girl, still at school?'

To Kate the night became dense. She moved slowly out of

the shadows and walked along the verge as if sleep-walking . . . Steve . . . poor Steve. There was no blame in her mind for him. *This* was what was worrying him. Oh, that girl! She was evil. Evil. She was quite capable of doing or saying anything. Kate began to hurry. She must see Rodney and tell him; he would understand. And if Cathleen were exposed it would free Terence . . . Surely Terence wouldn't even look at her if he knew . . . And Rodney – he would know at last what Cathleen was really like . . . But what was it Cathleen said she would say? That Steve was in love with her? Cathleen's numerous hints and insinuations during the past years flooded back to Kate in all their meaning. She thought of the day last month when they met on the Jarrow road. Cathleen would tell Rodney this, as an illustration. But Rodney wouldn't believe her. No, he wouldn't. Of course he wouldn't. She began to hurry, her feet moving with her mind. Rodney would laugh . . . But would he? He couldn't bear to think of her having even a friendly interest in any man other than himself. Was Steve really as fond of her as Cathleen said? Of course not. He had never shown her anything but the deepest respect. It was utter nonsense. Poor Steve!

She started to run, then pulled herself up, thinking: I mustn't do this; I mustn't be silly. Almost as she stopped her foot slipped into a shallow ditch, and to save herself from falling she grabbed at the nearest thing to hand, which was a young silver birch. It bent with her weight, twisting her sharply. Every pore in her body registered the flash of pain that shot through her. She lowered herself slowly on to the grass. Her breath came in gasps. What had she done? Oh God, what had she done? She remained still, waiting. It came again, more terrible in its intensity and sharpness; it shot through her brain, and blotted itself out with its own force. When it passed, she was lying along the grass, her fingers deep in the earth. She was conscious of thinking, I am dying;

Rodney will be too late. Then she grasped at a straw: But Steve's here. Steve will help me.

When the pain came again she screamed, 'Steve! Steve!' She continued to scream, 'Steve! Steve!' She knew she couldn't bear this and live.

It seemed a long time before she returned from some deep, deep place and heard Steve's voice, coming as if from the top of a high mountain, repeating, 'It's all right. It's all right. They're coming. They're coming.' As the agony seized her again she clung to him, and the last thing she remembered was the grip of his arms about her as she went down.

8

 ∽

They took the baby out of Kate's body at four o'clock in the morning. While Peter, a gynaecologist and two nurses worked in the room above, Rodney and Annie waited below. All night they had been together, not moving far from each other. Whether sitting, walking or standing, Annie kept near her stepfather. Rising above the sick terror in her heart was the desire to help and comfort him; never had she imagined that this god-like man, as he had always seemed to her, could be afraid, yet his fear was so apparent as to make him appear young in her eyes.

Mrs Summers came in with a tray; her face was red and swollen. 'Try to drink this strong cup of tea, doctor. It'll do you good,' she said. As Rodney didn't answer, she motioned to Annie to press her point, then went heavily out.

Annie placed a cup at Rodney's hand, then sat down beside him and continued to say her rosary, her fingers moving over the beads in the pocket of her dress.

Looking out of the window into the chill bleakness which precedes the dawn, Rodney cried silently, Kate! Kate! Don't leave me! Oh, beloved, don't leave me.

The aeon of pain-filled time which had passed since last

night would, he knew, leave its mark on him for ever. If only she had spoken to him between her spasms of excruciating torture. But during the brief spells of consciousness it was Steve's name she called. The gynaecologist asked who Steve was. His manner of assumed disinterest when told Steve was the chauffeur so annoyed Rodney that he felt compelled to explain that it was Steve who found Kate, and that, as he was the last person her conscious mind registered, she would naturally repeat the name. The gynaecologist had said soothingly, 'Yes, yes. Of course.'

But now she wasn't calling; they were cutting her up. The flesh would be folded back over her stomach; there would be the tangle of intestines . . . One little slip! One little slip! Oh God, if only he didn't know it, step by step! He buried his face in his hand and groaned, and Annie stood up and put her arms about him, cradling his head on her breast and soothing him. She kept murmuring, 'There . . . there,' very much as Kate herself would have done.

After what seemed another eternity the door at the far end of the room opened, and they both turned to stare at Peter. Rodney got to his feet, and Peter, coming towards him, said, 'It's all right, man, it's all over. It's a little girl, and she's alive.'

Rodney gave an impatient shake of his head.

'Kate'll be all right too,' said Peter, with a casualness he was far from feeling; 'that fellow's a marvel. He's coming down now, and we both need a drink.' He didn't add that he had witnessed what was, even to his professional mind, a miracle: Kate should have been dead an hour ago; she'd never be as near again. Was it the will to live, or someone's prayers? He didn't know. Only one thing was sure: she'd had her last baby.

Rodney closed his eyes. To some unseen force to which he had been pleading for hours he said, simply, 'Thank you.' Then he turned to Annie, and they smiled wanly at each other.

'Can I see her, Uncle Peter?' Annie asked eagerly.

'In a couple of days' time, perhaps,' he said, patting her shoulder comfortingly.

Left alone, Annie went to the window-seat and knelt down. She took her rosary from her pocket and began to recite the five Glorious Mysteries. All night she had said the five Sorrowful, dwelling on Christ's Agony in the Garden, but now the agony was over and she prayed with deep thanksgiving.

When she at last rose to her feet she stood and leant her head against the windowframe . . . Never again would she say she hated anyone. The blinding hate she felt for Cathleen last night was, she imagined, in some way responsible for what had happened to her mother, as if God was showing her there could be greater pain and greater losses than her own little personal ones. And her hate was a greater sin, too, because of what she had already promised to God. To promise to give Him your life, then to let hate consume you through jealousy, was dreadful. Oh, she would try to be better. She would.

She gazed at the room's reflection in the windowpane. Everything stood out in minute detail: the large open fireplace with the firedogs glinting in the reflection of the flames, the white bearskin rug on the red carpet, the two small railing-topped tables, the deep armchairs, all combining to make a picture of comfort. It's beautiful, she thought, but I would never have wanted to see it again if Mam had died. And she nearly died, I could feel it. I have so much, and I am so ungrateful. Oh God, make me grateful and content.

The night had seemed endless, but now it must soon be dawn. She had never seen the sunrise. She had a sudden desire to go outside into the chill air and to see the sky lifting its dark curtain to light and warmth. Taking her hooded coat from the hall-stand, she went outside and walked slowly down the curving path to the gate. But even before reaching it, even before she saw the glow of the cigarette, she was aware of someone standing there. She paused, and a voice said, 'It's all right, it's only us.'

'Oh!' she said, and put her hand to the neck of her coat and pulled it tighter about her throat.

'How is she, hinny?' It was Mr Macbane's voice.

Annie replied, 'The baby's born, it's a girl. And the doctor says Mam will be all right.'

'Ah! Thank God . . . Well, that's summat to know. Now I'll get back an' tell the missis.'

Annie stepped nearer to them. 'Oh, Mr Macbane, you should have come in; you shouldn't have stayed out here all night.'

'Well, we wor a bit worried, ye know. We haven't been oot all the time; we took our turns.' Mr Macbane had helped Steve to carry Kate on a stretcher to the house, and her groans were still ringing in his ears. He said, 'Well, I'm glad it's over . . . I'm off, lad.' His steps crunched away, and Annie stood watching the glowing tip of the cigarette as Terence inhaled.

'It was good of you to wait,' she said.

And he answered, low, 'It would have been dreadful if anything had happened to her.'

In the silence between them the cigarette glowed more deeply, until Annie hesitantly said, 'I came out to see the sunrise.'

It was some time before he replied, 'You won't see it from here, because of the trees. You'll have to go to the end of the lane; it rises over Thorpe's cornfield.'

Into their silence a faint rustling sound came from the woods, followed by definite movements in the hedge opposite and to right and left of them. A bird called. Then another. There were answering calls. Then the birds all seemed to speak at once, a crescendo of sound filling the air, blending into a chorus which soared up to the paling stars.

Annie looked up into the sky. It seemed to be getting higher and higher, as if the birdsong was pushing away the black night; the dawn was breaking.

When she again looked at Terence, she could see the sharp outline of his face. He was gazing at her. The hood had fallen back from her head, and to him she appeared as she had done that night on the step of the cottage when she came to ask him to the party. Only now, even in the dim light, he could see she looked tired and her face was strained.

'I've never heard them make such a noise before.'

'You must sleep well,' he said, 'for they always do. This is the dawn chorus. Some of them start much earlier, but they all get going with the light.'

'Do you often hear them?' Her voice was impersonal and calm.

'Yes, often. Are you going to the end of the lane?' he asked gently.

She didn't answer for a moment. Then she said quietly, 'Yes.'

He opened the gate, and she passed through, and they walked down the lane together, neither of them speaking. Studiedly, they kept their distance.

When the silence became almost unendurable Annie ventured, 'Term will soon be starting again.'

'Yes, two more days and I go up. When do you go back?'

'Tuesday.'

'It's my last term,' he said.

'Are you sorry?' she asked.

'Yes and no. I'll be glad when I'm teaching.'

They were talking like polite strangers. There seemed nothing more to be said, and again silence fell between them until they reached the end of the lane. And there Terence exclaimed, 'We're just in time. Look at that!' His voice was full of wonder, as if he were beholding the scene for the first time.

Annie looked across the cornfield on the opposite side of the main road. Over its far edge came the heralds of the rising sun: rays of purple, red and green, spreading out into a fan of flame, sweeping up into the sky and sending the stars to their night.

'It's wonderful!' she breathed, entranced, wondering why she had never seen this before. Every morning this happened, and yet she was seeing the sunrise for the first time. She realised dimly that one of nature's greatest wonders was witnessed each dawn by only a handful of the world's millions. Sleep claimed weary bodies, and most people who were about at this hour were, like herself, only there through some unusual occurrence. Of course there were exceptions, like Terence, who got up to see the sunrise, or walked all through the night to meet it. Yes, he was different. She looked at him and found his eyes fixed on her face. His lips were apart as if he were on the point of saying something. She would not meet his eyes, but turned back up the lane, saying, 'I'll have to be getting back, Rodney may be wanting me.' That's how he had looked at her in the hall at the party, and then kissed Cathleen afterwards.

She mustn't let it affect her, she must keep cool and calm.

He walked by her side to the gate, and there she turned to him and smiled gently, saying coolly, 'Thank you, Terence, for being so thoughtful about Mam . . . Goodbye.' And as she walked up the path she was conscious that he was standing watching her, and her heart suddenly leapt, in spite of her efforts to remember that it meant nothing.

It was about eleven o'clock when Mrs Summers bent over Annie and gently shook her. 'Miss Annie! . . . Hinny! Miss Annie, wake up!'

Annie sat bolt-upright in bed. Wide-eyed, she stared at Mrs Summers. 'It's Mam! She's worse?'

116

'No, no. Nothing like that. She's sleeping peacefully. No. It's young Macbane. He called at the front door and asked for you. He's all ready for the road. I didn't tell him you were in bed, I just told him to wait . . . It won't take you a minute to get your clothes on. Come on now.'

Mrs Summers didn't leave the room until Annie was out of bed and clambering into her clothes.

Every little counts, she said to herself as she went downstairs. Very little escaped Mrs Summers; she went about, as she was apt to say, with her eyes wide open, and she'd had them open for years where Annie and her interest in Macbane were concerned.

Still dazed with sleep, Annie rushed to the bathroom and douched her face with cold water. She decided there wasn't time to do her hair, so she just combed the top smooth, threw the tousled plaits behind her back and hurried downstairs.

Terence wasn't in the hall, but she could see him through the open doorway, standing on the path and talking to David. The sight of him made her pause, and ask herself, Why am I hurrying? What does he want?

She walked slowly towards him. He had his back to her and was saying, 'I sleep in a field; my little tent's in here.' He patted the bulging knapsack on his back.

'And is your bed in there too?' David asked.

'Yes.'

'Oh! . . . I wish I could go with you and sleep in a field . . . Oh I do, Terence. Could I come?'

'Yes, when you're a little bigger.'

'How much bigger?' asked David. Then, catching sight of Annie, he exclaimed, 'Oh, Annie, Terence is going to sleep in a field . . . I want to go and sleep in a field too.'

Terence turned and said hurriedly, 'I called to see how your mother is . . . and . . . and to say goodbye.'

Annie didn't answer. He had never before called to say

goodbye. She stared at him, and he continued, 'I do hope she is better soon.'

'Thanks,' she murmured. 'Apparently she is still sleeping.' And after a pause she added, 'I thought you had another two days?'

He hitched the knapsack further up on his back. 'I've decided to cycle back,' he replied. 'It'll take me a couple of days . . . And my friend returns home today. There's nothing much to stay for.' As if realising what his words implied, his face flushed, and he bent down to put on his cycle clips.

David cried, 'Let me! Let me help you, Terence!'

Terence laughed, and allowed David to turn the clips around his trouser legs. Then he straightened and looked at Annie once more, and his steady, intent gaze seemed to be asking her something. She turned quickly away and walked towards the gate. He followed, with David hopping along beside him.

'My Mammy's sick,' David was saying. 'And there's a thing in the nursery squealing. Daddy says it's our baby, and wanted me to look. But I wouldn't. My puppy doesn't squeal like that. I'd rather have him, he's fat, and I'm going to call him Hannigan, like me . . . Would you rather have a puppy or a squealy baby, Terence?'

'I'd rather have a puppy.' He caught Annie's glance and smiled, and her eyes dropped before the look in his. 'I hope you enjoy your term,' he said.

'Yes, I hope I do. And you too.' She would remain cool, nothing would disturb her.

'Goodbye, Annie.' He was standing before her. She could scarcely bear to look at him; the nearness of him, the tenderness in his eyes, the thinness that always aroused her compassion were unnerving her. What could he mean? There was still Cathleen. But his voice was low, and saying more than just 'Goodbye, Annie.'

When she did raise her head she returned his smile: 'Goodbye, Terence.'

They looked at one another for a moment longer. Then without another word he mounted his cycle and rode off. He had gone some little way when he turned and called, 'Goodbye, David.'

David ran wildly down the lane after him, shouting, 'Goodbye, Terence! Goodbye! Goodbye, Terence!'

Annie walked slowly up the path, thinking: It means nothing, nothing at all . . . Oh, but if it did! She suddenly skipped the remaining distance to the front door, and there pulled up abruptly with the thought that there was her promise to God – what about that?

It was about seven o'clock the same evening when Cathleen came in, her face a mixture of various emotions. She went straight to Rodney. 'Oh, pet, I'm so sorry. How is she?'

'Still very ill, I'm afraid, Cathleen,' he replied.

'Oh my dear, how awful! And you look quite done in. Haven't you been to bed at all?'

'No,' he said. 'No, I haven't. But I'm going now to try and get an hour.'

'That's right, darling.' She bent and kissed him. 'You mustn't crock up; whatever would Kate do?'

He smiled at her gratefully and patted her cheek. On rising he turned to Annie, who was sitting by the fire, and asked, 'You'll call me, won't you, dear?'

'Yes.' Annie nodded.

'Goodbye, Cathleen. It's good of you to come up.'

'Good of me! . . . Don't be silly' – she kissed him – 'I was worried to death. Now go and have a good sleep. Don't worry, pet, everything will be all right.'

When Rodney had gone Cathleen took his seat and lit a cigarette. She handed the case across to Annie: 'Want one?'

Annie made a motion with her head, and Cathleen laughed. 'Of course you wouldn't, you're not alive yet.' Her voice held none of the softness of a few moments ago. 'What are you staring at?' she asked, then exclaimed, 'Oh! Can you notice it? . . . I don't really need anything on my lashes, but it's fun.'

Annie saw that besides the lipstick Cathleen always used there was colour on her cheeks, and her eyes were darkened with a kind of grease. The lids looked blue and weird.

Cathleen began to ask particulars about Kate. Had Annie seen her when she was brought home? Was she conscious? Only partly, Annie said, and she had kept calling for Steve.

Cathleen raised her eyebrows and said, 'Really!'

After a few moments she stood up, saying, 'Well, I must go and see what's happened to my Terence, there isn't much time left . . . I'll be glad when he's finished and gets a post nearer home.' She looked down on Annie, who was staring at her, and went on, 'What do you think! We may go to Paris in the summer. Isaac Holt, he's a teacher at school, has a studio there, with a couple of rooms attached. It's let up to July, but he says we can pig in with him during the vac.' She gave her deep laugh. 'He'd prefer to pig in without Terence, but I said, "Oh no! Terence or nothing." And do you know John Dane Dee's coming through? He's some boy, that!' She stopped and exclaimed impatiently, 'Why on earth are you staring like that? What are you gaping at?'

Annie stood up and, try as she might, she couldn't keep her voice casual as she said, 'You don't know Terence has gone?'

Without taking her eyes from Annie, Cathleen flicked the end of her burning cigarette at the fire. 'What did you say?' she asked quietly.

'He went back to Oxford this morning, on his bike.'

The cigarette hit the low bar of the grate and bounced back on to the rug. Annie stooped swiftly and tossed it into the fire.

'How do you know?' asked Cathleen. Her dark eyes seemed lost behind the narrowed lids.

A thrill which Annie had no power to prevent made itself evident in her tone: 'He came this morning to see how Kate was, and told me he was going.'

They stared at one another, all their feelings evident. Mingled with their mutual dislike was Annie's triumph and Cathleen's astonishment.

With Terence's renewed interest foremost in her mind, Annie forgot her resolution of the early morning, never to hate again. She had only to see Cathleen for the feeling to rise naturally to the surface. It was now making her imply, through her expression, an affinity with Terence. It was giving her a poise that she knew would madden Cathleen.

Suddenly Cathleen threw back her head and laughed loudly.

'Sh!' cried Annie in alarm. 'Kate's asleep. You might waken her,' and as the thought of Kate came into her mind again she chided herself for forgetting her for the moment because of her own small problems.

Cathleen stopped and, putting out her hand, tapped Annie's cheek sharply: 'Don't get any ideas into that innocent head of yours, darling! Because they'll only have to come out again. Terence and I understand each other . . . Do you see? Do you understand what I mean?'

Annie felt her colour rising, and with it the desire to fight back. 'If that's the case, it's a wonder he didn't let you know he was going, isn't it?'

'See here!' Cathleen, her mouth narrowing, leant forward menacingly. 'It will serve you right if I open your eyes for you. What would you say . . . ?'

She got no further, for the drawing-room door opened and Michael and Rosie came in. Both Cathleen and Annie turned towards them, and Annie said, not without some relief, 'Oh, hello, Rosie. Hello, Michael.'

Cathleen stood looking at her brother and Rosie Mullen. The rage that was consuming her was evident in her face, and Michael unfortunately released it on himself by saying, 'I didn't expect to see you here. I thought you had gone to meet Macbane.'

'And I didn't expect to see *you*!' rapped out Cathleen. 'You are supposed to be at night school.'

Michael's face darkened: 'I asked Father if I could skip it; I wanted to come up and see Annie . . . about Kate,' he ended.

'See Annie!' Cathleen sneered. 'See Annie!' She turned to Annie who was looking anxiously from one to the other. 'It looks as if you've lost your childhood sweetheart as well. Too bad, isn't it?'

Annie flushed scarlet, and Michael took a quick step forward, his boyish face glowering darkly. 'If I were at home,' he gulped, 'I'd . . . I'd . . .'

'Michael! Michael!' Annie cried. 'Be quiet! You know Kate's ill.'

He turned away, saying, 'I'm sorry.'

Cathleen looked at Rosie, who was staring at her. She dropped her eyes in a scornful sweep and, picking up her gloves from a chair, said to no-one in particular: 'Baby-snatching's a criminal offence.'

Michael turned sharply, muttering, 'You . . . You . . .!'

He made to go after Cathleen as she went from the room, but Annie laid a restraining hand on his arm, entreating him: 'Michael . . . not here, please.'

Rosie said nothing. There was a bleakness about her face; it looked cold and pinched, and she seemed to have shrunk. She looked at Michael. He was standing unhappily moving his tie from side to side; his eyes were downcast, and his whole attitude hurt Rosie.

Breaking the uncomfortable silence with an attempt to appear casual, Rosie asked, 'How is Kate now?'

'Just about the same,' Annie replied.

'Is David asleep? Can I go up and see him?'

'He may not be. You can go and see if you like, only don't let him get excited.' Annie felt tense and upset. She blamed herself for the scene that had occurred; she should never have told Cathleen about Terence – causing all this upset, and Mam so ill. What could she have been thinking about?

Rosie went quietly out, while Michael stood looking down into the fire. He would be a big man, like his father, and already had many of his habits, but none of his even temper. He stood now, as his father often did when perplexed, rubbing the back of his neck with his hand. Annie, feeling sorry for him, said soothingly, 'Don't worry, Michael.'

He turned to her. 'Oh, Annie, she spoils everything. There's no peace where she is . . . Annie,' he went on haltingly, 'what she said wasn't true. I still like you, I'll always like you . . . But Rosie . . . well, she's . . . well, you see, she understands music, and . . .'

'Michael, dear, I understand. Oh, I do. And it would be lovely, Michael, if you could like Rosie. She's wonderful when you get to know her.' She had taken his hand, and at this moment she felt old enough to be his mother.

'Oh!' he said, embarrassed. 'Oh! Well, not like that . . . But she's nice to talk to.' He looked at Annie steadily and he didn't sound as boyish as he appeared when he said, 'I'll always like you, Annie. Always. There'll never be anybody like you.' He covered her hand with his other, and finished, 'But somehow I've always known it's useless.'

They hastily drew apart as Rosie came back into the room. She did not look at them, but said, 'He was asleep. Kate's nurse showed me the baby . . . She is tiny!'

'Yes, she is small,' said Annie. 'We are going to call her Angela.'

'Well, I'll be getting back; my mother is anxious to know.'

She turned to leave the room, without appearing to notice Michael.

'This is the second time you've been today,' Annie said; 'you must be tired. Stay a little while, Rosie.'

'Not tonight.' There was a sadness about Rosie's voice that hurt Annie, and as she followed her into the hall she raked her mind to find words to explain about Michael and herself.

Michael, too, followed. He took his coat from the stand, and put it on with an air of bustle.

'You needn't . . .' began Rosie.

'Oh, I may as well go now,' he said offhandedly; 'you can't go all that way by yourself.' He was very much the man.

Rosie glanced at Annie, and was greeted by a swift, reassuring smile. She returned it, and went out saying, 'I'll see you tomorrow then.'

'Me too,' said Michael. 'And give my love to Kate when you see her.'

'I will. Good-night, Michael. Good-night, Rosie.'

Annie went back into the drawing-room, thinking: Oh, why did any of them come? Such an upset, at a time like this . . . But I could have prevented it, if only I had kept quiet. Yet I couldn't keep quiet any longer . . . I've never before been able to hurt her; but I did tonight. It was just a little of my own back for all she has done to me, not only recently, but for years. And she'll spoil Rosie's happiness too; she'll never let her have Michael . . . Poor Rosie. Poor anybody who's unfortunate enough to cross Cathleen's path.

For days Kate lay in a world of dim, moving shapes and faint voices; even the bed seemed to be detached from her. She was only aware of her body as it floated in pain. She remembered faintly the desire to leave it there in the thick mist and to escape beyond to a place that would require no effort from her; she knew that once she was beyond the mist everything

124

would be easy, and she would need to struggle no more. But Rodney wouldn't let her go. This puzzled her, for if he loved her greatly then he should let her go.

It was a week before the mist finally cleared and she awoke one morning to find the shapes clear and sharply defined in the sunshine which filled the room. Rodney was looking down on her, his eyes full of love and relief. 'Darling, you're better this morning.'

She reached up her hand and touched his cheek. 'Quite better, my love.' When she saw the glistening brightness in his eyes she moved her head on the pillow. 'Don't. Oh, don't, my dear. I'm all right.'

He took her hand and pressed his lips to it; and his heart was filled with thanksgiving that at last he could tell himself this was the turning-point . . .

Day followed day in quiet routine: being washed, being fed, lying at peace with her hand in either Rodney's or Annie's, and having an occasional glimpse of the baby.

It was some time before she was allowed to see visitors. And when they did come, the nurse saw to it that they stayed only a matter of minutes. Cathleen called every night. She seemed greatly concerned over Kate, which touched Rodney . . . and puzzled Annie. She hadn't expected Cathleen to call again for some time at least, after the scene in the drawing-room. Cathleen could have learnt of Kate's progress from her father, but she still came every evening, and from the first spoke to Annie as though nothing out of the ordinary had passed between them. A few days ago she had mentioned Terence, saying, 'Annie, my love, it's all been explained. I've had a letter from my bad boy telling me why he went off in a hurry.'

With a sick feeling in her heart Annie wondered what the explanation was. It couldn't have upset Cathleen, for she was very bright, in fact more vivacious than ever.

Annie had cause to wonder still more when Terence's first

letter came. The old racing and leaping started within her, and she read reams of unspoken thought into the few stilted lines. In a daze, she went up to her room, holding the letter to her. Terence had written . . . he had written to her! Would he write to her if he were still writing to Cathleen? Was Cathleen telling the truth? This wasn't a love letter, she knew, but she felt it meant more than it said. And there still remained the fact that he had gone away without seeing Cathleen.

Sitting on the side of her bed, she read the letter again:

Dear Annie,

I do hope by now your mother is better. She has been very ill, my mother tells me. She also tells me you are still at home. This means you will miss some of the term; but I don't suppose you mind very much, as your mother will naturally be your first concern. I should like to hear of her progress, if you have the time to spare and feel so inclined.

Yours sincerely,
Terence Macbane

He would like to hear from her! She stared unseeing at the little altar.

It was the slant of the sun, glinting on the nails prominent through the feet of Christ, that brought her to the fact of where her thoughts were leading. Looking with a shamefaced glance at the altar, she whispered, 'You understand, don't you? I can't help loving him. I've tried.'

Jesus still hung his head from the cross, and St Anthony stared back at her with a look of sadness on his face. With a feeling of guilt, Annie left the room and went into Kate's. Standing by the bed, she said simply, 'I've had a letter from Terence.'

Kate said nothing, but took Annie's hand and squeezed it tightly.

'It isn't a . . .' Annie began. 'Well, it's just . . . Well, it's about you really,' she laughed. 'Read it.'

Kate shook her head. 'No. I don't think one should read someone else's letters . . . Are you going to answer it?'

Annie nodded, her eyes soft and bright.

'Don't tell anyone else you have received it,' Kate said. 'You understand?' They looked at each other, then Annie went swiftly from the room and back into her own. She sat down at her writing-table, and after staring at a blank page for some time suddenly began to write . . .

Kate relaxed against the pillows; Annie's news had solved a problem for her. With returning strength, the events of the fateful night had gradually come back to her, and she was torn between telling Rodney or keeping silent. If she told him he would sack Steve, his faith in Cathleen would be shattered and he would never treat her in the same way again. This, through time, would be noticed by Peter and Peggy, and would result in strained relations. Then again, Steve might come into the open and say he wanted to marry Cathleen. This would free Terence. She felt in her heart that Terence more than liked Annie, that he had always liked her, and had it not been for Cathleen they would have come together naturally. But now, in spite of Cathleen, Terence was showing an interest in Annie.

This decided Kate to keep silent, and so eased her mind about Rodney's attitude towards Steve. Terence's interest in Annie would also erase another worry: Brian. She shuddered at the thought of Brian having Annie. Annie's slender fragility against what was fast becoming a mountain of flesh made her a little sick when she even imagined the possibility.

She wasn't prepared for Cathleen's visit. Even with her decision made, which meant she would have to act as if nothing had happened, she found she couldn't look at her. The nurse showed Cathleen in, saying, 'Only two or three minutes, mind.' And there she was, standing by the bedside.

'How are you?' Cathleen's voice was level and strangely cold.

Kate's eyes travelled over the expanse of the eiderdown before she lifted them to meet Cathleen's. She found herself unable to answer, or to pretend normality. She was thinking: She's bad . . . bad.

Cathleen's eyes, like polished black stones, bored into Kate's. She knew for certain now that Kate had heard all that was said in the wood that night, and as she had obviously said nothing about it, she concluded with satisfaction that Kate was afraid. She kept her eyes, unblinking, fastened on Kate's, putting into them all the menace of which she was capable.

Kate began to tremble. She said weakly to herself: I'm not fit to cope with her. Oh, why did they let her in? She made an effort at control and forced her eyes away from Cathleen's.

But when Cathleen spoke, a wave of fear passed over her. 'Steve is very concerned about you,' Cathleen said softly. There was a pause, during which Kate shook her head. Then Cathleen went on, 'He's always concerned about you. I shall tell him how you are; it will relieve his mind. I don't think he likes to ask Uncle Rodney.' She stood for an instant longer, then went quietly out.

Downstairs, Cathleen found Annie in the dining-room, helping Mrs Summers to clear the table. Annie didn't turn to meet Cathleen, but went on piling up the plates. The brightness of her face did not escape Cathleen, who said casually, 'I've been clearing out my locker at school, and I've brought some of my sketches to show Uncle Rodney . . . Like to see them?'

'Yes,' said Annie politely. 'Yes, I would.'

'Just a minute then.'

Cathleen went into the hall and brought back a large portfolio, and put it on the now cleared table. She handed Annie a study of two boys climbing a tree. And Annie's praise was genuine when she said, 'I don't know how you do it. This is splendid! You have even got the stretch of the leg muscles under the skin.'

'Yes, I like that one,' said Cathleen. 'And look at this.'

'Why, it's Michael's head . . . Oh, that's wonderful.'

'Here,' Cathleen pushed the heap of sketches towards her: 'go through them yourself.'

Annie drew a chair up to the table and began to look at one sketch after another, making comments on the merits of each. Cathleen stood with her elbow on the mantelpiece, smoking and waiting. She hadn't long to wait. There came a break in Annie's comments. The break lengthened into a tense silence. The fire fell inwards with a *plop* and Cathleen said languidly, 'Have you found a bad one? They can't all be masterpieces, you know.'

Annie stared at the sketch before her. It was of Terence . . . Terence quite naked. He was standing on a rock with his hands above his head, poised for a dive; his black hair was dripping with water, and the water was gleaming on his thighs; the shadow of a cliff behind threw him into relief.

Annie sprang up from the table, tumbling the chair backwards in her haste. She turned to Cathleen, her face bloodless and her eyes blazing: 'You did this on purpose! I know you did!'

'What on earth—' began Cathleen. 'Good heavens! What's the matter with you, girl?'

She came to the table and looked at the sketch. 'Don't tell me *that*'s upset you. Haven't you seen anyone naked before?' She stubbed out her cigarette with deliberation. 'You must remember, Annie, I'm an artist. I see nude bodies every day.' She gave her deep laugh and threw her head back, as if in

129

surprise: 'Oh! I see. It has shocked you to see old Terence in the nude . . . Well, he's made the same as everyone else. You may not believe it, but he is . . . He'll laugh about this when I tell him. He often poses for me. Why look, I can show you . . .'

She raked among the sketches, and Annie cried out, 'I don't wish to see any more.' She righted the chair, and stood gripping the back.

'You're being silly,' said Cathleen. 'Why don't you grow up, girl? Over eighteen, and afraid to look at what God made!' She gathered the sketches together in feigned annoyance. 'Anyway, why should you mind how I do Terence? It's no business of yours, as I've told you before. And he likes posing for me. He certainly likes the sketches I do of him, for he's asked for this one. I'm taking it with me when I go to see him at the weekend. I suppose you consider that's wrong, too, going to see your boyfriend for a weekend without a chaperone?'

Annie's eyes were blind to everything about her; she was looking at Cathleen, but the intense feeling moving through her blotted Cathleen out. She could see only the naked body of Terence, as Cathleen must have seen it often and often to draw it like that. Her stomach gave a heave, and she thought: I'm going to be sick.

Her vision cleared when she heard Rodney come into the room and say, 'Ah, there you are, Cathleen. I thought you might have gone.' He seemed agitated. 'What happened upstairs, Cathleen? After you left, nurse found Kate in tears, and she had to call me.'

'Happened?' repeated Cathleen in surprise. 'What do you mean, Uncle Rodney?'

'Well . . . what did you talk about? What did you say?'

'Nothing.' Cathleen adopted the attitude of thinking. 'Why, nothing . . . I only asked her how she was, and the usual things one says to sick people.'

'Can't you think of anything that might have upset her?'

'No, of course not . . . Only . . . well, I mentioned Steve.' Cathleen saw the tightening of Rodney's jaw, and went on, 'I said he was worried about her.' She looked up at him, her eyes innocent and childlike in their perplexed stare.

'Why did you say that?' asked Rodney grimly.

'Oh, just because the other day he told me that he was concerned about her. I suppose it's natural, since it was he who found her that night.'

That was it, then: Steve's name was mentioned, and Kate cried . . . In the name of God, why? he asked himself. Surely . . . No, no, he wouldn't even think of it . . . Yet when he asked what the trouble was she would only say, 'Don't let Cathleen Davidson up here again. I don't like her.' He knew that Kate had never liked Cathleen, but she had never before been so openly hostile to her.

He tried to read behind Cathleen's limpid gaze. Did she know something about Steve and Kate? Great heavens! what was he thinking? . . . His Kate, who loved him as no man had ever been loved before! But there *was* something. What was it? Kate's continual crying of Steve's name that night, then Steve giving a week's notice . . .

He said, 'Do you know Steve has left us?'

'What!' Cathleen's exclamation was sharp. The pose of the child dropped from her. 'You say Steve's left? That's impossible. I saw him . . .' She pulled herself up. 'When did he leave?'

'Today.'

'Today?' repeated Cathleen. 'Did he just . . . go off?'

'No, he gave me a week's notice.'

Cathleen's incredulous look was genuine. 'Does Kate know?' she asked softly.

'No' – Rodney's voice was curt – 'I didn't tell her. It might have upset her that he should leave us at this time.'

131

'Yes . . . yes,' said Cathleen slowly. She was recovering from her surprise.

Rodney, watching her closely, thought: What is it? She knows something. What can there be to know?

Cathleen turned away, tied up her portfolio and asked casually, 'Did he say where he was going? Has he got another job?'

'He said his brother in Harrogate wanted him to go into his garage business.'

'Oh,' said Cathleen evenly. 'I didn't know he had any family; I thought he was a lone man.' Then she added, rather pathetically, 'I seem to have caused quite an upheaval with my visit tonight. I had better cut them short in future.' She tucked her sketches under her arm and made for the door, looking for the moment like a small, bewildered child.

'Don't be silly, Cathleen!' Rodney said hastily. 'You know you are as welcome here as you are at home.'

'Oh, Uncle Rodney, that's funny!' She gave a shaky laugh. 'If you only knew how welcome I am at home sometimes.'

Rodney followed her, saying, 'What utter nonsense, Cathleen!'

Annie watched them both go out. She was still holding on to the back of the chair. Into the upheaval of her mind there was creeping a terrifying thought: Rodney suspected something which implicated Steve and Kate. Why had Steve left, at this time when they needed him most? Cathleen knew why. This last thought made the terror so alive that for the moment it blotted out her own misery . . . Let what might happen to her, but nothing, nothing must happen to mar Kate's and Rodney's happiness.

On this thought she hurried upstairs, and found Kate lying back on her pillows, with the colour she had regained during the last few days drained now from her face.

'Has she gone?' Kate asked.

Annie nodded and took her hand.

'What did Rodney say to her?'

'He asked what she had said to you, and she told him she said Steve had been asking after you.'

'She told him that!' Kate sat up.

'Yes . . . Oh, Mam, don't get excited. She didn't know Steve had left.' Annie pulled herself up too late.

Kate stared at her: 'You say Steve has left? When? When did he go?'

'Just today . . . Oh, I'm a fool; Rodney didn't want you to know . . . Oh, Mam!'

Kate lay slowly back. That finished it. She couldn't tell Rodney now, even if she wanted to. There was only her word against Cathleen's, and although Rodney would believe her, Cathleen, in her own defence, would sow seeds of distrust in his mind. She was clever and dangerous. She thought of all the time she had spent alone in Steve's company, when he was driving her to Newcastle, or on shopping expeditions. There had been ample opportunity for what Cathleen, in her clever way, would imply. She wouldn't be above suggesting that the mistake that bred Annie could happen again . . . That girl! She was a devil! If only she felt stronger so that she could stand up to her. Oh, poor Steve, where had he gone? He had no-one belonging to him . . . And he was so happy here, until that . . . Tears overwhelmed her again, and she said aloud, 'Oh, poor Steve.'

It was unfortunate that Rodney should enter the room at that moment. He stopped just inside the door and said quietly, 'Why so much sympathy for Steve, Kate?'

Before Kate could reply, Annie said, 'It's my fault, Rodney; I blurted out that Steve had gone.'

Rodney limped past the bed and stood looking out of the window, and Kate called softly, 'Darling, darling, come here.'

He went to her and took her outstretched hand, and she

continued, 'I'm silly, darling . . . It's only that he's been with us for so long. He was like one of the family, and we'll miss him.'

Annie, watching Rodney's face, saw him smile at Kate. But it wasn't his usual smile, and she knew he didn't believe this to be the full explanation. She went out, her heart like a dead weight in her breast. In her own room she picked up the letter she had written earlier, and began to tear it slowly into tiny shreds. But no matter how small the pieces became they did not erase the drawing of Terence from her mind. What an utter fool she was! She read his letter again; it was now merely a polite note. But the other morning in the dawn, and when he came to say goodbye as well, that hadn't been mere politeness; it was a repetition of the night of the party. He was playing with her – and he had stood like that before Cathleen.

Oh dear God! She threw herself across the bed and buried her face in the crook of her arm. Oh dear God, stop me from loving him. Make me hate him as much as I do her. Yes, yes, do that; then I can bear it.

9

Annie's hair was up; the silver braids were coiled into a bun in the nape of her neck. The colour of the hair and the size of the bun alone would have drawn eyes in her direction. But the addition of the fringe lying above her dark, arched brows and green eyes caused heads to be turned. Men stopped talking; their eyes, hungry but still kindly, would follow her. But most women looked sideways at her, or pretended not to see her at all. A few months ago they would have said, 'Aye, she's a bonny lass,' but now she didn't look a lass, she looked a woman, and she presented a danger and a challenge to some hidden thing within them, as her mother had before her.

Three women from the fifteen streets were standing at the corner of Shields marketplace watching Annie without apparently looking at her. They didn't mind a woman being bonny, no, but there was a limit to the combined beauty their minds would receive without turning on the beauty itself and rending it. To have a skin like alabaster and an alluring slimness, and then that hair, was a bit too much of a good thing. No good would come of it . . . And it was looking that way already, for she didn't pick her company, did she? They commented aloud on her companion, and, as one of them said, there was nowt much good to know of him, for if everyone had their due he would soon be paying a maintenance order to one of his father's factory lasses, dirty upstart that he was! One, contemplating a stall of fruit, said to the others under her breath, 'They're 'avin' a row, look. She's not going to wait for the tram, she's off like the Devil in a gale of wind. Aye, and there he goes too . . . He's like a bloody pontoon. God, how some women fall for flesh!'

As she hurried out of the marketplace, Annie felt Brian's hand on her arm, and she was jerked to a stop. 'Look here!' said Brian. 'I'm going to have my say out . . . Why, you'd think I was insulting you instead of asking you to marry me.'

'You choose very odd places to have your say out. I've told you before I'll not marry you now, or ever.' Annie had spoken without looking at him, then walked on.

Striding by her side, Brian said, 'Tell me what else I can do. When do I get a chance to see you alone, eh? It's "I'm going here with Mam" or "I'm going there with Rodney" . . . It's always Mam and Rodney. God! it gets me down!'

'I've told you not to come up. I'm getting tired of telling you.'

'Well, I'm getting tired too, but in a different way.' His voice dropped low in his throat: 'I'll have you in the end, Annie, and you know it, so what's the good of fighting? You've always been mine since you were a kid, and you'll be mine in the right way before I'm finished.' Or in the wrong, he added grimly to himself.

Like Kate, Annie walked with a swinging stride from the hips, and with each step the line of her thigh was evident, and her slim legs stirred Brian as no voluptuous curves could.

'Why this touch-me-not attitude?' he said. 'You weren't like this before Christmas.'

She turned on him, her eyes deep green with sudden anger.

'I've always been like this where you're concerned. Before you went away I told you I wouldn't go with you, and since you've come back I've kept on telling you. Haven't I told you to stop coming up? But you will come!'

He walked along in silence for some way before saying, as if to himself, 'If the Oxford don wasn't going with Cathleen Davidson I'd maybe get ideas in that quarter . . . It wouldn't be him, would it, Annie?' His tone was quietly ominous.

Her pace quickened. 'No, it wouldn't be him! It isn't him or anyone, for you see . . . Oh, I'll have to tell you this to make you see. I'm not going to marry. I'm . . . I'm going into the Church. I'm going to be a nun.'

In and out of the people on the crowded pavements they went, sometimes together, sometimes separated. It wasn't until they were in a comparatively quiet street, leading to Leygate, that Brian started to laugh. It was just a low rumble at first, but, gathering force, it became a bellow, in which passers-by joined, saying, 'Tell us the joke, man!' His huge body shook, and the quivering of his flesh was evident through the thin suiting of his jacket.

Scarlet of face, Annie appealed to him, 'Be quiet, Brian. Please, Brian, be quiet!'

Gradually he stopped and, wiping his eyes, said, 'So you're going to be a nun?'

The very mention of the word threatened to set him off again, and Annie cried, ' There's nothing to laugh at! Anyway, I'm quite serious and I shouldn't have told you – no-one knows yet. I can't tell Mam until she is herself again . . . You won't mention it, will you, Brian?' she entreated him. 'Please don't say anything. Please.'

'No, no,' he said. 'You can trust me. Remember, I used to keep your secrets when you were a kid?' He gave her a sly glance. But she didn't pick up the reference in his last remark; her mind was too full of the present.

'You don't mind what I've told you?' she asked, a little bewildered.

'Mind? Not me. I've only got the Church to fight now, and I thought it was Macbane, or young Davidson, or half a dozen others . . . No, I don't mind.' No, he thought to himself, there's one sure way to fight the Church . . . A nun, by God! Well, I'll give her something that'll make her come yelping if she doesn't want to be in the same boat as her mother was . . . A nun, by God! That's funny, with a mouth like hers, and those legs.

After failing to persuade her to go to a show with him in Newcastle that evening, he left her at Tyne Dock on her way to the Mullens'. It was Saturday, so the trams were full, and hot as it was she preferred walking to sitting crushed in a tram. Steam was rising from the pavements under the arches, and as she walked it swirled around her ankles like mist from a marsh. She felt tired and weary after her conflict with Brian. If only he would stop pestering her; she seemed unable to combat him. Well, perhaps it wouldn't be for much longer.

Out of the shade of the arches the sun struck the lead-coloured pavements, and the glare hurt her eyes. This time last week she was in Paris. Yet it was odd: even with all the dirt and drabness and heat, she preferred to be here. Why did people rave about Paris? To her, the Champs Elysées was just a wide street, and the restaurants were just places where one paid treble the value for everything. Would she have enjoyed it more had she not forever been on the look-out for Cathleen and Terence, she wondered. Although Rodney had Cathleen's address, he never suggested they should pay her a visit. Cathleen had gone to Paris with another girl artist, while Terence started for France a few days later, presumably on a cycling tour.

She had not seen him once since the start of his summer vac. It was a passing remark of his mother's that gave her the information that he might be going to Paris: 'Awful weather, Miss Annie,' she said. 'I hope it clears up soon, for Terence started on his cycle tour this morning. He's going all the way to France.' They had smiled at each other sadly, and Annie said she hoped it would clear up.

In Notre Dame, in the Louvre, looking at the priceless paintings that had no power to stir her, walking in the grounds of the palace of Versailles, scanning the people from the terraces, everywhere she went she found herself looking for them.

Nor, Annie guessed, did Kate enjoy the holiday either. She was anxious all the time about the children, and although she appeared gay there was an undercurrent to her gaiety. She had not returned to her former strength or sparkle; only once during the holiday did she appear to act like the old Kate, and the righteous indignation she showed on this occasion upset Annie. It was during a visit to Notre Dame. Having passed the beggars on the steps and looked around for a while inside the church, they joined a group who were buying tickets to view the treasures. At the cost of a few pence fabulous wealth in the form of gold and jewels, vestments studded with gems, chalices and church plate could be viewed. Annie had been upset at the time by Kate's attack on the wealth of the Church in striking contrast to the beggars on its steps and the poverty outside; the bare-facedness of selling tickets to view the wealth aroused her wrath. She quoted Christ throwing the money changers out of the Temple. Rodney agreed with all Kate was saying, until he saw Annie's face. A signal was passed to Kate and she became silent. Then later, in the street, she took Annie's arm and became gay again. But Annie was hurt; it was as if the attack had been made on her. She had wanted to say, if the jewels were turned into money to be given away, the people would only come back for more and more. There would always be poor people, for some were

139

born shiftless. Sister Ann had explained a similar situation in that way, and Annie could see that it might be right.

No, Paris had not been a success. In just one more week the holidays would be over and she would return to college. She wasn't looking forward to it very much. Sister Ann, she knew, would be delighted to hear she wanted to be a nun. Would she be allowed to do her novitiate near her, she wondered, or would she be sent to another house? That depended on the Mother Superior.

The thought of the Mother Superior chilled her a little. She would have to go to her and tell her everything, and once she did that the die would be cast. The finality of this acted as a deterrent. She felt she must think very carefully about the whole situation, and have everything straight in her mind before telling anyone.

But Brian knew. Of all people, he had been the first to be told! And the effect was entirely lost, for it did not put him off at all, only amused him. She was beginning to dislike Brian, and even to be a little afraid of him. Up till last Christmas she had found him amusing and good company, but now nearly every time they met he did something to upset her. Just the other day, coming upon her unexpectedly from behind in the wood, he put his arms about her, and his hands covered her breasts, squeezing them tightly. They hurt all day afterwards. He was forever wanting to touch her. What could she do to be rid of him? If what she had told him would not deter him, what would?

As she neared the fifteen streets, she was thinking life was very difficult. Once she had imagined that with a nice house and money life couldn't be other than wonderful, but now she was learning that happiness depended very little on material things. It was what was going on inside one that counted. For instance, look at the Mullens: they had nothing – at best they lived from hand to mouth – but they all seemed happy. At least, they derived happiness from the little they had, whereas she, who had everything, wasn't happy. No, she told herself, I'm not happy . . . Why can't I be happy with what I have?

Her thoughts were dragged away from herself by a yelping sound of anguish, and looking ahead she saw two small boys, one of whom was rhythmically knocking the other's head against a telegraph pole. She recognised the aggressor as the youngest Mullen, and she ran to him, calling out, 'Jimmy, stop it this minute!'

Jimmy stopped, but still held his victim against the pole. He turned a dirty, impish face to Annie and grinned. 'Hello, Annie.'

'Let him go,' said Annie. 'You're a bad boy, Jimmy!'

'Aa ain't, it's him. He's tuppence and he won't stand me a treat to the Crown, an' Aa'll miss the serial.'

'Here,' said Annie, opening her bag and handing him sixpence, 'let him be, and get off to the Crown.'

The snivelling victim was released, and didn't wait to be told to run. Jimmy grinned widely at Annie and said, 'Ooh! sixpence! But its too late to gan noo, Aa'll walk back home with yer.'

Annie smiled to herself as she looked down into the cheeky face of the seven-year-old. He was already labelled a devil by the inhabitants of the fifteen streets; never did she visit the Mullens but she heard another of his terrible exploits, the last of which had been climbing on to the roof of Grannie Minton's old tumbledown cottage and dropping her equally old cat in a sack down the chimney. It took half a dozen men to get it out and the poor demented thing dashed away as soon as it was released and had not been seen again. Jimmy had since presented Grannie Minton with numerous cats, even though each presentation was received with something being thrown at his head.

Something was always happening in the fifteen streets,

Annie thought; things that made you laugh and cry. In the higher stratum of society in which she now moved, life was ordered; nothing happened that was surprising. At home there was sure to be food to eat, and new clothes to wear, and money for the asking. Here, food was the pivot around which life revolved; if the man of the house had a short week, there was less to eat; if he had a full week, there were full stomachs, and now and again perhaps a change of clothes, if the tally man was cleared . . . If not, second-hand ones – that misused word for countless previous owners – were a welcome change. Yet the people laughed more. Without knowing what life was all about they seemed to enjoy it. In the struggle for their existence they were in the very marrow of living.

As Annie went up the street to the Mullens', every few yards she had to sidestep people sitting on the doorsteps or on chairs on the pavement, trying to get what air there was. The water cart had been up the street, but the cobbles were almost dry again. The grey dust in the gutter was being mixed into mud pies by the small children. The bigger ones had an old tin bath full of water and were scrambling to get their feet into it.

Annie said, 'Go on, Jimmy. Why don't you go and play with them?'

He looked up at her engagingly and replied, 'Aa'd rather be with you.'

He walked beside her with a proud air of possession. On entering the Mullens' front door, Annie could not help but feel sorry for her cavalier when he was rudely shooed out by Rosie: 'What do you want, coming in the front way? Get yourself round the back! Or better still, stay out altogether . . . Come in, Annie,' she added, laughing. 'Mam's out, so I can stop that little devil having his own way. Do you know what he did last night? He put tar on all the door knobs in

142

Bleydon Street. Everybody was up in arms. You should have seen them coming here, one after the other!'

Annie's efforts at trying to keep a straight face resulted in them both bursting out laughing. Episodes from their own childhood, played around these doors, came back to them. Annie dropped into a chair by the table and buried her head on her arms, and laughed as she had not done for a long time. 'Oh, Rosie,' she gasped, 'I always get a good laugh when I come up here.'

'But it's no joke really,' said Rosie, still laughing; 'he's got us all nearly daft . . . Oh, isn't it hot!' she added. 'Would you like a drink of ginger beer? I just made it last night.'

While she was drinking, Annie looked around the kitchen; today everything was unusually neat and shining. It was almost an impossibility to keep things neat in the Mullens' kitchen, so she remarked, 'You're all very smart, Rosie; you'd think you were going to have a party.'

Rosie, with her back towards Annie, answered, 'Michael's calling for me; he's asked me to go to the pictures.'

Annie sprang up and swung her about: 'Oh, Rosie, I'm glad! I knew he was struck on you.'

'Did you?' asked Rosie, her chubby face looking almost pretty in her happiness. ' He's taking me to Newcastle. I'd just as soon go to Shields, for I know he can't afford it . . . they don't get a wage, do they, when they're articled?'

'No, but his father doesn't see him short.'

'Do you think I look a lot older than him?' Rosie asked, her small, bright eyes looking fixedly at Annie.

Annie sensed the appeal for negation, and immediately replied, 'No, of course not.'

'But I'm two years older.'

'Well, who's to know that?'

'Cathleen does, and she'll make the most of it . . . Annie,' she said quietly, 'I've never been afraid of anyone in my life, but I'm afraid of Cathleen Davidson . . . I can't tell you why, I only know I'm afraid of her. You know me: I could always stand up to anyone, but somehow she puts the fear of God into me. I used not to be afraid of her; it's just lately I've felt like this. You know, Annie, sometimes I have the feeling that she's going to wreck my life.'

'Oh Rosie, that's silly.' Annie's words sounded unconvincing to herself, for she already had knowledge of that feeling.

Rosie said, 'Yes, I know it is, but I can't help feeling it.'

'You have your singing. She can't touch that.'

'No,' said Rosie, 'she can't.' She stood by the table, twisting the curly fringe of the cover around her finger. She shook her head in perplexity; she hadn't been thinking of her singing at that moment, she had been thinking of Michael, the only boy who had ever asked to take her out, the only boy she had ever wanted to take her out. It was odd and a little frightening, but her singing had taken second place in her life since Michael had begun to show an interest.

'Forget her and go and get ready,' said Annie, 'and I'll pass judgement on you.'

'All right.' Rosie threw off the cloak of depression and became her perky self again. 'But let your judgement be tempered with mercy,' she called as she darted away up the narrow, dark stairs to adorn herself for Michael.

Annie sat down. 'Forget her,' she had said. What would she give to be able to follow her own advice . . . to forget them both, blot them out as if they had never existed!

10

~

Sunday morning started early for Annie. But no small detail of this day would ever be forgotten. She woke at four o'clock, feeling shivery, and pulled over the sheet she had tossed back earlier in the night. She lay for some time thinking of nothing in particular, wishing she could go to sleep again but knowing she was too wide awake. The house was steeped in quiet, a deep, thick quiet. Once she heard David cough, and her mind turned towards him and little Angela . . . She was so sweet, very small and not overstrong, but lovely. Oh, wouldn't it be marvellous to have a—

She turned swiftly on her side. She'd get up and go for an early walk. No; she'd go to first Mass at Shields. But first Mass wouldn't be for hours yet . . . What about Jarrow? It was early there, round about six o'clock. Yes, she'd go there, she'd always wanted to go to first Mass at Jarrow. She'd leave a note for Kate. It would be quite an adventure, cycling all the way to Jarrow in the early morning . . .

Half an hour later she was quietly pushing her bicycle through the gate. She pedalled away down the lane and into the main road, and on sighting three rabbits sitting perfectly still in the middle of it she smiled happily. Oh, it was good to be alive after all! There was so much to see and enjoy. If only she could forget just one thing then she could be perfectly happy. There beyond the fields was the sea, lying like a sheet of grey glass in the strange morning light, so still it was impossible to believe it was made up of movement; there were the stooks of golden corn in the fields lining the road; the air was like warm scented wine; and she was the only one in the world awake! She began to sing softly to herself: 'Kyrie eleison, kyrie eleison,' her feet turning the pedals in time with the chant.

She had reached the summit of the hill above the village when she saw she wasn't the only person awake; a man was pushing his cycle up the slope towards her. The back of the cycle was piled high with unwieldy bundles, and his bent back showed a bulging knapsack lying on it. Her feet and her heart seemed to stop their work at the same time. The man lifted his head at the sound of her approach, and immediately straightened himself and stood still, his expression showing his astonishment. But through it there threaded a smile, and as she came swiftly on him his grey eyes sent an appeal to her to stop. He went as far as to make a gesture with his hand, but before it was half completed she was past him and away.

Annie pedalled steadily on. She would not fly as her heart told her to, she would not let the sight of him effect her . . . no, she was not going to mind. Past large houses standing with knowing superiority back from the road, past smaller ones with neat front gardens and crazy-paving, past rows of semi-detached houses, which quickly gave place to attached ones, she went past them all and was actually on the main road to Jarrow before her hastily acquired reserve broke down, and she cried to herself: Why does he have to live so near us? Why doesn't he go away and never come back? . . . And he expected me to stop. After he's been in France with her! He's cruel, cruel!

A knowledge that he was not completely worthy of her love added a sadness to her already torn feelings. She could go as far as to understand him loving Cathleen, but she could make no allowances for him trying to attract her at the same time. And that was what he was doing. She began to recall now how he looked. She didn't recognise him at first, for he was deeply tanned and seemed very much older. She realised with a renewed stab that he looked very attractive, and that his thinness wouldn't evoke pity now, even from her . . .

She reached the church just as the Mass began. It was already crowded. Shawls covered nearly all the women's heads, except here and there where the sequins glistened on a worn black bonnet. Lifted for a moment from her own miserable feelings, she looked slowly about her; the men, young and old, all wore mufflers, ranging in colour from off-white to black. Those she could see were crossed inside the coats. As she glanced discreetly about her she knew a moment of intense pity that brought the stinging tears to her eyes. She knew why the mufflers were worn: very likely there was no shirt beneath the coat. This was the Mass about which her granny used to talk; she had attended it for years, walking all the way from the fifteen streets and back. Her own pet name for it had been 'the soul Mass'. Annie never understood what this meant, but now she knew. Only those with their souls very near to God could come to this Mass; here was poverty bare and literally naked; here too was the smell of the poor, that sweet, cloying, singed smell; these people brought everything they had to God, their martyrdoms and their vices.

Why then, Annie thought, with a wave of rebellion that shocked her even as she created it, why if they love God does He keep them as poor as this? The memory of Kate's outburst outside Notre Dame returned to her, and she chastised herself: I mustn't think like Mam; no, I mustn't.

147

By her side an old woman was murmuring, beating her breast and chanting, 'God be merciful to me, a sinner. God be merciful to me, a sinner.' And on hearing this, Annie asked herself the age-old question, Does God have to be asked to be merciful? Surely this woman's sins were all forgiven by her present suffering. Look at the rags she wore! Look at the bones sticking through her flesh, and the hands, twisted out of all recognition. Surely God couldn't ask any more of her?

She had never questioned in this way before. Why, she was thinking exactly like Mam! Burying her face in her hands, she prayed for forgiveness. The Mass went on; the people streamed up to the altar to take communion, but she couldn't join them, she couldn't take her expensive silk dress among all that drabness. The plate came round, and when she saw no bright silver gleam, her fingers refused to put her own two-shilling piece amongst the copper: she couldn't put a piece of silver in with those heart offerings. So for the first time in her life she let the plate pass. The old woman turned and smiled. The wrinkles on her face converged to the indrawn lips: 'Did ye cum oot withoot yer purse, hinny? Aa've dun that mony a time.'

Annie made no reply to the whisper, but smiled faintly, and thought with new understanding: Well, you must have something to cling to, something to love, when you get as old as that. Oh, dear Lord, she prayed fervently, help her! Help them! Only give them food and clothes, that's all they want . . . I'm sure that's all they ask.

As the Mass ended she pressed her silver net purse into the old woman's lap, and hurried away without waiting to see the impression made by her gift, regretting there was only seven shillings in the purse. Outside, the sun was hot and she was thankful for its warmth, for this experience had chilled her. Yet she felt calm, her own troubles being shelved for the time. She rode the long journey home thinking how

148

ungrateful she was for all the good things God had given her, and pushing back the nagging question of why He withheld them from all those poor people. Economics had not been part of her education in the convent, she knew nothing whatever about the subject. Had she done so, she would have still thought that the people's welfare was mainly a matter of the bounty of God . . .

'I had a shock when I found you weren't in your room,' Kate greeted her when she arrived home. 'I looked in before seven, and I didn't get your note till I came downstairs. But,' she added, 'I'm glad you went to Mass at Jarrow; I have it in me to envy the kind of faith you see there.'

Annie spoke of the people she had seen at the Mass, and of their condition, which was infinitely worse than that of the people of the fifteen streets. But she made no mention to Kate of the disturbing questions that had assailed her. She shelved the matter in her mind.

The day passed happily enough. Annie busied herself with David and Angela. In the afternoon they all went down to the pool and bathed, and had a picnic tea in the shade of the trees. Annie tried not to think that a mere thirty yards away, behind the high hedge, Terence was likely sitting in his garden, or perhaps bathing in the stream. But no, he couldn't bathe in the stream now, for it was almost dry.

A remark of Rodney's bore reference to her thoughts: 'You'd both better make the most of the pool, for if this heat keeps up I'll be unable to have it refilled. There'll be a water shortage, and this will be the first thing that will have to be cut.'

Kate said, ' If this heat keeps up, I won't have the strength to walk down here.'

'Are you feeling it so much?' Rodney asked, and Annie noticed a trace of anxiety in his voice.

Kate laughed, and replied: 'No, not really. Only it makes me limp.'

This was another thing that kept intruding on Annie's mind, the relationship between her mother and Rodney. To all outward appearances, it was the same as it had always been, but there were times when Rodney seemed moody and hardly spoke, and other times when he hovered round Kate with almost passionate attention. She wondered if his moods were associated with his foot and arm. But then again, these had always troubled him. She seemed to date the moods from shortly after the birth of Angela, from that night in the bedroom when Kate had cried over Steve leaving . . . Where was Steve now? No-one mentioned him, which was odd, when she came to think of it. Why didn't they? Why hadn't she? Oh, it was too hot to think.

She stretched out on the grass and laid her cheek against the warm earth, and presently the rich smell lulled her to sleep.

Sitting with her head leaning against the frame of the open window, Annie heard the hall clock strike eleven. The house was quiet again. It seemed a long, long time since four o'clock this morning. All day she had successfully managed to guide her thoughts along channels which would hurt her least, but the painful nagging thoughts that lay just beneath the thin veiling of her will would be dominated no longer and were again filling her with misery. The misery made her body move restlessly; it would be useless going to bed yet, for she wouldn't sleep, it was still so hot and she didn't feel tired. She looked down into the garden.

It was a place of dark shapes against a darker background, and the darkness seemed to be pressing the hot air into the earth. Where was the moon, she wondered idly; it should be out. Last night it had flooded the garden and tempted her to run out into the enchanted night. But what would she do out there alone, she had asked herself. It would be different were there someone for company, Kate or Rodney, or even David.

An owl, close to the window, startled her with its eerie call: 'Hoo-oo! Hoo-oo!' and mentally she quoted: Tu-whit tu-who, a merry note, while greasy Joan doth keel the pot, before springing up and whispering aloud to herself: 'I'm going out, I can't stay indoors! I'll go and have a bathe.'

She did not question what was prompting this exploit, but slipped into a bathing-costume, pulled a dress on over it and crept stealthily from the room. If Kate were to hear her, what would she think? . . . Well, she would likely imagine she was going to the bathroom.

Once through the side door, she ran swiftly along the well-known grassy path until she came to the cypress hedge. Here she went more cautiously. She passed through the orchard and into the small belt of woodland, which became a terrifying place in the darkness. When she was beyond the trees she started to run again: past the tennis court, over the grassy surround bordering the pool, right to the edge of the pool itself. There she stood holding on to the iron support of the steps, panting and afraid. She hadn't imagined it would be like this. It was the first time she had been alone down here at night, and it had not occurred to her that she would be afraid. There was an eeriness over the whole garden, all the shapes seem twisted and gigantic . . . Where was the moon? There should be a moon. If only it would show itself. As she stood her eyes grew accustomed to the darkness, and she saw that it wasn't, as she termed it, pitch dark; it was the semi-blackness that made the shapes stand out in relief. She comforted herself that the moon was only obscured by clouds, and that it would soon be out.

As she stood trembling, she heard a gentle movement below

her, as if a bird were in the water and was flapping its wings. She tried to still her breathing. After a few flaps the noise ceased and she took a deep breath. She was scared of her own shadow! Well, she was here, and she might as well bathe. She took off her dress and sandals, pulled on a bathing-cap, and let herself down into the water. Ah! it was deliciously cool. Oh, lovely!

Striking out from the steps, she did a quiet breaststroke to the other end. Eighteen times she flung out her arms before she was there. How strange it was, swimming in the dark; her body seemed light, not part of her, it was uneasy no longer. She swam back again, conscious only of her mouth swallowing air.

By the steps once more, she turned lazily on her back and floated. There was the sky above, much lighter now, and the moon would soon be out. And there, high above her, was the bushy head of the pine, like a floor mop dusting the heavens. As she had done earlier in the day, she assured herself once more how fortunate she was to have so much; how many girls were there who could swim in their own pool, play on their own tennis court? Was it just five years ago she and Mam had been living in the fifteen streets? What a lot had happened since then!

There came the flapping of the bird again, quite near now. Stopping all movement for a second, she listened. And in that second the terrifying knowledge assailed her that it was no bird: there was someone else in the pool. Her body stiffened. The flapping had stopped, but whoever made it was between her and the steps. She felt, rather than saw, the bulk of its shape. It must be a tramp off the road. The thought made her cold. Oh, why was she so silly as to come here at this time of the night? It was asking for trouble. He might kill her!

Unaware that she gave a cry of alarm, she turned and, thrashing the water with all her strength, made for the other side of the pool. Then her terror mounted to a scream in her throat as she felt the body of the man swimming alongside her. His hands came on her arms, his legs for a moment touched hers and, as she battled fiercely with him, she found herself swung upright. Her feet touched the bottom and her head just cleared the surface of the water. She was gathering breath to scream when a voice gasped, 'Don't be afraid, Annie. It's me, Terence.'

The night became still again. She could make out the shape of his head and shoulders, like something disembodied floating on the water. Like one soothing a child, he said: 'It's all right. It's all right.'

His hands were on her arms, holding her up. The stillness became intensified, so that she heard their short, gasping breathing. 'Let's swim to the steps,' he said.

She slowly dropped into the water, but could scarcely move her limbs; all strength had gone from her. So she turned on her back and floated gently towards the steps, conscious of the strong movements of his arms near her.

The moon was coming from behind a bank of cloud, and the water looked like a sheet of silver paper, crumpled a little by the ripples from their bodies. She could see the steps as she climbed heavily up them; then the green of the grass under her feet and his feet and legs, thin and glistening; they were very close to hers, the toes pointing to her toes. The moment came when she could no longer look at his feet, and she had to raise her head. Her eyes moved up to his and were held. She could see nothing, no other feature of his face, no sky above, no trees behind, only his eyes, dark and deep in the shadow of his face, and she knew they were filled with intense pleading.

'Annie . . .' Her name seemed to rest on the air between them. 'Annie,' he said again. His arms were about her; their bodies met and pressed close. His mouth was on hers, hard, not like flesh at all. She was conscious of her lips being bruised against her teeth and the breath leaving her body as he pressed her mouth against his . . . And all she could think was: Oh, Terence! Oh, Terence! . . .

His grip slackened and his mouth left hers. She felt him loosen her bathing-cap with one hand and pull it gently off, and as he moved his face in her hair she thought: I can't bear it . . .

In the brightness of the moon she saw the contrast of her arms against the dark skin of his neck. The wonder of it, to have her arms about Terence's neck! She leaned against him, relaxed, listening with an unreal, joyful wonder to him murmuring, 'Oh Annie, I love you. I love you.'

Something seemed to leap from her body and soar into the heavens . . . If she could only die now, at this very moment, and so be able to hold this feeling for ever! She hoped he would never stop talking.

'I've wanted to do this for years and years,' he whispered. 'I've tried to forget you. I've done everything to put you out of my mind. But it was no use . . . Oh, Annie! Annie Hannigan! You've been a torture.' His lips sought hers again, but more gently, and he murmured, 'Say something to me, Annie.'

But no word came, and he pleaded again, his hands stroking her shoulder blades, 'Annie, say you like me a little bit.'

She remained still, and he waited, his arms becoming hard like iron against her flesh.

'I love you. I've always loved you, Terence.' She could hardly hear the words herself – or believe she was speaking them. She felt his body quiver. Then she was caught up into an embrace that was neither gentle nor savage; she only knew that everything she desired was in it. It went on and on; it was like the beginning of eternity. And then she shivered, and he said, 'You're cold.'

'No, no,' she assured him breathlessly, 'I'm not.'

He took her face between his hands, and tilted it upwards to the moon. 'You're like the moon, Annie, gentle and mysterious, and a little frightening.'

She laughed shakily. How funny for anyone to think she was frightening and mysterious.

He rubbed his hands gently over her arms. 'You *are* shivering,' he said. 'You'll catch cold, you must go in.' There was regret in the words.

She didn't explain to him that she always shivered when she was happy, ecstatic shivers. But she said shyly, 'I've my dress here . . . there's a towel in the pavilion, I'll go and change.'

'Will you? . . . Yes, do. Then you won't catch cold. Oh, Annie' – he caught her hand as she made to go – 'is this true? Tell me it's true. Tell me again that you love me.'

She stood mute before the wonder of his request. He was begging her to say she loved him. She suddenly threw herself against him, and kissed him with a fierceness that surprised even herself. When she would have gone he swung her off her feet. His lips still on hers, he whirled her around in the moonlight.

It wasn't until she was standing inside the little pavilion, leaning panting against the closed door, that she thought of Cathleen. But then it was only a fleeting thought; it did not even scratch the surface of this new joy . . . He loved her! He had kissed her . . . Oh, how he had kissed her! Her body shivered anew.

As she stood drying herself, the memory of the drawing came back to her, and she said, as if to someone who was standing far off, 'He couldn't have posed like that. He couldn't. It was a trick of Cathleen's. And he couldn't have been with her in France.' She would let nothing, nothing touch the wonder of him.

When she went outside he was standing a few yards away, waiting for her. He was wearing a mackintosh that reached only to his knees, making his legs look longer and thinner than ever. She glanced at them, and started to laugh: 'Oh, in this moonlight you do look funny in that mac, Terence.'

He looked down at his legs. Then he too laughed, and pulled her to him, saying, 'Well, you'd better get used to them, for you're going to know them a long time.'

They stared at each other, their heads pressed back on their shoulders, and he burst out, 'Oh, why didn't this happen at the beginning of the holidays? And I must leave the day after tomorrow for Colchester! I've got a temporary job there.'

They continued to stare at each other, their eyes wide and searching, until Annie exclaimed, 'The day after tomorrow? Oh, Terence, why must you go so soon?'

He took her hand: 'Come and sit down by the pool; we must talk.' But they didn't go to the pool immediately. His arms went about her again . . .

Since when had she loved him? Oh, as long as she could remember, from the first time she had seen him in the wood . . . When had he first loved her? From the night he saw her at the window . . . she had looked so startlingly like an angel. He had dreamt about her that night, and he had wanted to kiss her that day in the Jarrow road. What would she have done if he had? . . . She would have kissed him back, hard, hard like this . . .

After a time she asked if he had ever loved anyone before, and he replied instantly, 'No, never.' Had she? Oh, no, no, never! They laughed and started to run . . . You see, she told herself, he's never loved Cathleen.

When she trod on a pebble he picked her up and carried her, unprotesting, to the bank above the pool. He went down on his knees, and as he laid her on the grass he bent over her, and her heart leapt, and something within her quivered and reared itself to meet what she knew must be in his eyes. He lay down, stretching his body close beside hers, and she met his embrace. Through the thinness of her dress she felt the hard warmth of his body. His foot touched her foot, it moved up and down her calf, his mouth covered hers, and her body began to rise and float away . . . upwards, upwards. Then, as if flung bodily out of an ecstatic dream, she found herself on her feet. She blinked at him, dreamily, questioningly, like a bewildered child. He was holding her hands and his face was twisted, almost as if with pain. He said huskily, 'It's nearly twelve o'clock. You'd better go; we've got tomorrow.'

Perplexed, she shook her head. 'Yes . . . yes. . . Oh, yes, I'd better go.' Then she smiled at him.

'Oh, Annie!' He bent and kissed her tenderly. 'You're so young, so dear, so . . . Oh, my sweet!'

'I'm not so young, I'm nearly nineteen,' she said.

He brought her sandals, and put them on for her, and she rested her hand on his head as he did so. They walked up through the wood, their arms about each other. 'You've never asked why I was in the pool,' he said; 'you know I was trespassing.'

'I'm glad you were . . . I've often longed for you to come over.'

They turned again to each other, and the smouldering fire flamed up once more. But again it was he who broke away and moved on, just holding her hand now, until they reached the cypress hedge. He continued to talk as if there had been no break in the conversation: 'I must confess I've often used your pool. But I've always waited until about twelve o'clock. But tonight it was so hot.'

'How do you get in?' she asked.

'I drop down into the stream from the bottom of our garden, plodge up, climb the bank, and there I am . . . Simple!

157

I won't come any further,' he added; 'someone might see me. And then what would they say?' He laughed down at her, and took her face between his hands once more: 'You're beautiful, Annie . . . too beautiful. Say again you love me.'

'I love you, Terence. Oh, I do, I do.' Then with a shy burst of candour she whispered, 'I think you're wonderful.'

He became quite serious. 'Annie, don't say that, don't even think it, for you'll be so disappointed. There's nothing wonderful about me, God knows.' He laughed ruefully: 'I've got a vile temper and I'm as stubborn as ten mules. And I'm still skinny! Remember? You were always so sorry for me. Take me as I am, Annie – please.'

'I'm stubborn too,' she cried. 'And I'll always think you're wonderful; there's no-one in the world like you.'

A cold hand was suddenly laid on his brimming happiness . . . This was what he had always feared from her, this whole-sale adoration. It would demand perfection in return. It was one of the things that had subconsciously kept him away from her. She must take him as he was.

If only he had told her he loved her last Christmas! Then he and Cathleen . . . Oh God! 'If, if . . .' That was done, past, forgotten. He loved Annie above everything in the world, he always had. There was nothing to stop him living up to her idea of him from now on. But he must make her see . . . The wonder of the night was a little dimmed; the old unsure feeling returned for a moment, to be swamped again by the intoxication of her. 'Go on in,' he said shakily, 'before I don't let you go at all . . . Good-night, my Annie.'

They stood close for a moment; then she was gone. But she had gone only a few yards when he caught her again and whispered urgently, 'How soon can you get out in the morning? . . . Will you come cycling?'

'I can be up by six,' she whispered back.

He laughed softly. 'No, you must get more sleep; make it

eight. I'll be at the gate at eight o'clock. Good-night, Annie Hannigan.'

Her feet skimmed the ground as she ran to the house, and they carried her body as though it were the lightest piece of thistledown. She quietly let herself in and stood listening. But only her excited breathing made any sound. When she reached her room she flung herself on the bed. Oh the joy, the joy of this night!

She lay with her face turned away from the altar. Tomorrow or the next day she would have to face that, but tonight there was only Terence. Her Terence – he was her Terence now – her wonderful Terence! He was so good and kind and gentle. She would think about him all night, she wouldn't sleep. She never wanted to sleep again.

When the moon was high in the sky it flooded the room and shone on her, lying on her back fast asleep, still dressed.

11

At seven-thirty Annie followed Mrs Summers into Kate and Rodney's room. She laid the tray with the early-morning tea on the bedside table with the remark, 'Some people are up with the lark these mornings! Good-morning, ma'am. Good-morning, sir,' she added.

Rodney grunted, and Kate said sleepily, 'Thanks, Summy.' Then, blinking at Annie, she said, 'Where are you off to at this time?'

Something about Annie's face made Kate sit up and shake the sleep from her eyes. But she waited until Mrs Summers had left the room before saying, 'What's the matter? Where are you going?'

'I . . . I'm going for a ride . . . And, Mam . . . I may not be back for breakfast.'

'Must have your breakfast before you go out,' Rodney grunted from the pillow. 'No breakfast yesterday . . .'

'Where are you going?' asked Kate.

'I . . . I don't know. Oh, Mam, I'll tell you after.'

Kate looked at her enquiringly. 'What time will you be back then?'

'I don't really know.'

'She doesn't know,' grunted Rodney again.

Annie moved close to Kate and whispered, 'I'm going out with Terence.'

'Terence?'

'Yes.'

'But when . . . ?'

'I saw him last night.'

'Last night?'

'Yes. I went down to the pool. I couldn't sleep . . . He was there.'

'But, Annie, you didn't go down there at night? Why . . . Why, anything could have happened to you. You never know who is in the . . .' She stopped as she felt Rodney's hand under the bedclothes, pressing a warning into her back. And Annie was smiling mischievously at Kate when Rodney muttered, 'Macbane in our pool! Aah, I'll have to look into this, the cheek of it! He gets about, does that Macbane.'

Kate looked hard at her daughter. Behind the pleasure of knowing that Terence and she had at last come together she felt a momentary fear at the apparent vulnerability of Annie. She was so young and fresh; her strange beauty at this moment was breathtaking. Kate knew that all Annie's being would be offered together with her heart; where she loved she would hide nothing. She'll suffer for it, Kate thought, as I did. Oh, the heart-rending youngness of youth! Unless he loves her very much there'll be no limit to her suffering. Oh God, make him love her well. And keep Cathleen Davidson away, she prayed, almost childishly. She remembered Terence's letter which had borne no fruit, and again she repeated, Keep Cathleen Davidson away.

She reached up and kissed Annie, then pushed her away, saying, 'Go on, and take a snack with you; you are bound to feel hungry.'

Annie sped downstairs and packed some bacon sandwiches

under Summy's comments about people ruining their health by riding bikes on empty stomachs. She hugged Summy, saying, 'Darling, I think you are old enough to know people don't ride on their stomachs, they use their other sides.'

Laughing, she dashed out and upstairs again to pay a flying visit to the nursery, where the sight of Angela added in some strange way to the total of her happiness.

It was ten minutes to eight when she took her bicycle out of the garage, but eight o'clock seemed an eternity away. She was standing undecided whether to go to the gate and wait when a bell rang discreetly from behind the hedge. For a second she was overcome by shyness, and felt she would be unable to face him; she wondered why she had found the minutes dragging, for now she wanted to go back into the house, or anywhere so that there would be time and space between them. Yet she hurried down the path. And the sight of him made her feel faint with happiness.

He opened the gate and took her bicycle. They smiled at each other but didn't speak. He pushed the two cycles some way along the road before he said, 'Now I know I'm not dreaming.'

She looked away, unable to meet his eyes . . . He looked different in the daylight, taller, more tanned, more alert. All his body looked hard and taut, only his eyes were soft.

At the curve of the lane he supported the cycles against each other, and turned and took her into his arms. He kissed her slowly, reverently, the passion of last night gone; they murmured each other's names; then, laughing a little self-consciously, they mounted their cycles and rode away into the sunshine.

All day they were together, Terence accepting Kate's invitation to lunch and tea. There was a mounting feeling of pride in Annie as she listened to him talking with Rodney. Although there was a certain deference in Terence's manner, he expressed his opinions quietly and fearlessly, and Annie could see that Rodney liked him more than a little. The day seemed packed with endless joy.

It was after tea that Terence said to her, 'Come along, I want to show you my cave.'

'Your cave?' she enquired. 'What cave?'

'It's a magic cave, and it's entirely mine . . . I feel sure of that.'

'But where is it? All the caves along the coast are well known.'

'You wait and see. Come on.'

He took her hand and they ran down the lane like children let loose, laughing and shouting at each other. When they reached the stream he said, 'If we cross the stream here it will cut off half a mile.'

'Is it far?'

'No. About twenty minutes' walk.'

But as they went across the fields and he helped her over fences, the journey was continually being interrupted, and she cried, 'The twenty minutes is up, where's this cave of yours?'

Again laughing and running, he led her along narrow tracks through the scrubland, until they emerged abruptly on the cliff-top. And Annie exclaimed in surprise, 'Why, I never thought it was possible to reach the cliffs this way. I've always gone by the main road!'

'Ah! but this is the prowler's route,' he said.

'But, Terence, we can't get down to the beach here; these cliffs drop straight, and . . . and they're dangerous!'

'In parts they are, yes. But there is a way down . . . Don't be afraid. Look.' He took her to the very edge of the cliff and pointed.

She stepped quickly back, saying, 'Oh, Terence, I'll never get down there! I'll be terrified . . . I'm a coward about heights.'

'You're no coward; come on, I've got you. Do you think I'd ask you to come this way if there were any danger? Now do you? Give me your hand.'

She put her hand in his and they began the descent and, as he had said, she found that it was much easier-going than it looked. But when they reached the bottom she could not hide her disappointment that this part of the beach did not merit the difficulty of reaching it, for it was strewn with great boulders, some like miniature cliffs themselves.

Seeing her expression, he said, 'Wait, wait!' and led her to the water's edge. Mystified, she looked at him when he pointed to a massive rock jutting out into the sea. 'See that? In another half-hour we'll be able to walk round it, but if you take off your shoes and stockings we can do it now.'

Still looking mystified, she allowed him to take off her shoes, which he slung about his neck with his own by their laces. She turned from him as she undid her stockings. This was daylight and there was, she imagined, something immodest about the undoing of a suspender.

'Don't be afraid for your feet,' he said as he led her into the water; 'you won't find any rocks, there's smooth sand all the way now.'

Bewildered, she followed him until they came to the very point of the jutting rock. Here his grip on her hand tightened, and as they rounded the point he watched her expression, and it made him laugh. 'Was it worth it?'

'It's wonderful! It's like a fairy-tale picture.' She stood still in her amazement, unable to take in the scene.

For about thirty yards there showed a narrow stretch of sandy beach, rippled by the tide into lines of almost mathematical precision. It lay between huge boulders. And overhanging it like a roof was a sloping shelf of rock, perhaps twenty feet in height at its point nearest the water. From where they stood it looked like a gigantic wedge, attached at its base to the main cliff. The beach and the under-surface of the wedge rose and fell to meet each other far back in the shadows. And out of the shadows came glints of gold and red and brown where the sun caught the wet sheen of the seaweed hanging from the underside of the rock.

'Terence, it's wonderful!'

'Ah, but wait. There's still more.' He was as excited as a boy.

They left the water, and in a few steps were beneath the roof of rock. Soon it was impossible to walk upright, and as she bent double and walked further into the gloom the seaweed trailed over her hair, and she shivered. 'Why are we going further, Terence?'

He said nothing, but went on, almost on his knees now, and she saw him disappear through a black vertical slit in the wall of rock ahead. As she neared it, his arm came through and guided her in.

She straightened and gazed around her. They were in a tiny cave. It was lit by a strange light, which came from the top of the cave about a foot above her head and which was reflected in gleams of pink and pearl from the shells studding the cave walls.

'It's unbelievable! How did you find it?'

'By accident. I was climbing down the cliff on the other side to where we came down, and it was this gulley in the rock I found first. Look.' He pointed to the roof, to where a gap about a foot wide showed along its entire length. 'It's a fissure, and it goes straight up through the wedge of rock.'

She looked up through the crevice, and miles and miles away, it seemed to her, was the sky.

'The sloping shelf was too smooth to venture down,' went on Terence, 'and I had no means of knowing how far I should have to drop to the beach if I did slide down, nor how I should get back again. But I made a note of the position of

165

those rocks out there in the sea, and I worked my way round to them from the shore. But it was an awful journey. Then I found the way we came down today . . . I don't think anyone else could ever have been here. You see, it's all so hidden and camouflaged . . . I call it Davy Jones's locker.'

'Oh, what an awful name for it! It's so lovely.'

'Yes, it is lovely' – his tone changed – 'but it could be dangerous too. Deadly, I should say, on certain occasions. Come and see what I mean.'

Outside the cave again, they made their way under the roof of the rock and into the sunshine, and Terence pointed seawards: 'You see that? Nothing can get into this bay, and nothing can get out.'

She looked to where the tide was dancing and surging about the points of a continuous half-circle of rocks. Each end of the half-circle touched the gigantic rocks bordering the bay, and Annie saw that the rock round which they had paddled was really one end of the half-circle, and the only place showing a gap.

Terence, following her gaze, said, 'At high tide the water swirls over those rocks like mad and dashes up this beach and fills the cave. I've been on top at the opening of the fissure and heard it roaring like millions of demons . . . So you see why I call it Davy Jones.'

Annie shuddered. 'I don't think I like it so much now . . . Do you often come here?'

'Yes, when I want to escape.'

'Oh, I'd be terrified if I knew you were here alone . . . You might fall asleep, or anything, and get cut off.'

'Well then, you must see I never come alone.'

Their eyes met and held; and they laughed and fell into each other's arms, and kissed, hot, hard kisses.

After a while they found a patch of sand where the sun had dried the surface, and they lay close together, face down-

166

wards, resting on their elbows and looking out to sea. A warm thoughtful silence fell between them for a time, until Annie said, 'Terence, why must you go tomorrow morning when school doesn't start for nearly a week?'

He rubbed his chin over his linked knuckles: 'I've got to cycle, and it will take me three days at least . . .'

'But must you cycle? You could get there in a day by train.'

He looked at her steadily for a moment, then turned his gaze seawards again and started to aim pebbles at an imaginary object. Stopping abruptly, he laughed and said slowly: 'Miss Hannigan, I think I'd better put my cards on the table and see how you react to the shock.' As he spoke they turned on their sides and faced one another. 'First of all, I cycle from necessity, not from pleasure; I haven't the money for the train fare—'

'But Terence . . .'

'Now, now, don't say it. I know you could give me the money, but don't . . . don't offer it, please.' There was a grim firmness about his voice that silenced her; he was suddenly the other Terence of long ago. He went on, 'It seems early days yet to speak of ways and means, but I think I'd better let you know what you're in for, so you'll know whether you want to go on or not.' The tone of his voice and the expression of his eyes were at variance. 'You see, it's like this: I've always had a sort of inferiority complex about you and your money.'

'But I haven't got any!' she burst out. 'Only my allowance.'

'Only your allowance,' he said quietly. 'And anything else you may want. But that allowance', he went on, remembering the amount Cathleen had mentioned, 'is likely very near to what I'd expect you to keep house on.'

The sand seemed to withdraw its support from her body; there was the sea before them, with its trap of rocks; there were the towering cliffs behind them; but her heart took flight at his words and soared away over and beyond them all. And the clear, blue sky did not seem high enough for its soaring. He hadn't said, 'Will you marry me?' He had passed all that, and said, 'Your allowance is very near to what I'd expect you to keep house on' . . . Oh Terence! Terence!

'You mightn't believe it, but my salary will be four pounds ten shillings a week. And that after five years at a university! If I'd left school when I was fourteen I'd likely have been making as much now, besides having been earning all the time since. But here I am, lucky to get this temporary post at four pounds ten, out of which I'll pay my digs and send something home. This last is very important, Annie: I owe my parents so much.' He looked at her steadily whilst saying this.

'Oh yes, yes,' she murmured slowly, while her thoughts were clamouring: I'd live with him anywhere . . . back in the fifteen streets . . . I'd go out to work . . . anything, anything . . . What does money matter? The crowded mass of poverty she had seen the previous morning was entirely forgotten.

'Posts are hard to get,' Terence was saying. 'There are dozens after every one. If it hadn't been for a friend of mine, John Dane Dee, I shouldn't have got this. He happened to know the headmaster. Incidentally, it's him, John, I'm to meet in three days' time. I'm staying overnight at his place, it's only a few miles from the school. He wants me to live there, but I couldn't do that. I intend to get digs of some kind, which is why I'm going early, so that I can have a look round. So you see, Annie, how matters stand. It will be months before I'm even straight, for I've borrowed money to live on for the next few weeks; you don't get paid until the end of the month.'

'Terence . . . Oh, my dear.' Love, pity and tenderness filled her. She knelt up and bent over him, as a mother over a child.

'But Terence, there is no need. Why, Rodney would—'

In a flash he was up on his knees and facing her. She was utterly taken aback by the sudden hardness of his eyes and mouth, so grim and tight that the words were released only with an effort: 'That's what I was afraid of . . . I don't want any help from Rodney. That's what you must understand. I don't want it now, or ever . . . I like him, I like him very much, but I'm not going to become the recipient of his philanthropy through you. If I'm to have you, then I'm going to keep you. But it will have to be my way . . . I'll work, I'll get on. At least, I hope I shall. But you'll have to take that chance. You've also got to know this: even if I do get on, I'll never be rich; there's no fortune to be made from teaching. You'll never be able to dress as you do now, or have half the comforts. Why, we'd be lucky if we could set up in a two-roomed flat.' He stopped abruptly, knelt back on his heels and passed his hand over his brow: 'What am I talking about? Why am I yammering on?' His voice lost its cutting edge and became weary. 'I've never even asked you . . . You never even said . . . God, what a fool I am to get all worked up!' He looked at her and murmured, 'Oh, my dear, don't cry. I'm a beast. What possessed me to go diving into the future like that? Don't, oh don't, Annie.'

She was crying silently, as she had done that day in the wood.

He pulled her to him: 'Annie . . . Annie, I wouldn't hurt you for the world. Don't. Don't cry like that. Only I had to tell you, and I warned you I'm a bad-tempered beast. Here am I dictating and bullying you when I don't even know if you will marry me. All I want is to love you . . . always to love you.'

He kissed her so fiercely they lost their balance and fell over. They lay where they fell, and she murmured, 'I'd live with you anywhere. Anywhere. I'd do anything for you, anything in the world you want. I don't care where we live, I only want you.'

They lay as one, silent, not moving. The tide went out and the sun went down. And he thought: This must not happen. It mustn't! But he lay on, pressed close to her.

12

Terence had been gone three days, days in which Annie flitted about the house and the garden like one possessed of the very essence of the joy of living. Kate, Rodney and David, and even the baby, seemed to be caught up in the reflection of her happiness. On the morning of the fourth day Terence's letter came, a pencilled note written at dawn after his first night of camping. She flew up to her room with it, and read the beginning with dismay:

> *Dear Miss Hannigan,*
> *This is just to inform you there are times when I earnestly wish I had never set eyes on you. Apart from interfering with my sleep, you are also interfering with my sense of direction. Twice I have taken the wrong road, an unusual occurrence with me, a map expert. Also I've had the strange urge to sing, with embarrassing results, for I am tone-deaf.*

Annie fell across the bed, laughing and clutching the letter to her. This was another side of him . . . a funny side. She lay on her back and continued to read:

. . . So you see what you've done to me. Oh Annie, Annie, Annie. Now I'm away from you I really can't believe it . . . Do you love me? Do you – this long, lanky, plain individual? I have a colossal nerve to expect it. But I do expect it, remember that . . . I expect you to love me, Miss Hannigan.

Oh, Annie, I keep repeating your name; the pedals of my bike beat it out as they take me further and further away from you. And to think I won't see you till Christmas! Annie, I love you. I couldn't put into words all I thought of you when we were together. I don't think I ever shall be able to. You're made up of all my dreams from a boy; you're so wonderful. Yes, you are the wonderful one – not me, Annie. Try not to class me in that category . . . it frightens me. I'm just a very ordinary chap, but a very lucky one, the luckiest one alive . . . Do you realise how beautiful you are?

At this point Annie turned on her face and lay still, the letter crushed beneath her. It was too big to take in; that Terence should care for her like this, as much as she did for him . . . Who was it said two people couldn't love each other equally, that one must love more than the other?

The bell rang for breakfast, and she hastily read the rest of the letter, then went to the dressing-table to tidy her hair. And as she passed the window she caught sight of Mrs Macbane standing uncertainly in the drive below. Eagerly she hung out of the window and called, 'Good-morning, Mrs Macbane!'

Mrs Macbane looked up, relieved, and said, 'Oh, good-morning, Miss Annie. Could . . . could I speak to you a minute?'

Annie was out of the room and down the stairs and on the drive so quickly that Mrs Macbane exclaimed, 'Why, Miss Annie, you'd think you flew!' She gave her a happy, warm smile. 'It was just this, Miss Annie,' she went on: 'Terence has a little book that he writes things in – you know, bits of poetry and things – and he's gone and lost it. He posted a card in Newcastle on Tuesday morning, just after he left, to say he must have left it behind in his room and would I send it on to him. Then this morning I get another letter to say he hadn't left it in his room, he remembered writing in it in . . .' Mrs Macbane hesitated. 'Eeh, Miss Annie, I don't know how to tell you this, 'cos the doctor'd likely be vexed if he knew, but Terence sleeps out most nights when it's fine, and on his last night home he slept in your grounds. He said he lay in a little copse near the pool, and he remembered writing in his book there. And he's asked me to go up the stream and look for it. But, Miss Annie, I couldn't plodge up the stream, now could I? And anyway, I wouldn't go into your place without asking . . . So I thought, if you wouldn't mind, Miss Annie . . .'

'Oh, Mrs Macbane! Of course, of course I'll get it. And, Mrs Macbane, call me Annie . . . Terence and I are . . . we're friends.'

Mrs Macbane nodded slowly: 'Aye, I'm right glad, Miss Annie . . . I'll get out of it, lass, through time,' she laughed. 'Yes,' she went on, 'I am glad; I've known there was summat wrong with him for a long time, and . . . it was you. He's a lucky lad.' She smiled her kindly smile. 'But he's a good lad,' she added, 'such a good lad. Eeh! now I must get on or I'll miss me tram. And you'll look for the book?'

'Yes, Mrs Macbane, I'll get it. And I'll bring it along to you tonight. Or shall I send it on to him?'

'You could, lass. Yes, you could . . . You know where to send it? To Mr Dane Dee's house.'

'Yes, I know.'

Annie's liking for Mrs Macbane was added to by the simple omission of the 'Lord' when speaking of Dane Dee; so few could have resisted that temptation, she thought.

As she ran back to the house, she wondered whether Terence had written about her in his little book.

Kate was at the telephone in the hall, and she held up her hand to Annie in a warning to be still and to wait. She was saying, 'I'm very sorry, Rosie. I'll come up later, but I can't see what I can do. You see, we've never spoken for years, and I'm sure the Jarrow relations will not let me do anything for the child.'

Annie heard Rosie say, 'My mother feels Pat will go off his head if anything happens to her. He's been looking after her; the granny from Jarrow's there, but she's so old, and partly stupid.'

'All right, Rosie,' said Kate; 'I'll come up later . . . Here's Annie.'

As Annie took the phone Kate whispered, 'Connie Fawcett's dying.'

Annie said, 'Oh, poor thing,' but she could feel no sorrow. Connie Fawcett remained in her memory as a mountain of drunken fat, and as a woman who had shamed her in the street. She said, 'Hello, Rosie,' and for a moment listened to her friend talking.

Then, turning round to see if the hall was clear, she whispered, 'I've got something to tell you. Terence and I, you know, Terence Macbane . . .'

She stopped, and Rosie said, 'Ah, yes.'

Annie went on, 'You know what I mean, don't you?'

Rosie started to chuckle. 'Yes, I know what you mean. And I'm glad, Annie . . . When is it going to be . . . ?'

'Oh, Rosie, don't be silly. We were only together one day; he had to leave on Tuesday . . . But it will be some day,' she added naïvely. 'He . . . well . . . Oh, I can't talk here. Look, I'll tell you when I see you.'

Laughing at a remark of Rosie's, she rang off, and turned to see Kate standing behind her. Kate was smiling, but her tone was serious when she said, 'Cathleen rang Rodney up first thing this morning; she'll be up later. I won't see her unless it's impossible not to, and if you see her I shouldn't say anything to her about Terence.'

Annie said, 'No, no. Of course not.' In her heart, though, she wanted Cathleen to know it was her whom Terence loved.

She found the place where he had lain. It was a small piece of grassland enclosed on three sides by low bushes. Its open side faced the stream, and the spot was only a few yards away from the pool. There remained quite clearly the impression of his body in the long grass, but not a sign of the book. The little alcove was narrow, and there was no place for it to lie hidden. She switched the long grass near the foot of the bushes, but there was no sign of it. Disappointed, she sat down on the bank of the stream.

It must be very precious for him to be so concerned about it . . . Had he written anything about her on his last night here? His mother had said 'poetry and things'; she couldn't imagine Terence writing poetry. She realised there were many things about him she didn't know; there had scarcely been time to talk, just a day together. All the time that had gone before seemed such a waste; every minute that wasn't spent with him seemed a waste. How had she lived before? What had filled her days? She couldn't think. And now they would never be really parted; nothing could come between them now, nothing.

On this vehement assertion, the thought of Cathleen rose like a black spectre. Cathleen's name had not been mentioned by her, nor by Terence. Was that odd? It wasn't that she hadn't thought of Cathleen during the time she was with Terence; she had quite often, but she had been afraid to mention her. She had been afraid of hearing Terence mentioning Cathleen's name, which was silly, but there remained with her still a lingering fear of Cathleen, in spite of

175

the knowledge of Terence's love. How, Annie asked herself, would she be able to hide her joy from Cathleen's sharp eyes when they met?

Cathleen's spectre faded as Annie watched a family of moorhens dart, one after the other, from a clump of reeds on the opposite bank and paddle away in formation up the stream, their little black bodies sending arrows of waves. The last ripple came almost to her feet as they dangled above the water. With the severe drought, the stream was only half its normal depth. In the winter it usually flowed to within a few inches of the bank top, but now the incurved banks were baked dry. It was her eyes following the path of the ripple which caused her to bend over, and there she saw the book; it was lying practically behind her legs, caught end-up in the thin root of a tree protruding from the bank. It must have dropped when he lowered himself into the stream. She had only to put down her hand to pick it up.

She laughed softly to herself. Oh, she was glad she had found it! She began to examine it, turning it over and over in her hands. She had never before seen a book bound like this. It was beautiful; no wonder he didn't want to lose it. How did he come by such a beautiful thing? She knew he could never have bought it. The covers were pieces of fine black leather, on which weird figures were embossed in delicate golds, greens and blues, while the back itself was a panel of exquisitely painted enamel with tiny rings down each side linking the leather covers and the pages together. Across the front were three clasps, in the same enamel as the back.

She went to undo the clasps, then hesitated. Would he mind her reading his poetry? No, of course not. But it was private, it was his own. Yes, but she was different; he would want her to know all he thought. What did Kate say about reading other people's letters? But this wasn't a letter, it was just a book of poems. His mother must have read it to be able to say they were poems. Well, if his mother had read it . . . She found that the two end clasps sprang back at a touch, but the middle one did not move. It couldn't be locked, she reasoned, for there was no keyhole. But, do all she might, it would not open to her fingering. There must be a secret spring somewhere. She began systematically to press the back and the rings, which availed her nothing. After a time she laid it down in exasperation.

But her curiosity began to eat into her, and again she picked it up and searched for a means of releasing the clasp. Finally, when she was admitting defeat, she snapped the two end clasps home together, and to her delight saw the middle one fly open. How simple, yet how ingenious! You could close one clasp after another, and nothing happened, but close them sharply simultaneously and there you had the secret.

On the flyleaf was the inscription: *From a Chinaman to an Englishman, with his deepest respect. Larry.* She paused before reading further; there was already a sense of privacy about those words. She fingered the paper. It was fine, like rice paper, but strong, and crackled like parchment.

On the next page Terence's writing met her eye, firm, rounded letters forming plain, intelligible words:

To the gods that be:
Should I be born again of your bounty,
Create me a Chinaman.

How funny, she thought. Before turning another page she paused: Should I? of course; he won't mind . . . it isn't as if it were a letter.

She turned a page, and read:

To an old woman of Wherry Street, who had
  geraniums in her window:

177

The windows are clean which she looks through
To gold-crowned trees dusting skies of blue,
And birds like arrows before her sight
Dart into immensity of light;
Fragile and wax-like the roses must seem,
Untouchable, like beauty in a dream,
Icy the chrysanthemums' frosty elegance,
Against whose beauty she has no defence;
She sees them all through her windows bright,
She sees them there by day and by night.
Don't say she looks on a back yard small
And sees nothing but a gaunt blank wall.

How quaint! And how nice of him to think of the old woman like that . . . Oh, her Terence *was* wonderful.

She turned another page and read:

Larry and I listened to two kids arguing with the pointlessness of all youthful argument. We were lying soaking up sun after a swim in Parsons' Pleasure. I scribbled the following, which tickled him; he translated it into Chinese to send to his sister:

He said it was a . . . bluebottle,
I said it was a . . . fly.
He said it was a . . . bluebottle,
And then I asked him why.
Just 'cos . . . he said,
Just 'cos . . . that's all.
Wasn't any answer,
Was it,
At all?

Simple things please Larry. Is this why he's so happy, I wonder?

As Annie read on, a sense of guilt began to steal over her. Some of the writing was not poetry, but little pen sketches of different people. And some of the writing disturbed her, as did the piece on 'Beauty'. She could not really understand it; it seemed rather far-fetched, and had very little connection with the mind she imagined to be Terence's. She read again:

Take from me the beauty I have craved; it is past my power to bear; only by pain can I live. How I have longed, cried and striven, pleaded night and day . . . Oh, give me the power to feel, to be conscious of beauty. Let the springs of my soul fling back its doors, and let me experience the ecstasy of beauty. It is here within me; once released it will flood each aching pore. But how to seek? Where to seek? By what road?

Unbidden of the moment it came to me, unthought of, unsought, in that second it floated out on the frosty air . . . A boy's voice, pealing high and clear, flying away through the stained-glass window . . . up, up from the muted organ, swinging me with it from the earth as it soared to the very feet of God Himself. And now I knew the power of beauty: no soothing balm this, but a burning, tearing, unbearable emotion; no vein left out, no sense forgotten, each torn apart and sent shivering away into realms unknown: I cried as I was flung into the world I had craved.

No! no! I am not big enough to bear it. I will take pain, localised and named; earthiness and squalor I will embrace; these I can bear, but beauty . . . no more.

Really, it was quite odd, and so intense! she shook her head. Not a bit like Terence!

She turned to the next writing, and this brought the blood to her cheeks. She read the words again; they were alive and molten, as if they were spilt from some overfull cauldron, and were headed 'The Sage of Youth':

For *what do I clamour? you ask . . . Not the surge of youth that springs and lashes the flesh to its task, conjuring bright pictures in the night of beauty masked in fleshy desire, over which your blood sings and wings to flight; nor the desire to barter all life for the touch of a body, and to work all my days to sustain it, maintain it, in strife, and watch the wrinkles slowly creep, and weep inside, and lash out in the end, crying, 'Why must I abide?'*

After this tirade I look at myself and laugh, and say, 'But this do I ask: Age and peace, and fulfilment within.'

But how can I complete a life without the things I spurn and the experience of sin? If I would reach this mellowness then I must fly, wasting not a day; I must seek me a woman right away.

Annie stared at the words, not believing what she read. She could see no satire, no subtle humour, no working of a mind fearful of yet grasping at life. I should never have opened the book, she thought; it's my own fault. But she did not close it. She turned another page as if the paper were burning her:

I watched an old Cullercoats fisherman gazing out to sea today. He was old, very old, and his eyes were colourless and had almost ceased to see the things of this world.

180

What does he see as he gazes afar?
The texture of the wind?
The material of a star?
The soul of a ship resting in the hull?
The spirit of Time's flight in the wing
of a gull?
He only feels, and knows, across the bar
Gone for ever will be the need to gaze
afar.

She made no comment on this one, except to say to herself, The metre's wrong!

She turned the pages hastily, scanning the writing, until she came to words that, she told herself, she had known she would find: words about Cathleen, words that made her sick and angry by turns, words that dimmed the sunshine, that took the sparkle from the stream and the wonder from a rising lark in the meadow beyond, words that blotted out the Terence she thought she knew and conjured in his place someone quite different. And she brought the final sentence down on him, the convent's and confessional's description of the dark and clamorous products of the mind: 'They are bad thoughts!'

She remained quiet; the moorhens came back to their nest; the shadow of a tree touched her and imperceptibly began to move across her. With a great intake of breath she at last moved, and turned and buried her face in the grass. Oh, how could he! How could he think such things? Even if he thought them, to put them into words was infinitely worse. And about Cathleen! He had wanted Cathleen in that way ... He said plainly in the writing that he wanted her. Then had they ... ?

She suddenly raised herself from the grass and, grasping the book as if she would tear it asunder, she read more:

The Bravery of Darkness

I lie near you in the night,
Pressed close against the earth
  Beneath a tree,
  Breast to breast
  And knee to knee,
And bless the myriad gods who gave you birth!
Your breath, your sighs, your senseless chatter,
  Your perfume, your sweat,
  Your endless repetition of 'my pet'
Are thickly varnished with the wonder of my body's
  flight.
They do not matter.
A seabird calls and wings into the night;
Your voice squeaks, twitters, raised in mock alarm,
Begging my brave protection from all harm.
Great warrior. I give it with my might.

Tomorrow when the sun shines fair
I shall face myself and find me there,
Disgusted, horrified that I lusted.
But that is tomorrow, and this is night!
  Dark earth, soft grass, and you,
  Who would not dare?

Cathleen Davidson . . . I hate you, I loathe you! With each
word she twisted clumps of dry grass around her hands and
tore them up by the roots. *My pet*! . . . It's you who have done
this, you who have made him like this! You have also made
me like *this*: capable of hating. I have never hated anyone
before, but I hate you! I wish you were dead! I've always
wished that. 'Yes, I have!' she cried aloud, defiantly looking
heavenwards.

Even in her rage she was aware of a feeling of surprise that she had not immediately begged God's pardon for her sin of hate and defiance. She didn't cry, which surprised her too. This cold, deadly feeling of hate scorned tears; she found strength in it, it bore her on through her bitterness and recrimination. Cathleen had always tried to spoil everything for her. Since the early days at the convent she had set out to take from Annie every friendship she made, to spoil anything she enjoyed . . .

Her mind completed the circle, and returned to Terence. These were *his* thoughts, not Cathleen's! It was he who said . . . What did he say? She looked at the book again, her eyes seeming to lift each word from the page. *Bless the myriad gods who gave you birth! . . . Varnished with the wonder of my body's flight . . .* Oh, it was horrible! How could he?

A question sprang from the detached part of her mind which stored her honesty: Had he written all that about you, would you have thought it horrible?

She gave a flick of her head, making no answer but asking herself: What has he written about me? Has he written anything about me? . . . There, on the last page he had used, she saw:

Derision of the Moon

Your strongest light is but a glimmer
To the reflection from her hair;
I see you flaunting it in envy
Of the pale beauty you see there,
Borrowing white clouds to enhance your beam
And hiding your face when she runs,
Her glinting hair like wind-blown water,
Her body a silver stream

In the eerie greenness of a dream.
You scarred crater,
A myth of light,
Torn from the sun
To light the night,
What can you know of pale gold hair,
The torments and laughter hidden there?

Just about her hair! No words of passion about *her* . . . She pulled herself up. Did she want words of passion? No! No, of course not!

But the small voice came again: You lay like that with him . . . 'I didn't! I didn't!' she flung back. 'It wasn't meant like that.' She bent her head on to her knees and rocked herself to and fro. And the sense of disappointment which she felt the night Terence pulled her abruptly to her feet when they were lying near the pool returned . . . And also the next night, on the sands, he had done the same . . . He clearly didn't want her as he had wanted Cathleen . . . He didn't love her like that; he thought her a child . . . Well! she didn't want him to love her like that. Didn't she know that sort of love was wicked! Hadn't she suffered all her life because of that kind of wickedness? She had been born of it!

She thrust the book into her pocket, got hastily to her feet, and walked up through the wood, conflicting emotions tearing at her. She asked herself what she would say about the book . . . Should she tell him she had read it? Oh, why had she read it? What could she do about it?

As she neared the bottom of the garden, David ran to meet her with outstretched arms, expecting to find her own arms flung wide to whirl him off his feet. She said, 'I can't; it's too warm.'

He stood away from her, his brown eyes full of surprise and enquiry. 'Have you got a pain in your stomach?' Since a secret

184

orgy of apples the previous week had resulted in severe pain in his stomach, he was apt to attribute any change in the disposition of those around him to this cause.

Annie shook her head; she could not even smile at him.

Taking her hand and walking by her side, he asked, 'Have you got a pain somewhere else, then?'

His sympathy was cutting away the feeling of bitterness. She turned her head from his childish gaze. Oh, if only one could stay like David, never, never to grow up and feel the hurts dealt by those you loved! But then, Terence didn't think she was grown-up, did he? He had said, 'You are so young.'

The pain in her heart seemed unbearable; all this beautiful new life to be spoilt by a little book! Why oh why had he to write stupid poetry? Why did people feel the necessity to expose their inmost thoughts? There seemed something odd about people who wrote poetry. Look at Rodney's first wife. She had written books of it, and got herself killed in the end. Cathleen once brought one of the books to the house – she said she had picked it up in a second-hand shop – and asked Annie if she would like to read it, adding slyly that perhaps Kate might like to see it. She remembered her feeling of panic when she thought Cathleen might show the book to Kate, and begged her not to. Cathleen had played with her like a cat with a mouse for hours. It was a long time ago, and now she knew that Kate wouldn't have minded seeing the book.

Cathleen! Always Cathleen. She was like a great black star in her sky, and nothing would blot her out. 'You *have* got a pain,' David said; 'I know you have. Mammy'll send you to bed . . .'

'No, no!' Annie caught him as he made to run off. Whatever happened Kate mustn't know how she was feeling; her sympathy might ferret out the cause, and nobody must know about Terence and Cathleen.

He was a fallen god; for years, in her mind, she had kept

him high on a pedestal. He had slipped off at Christmas, but she had gradually forced him back. And now he was once more on the earth, and as her hand touched the book in her pocket it was as if he were saying: 'This is my foundation. Don't try to lift me from it again. Remember what I said in my letter? I'm an ordinary chap.'

A little later Kate called from the house, and Annie went up, David dancing before her. She found her mother standing by the study window, dressed for outdoors. 'I'm off to the Mullens', dear,' she said, 'although I can't see what I can do for Connie now . . . You wouldn't like to come?'

'No, it's too hot.'

'You do look hot . . . and tired. Are you feeling all right?'

'She's got a pain, Mammy,' cried David.

'No I haven't!' Annie turned on him with unusual sharpness. Then, pulling herself up, she said, 'I'm sorry, dear. Go and ask Alice for your milk.' She turned to Kate: 'I'm all right, Mam, really; it's only this heat. It doesn't seem to ease up at all.'

On his way dutifully out of the room, David said to no-one in particular: 'She *has* got a pain, I know she has.'

Kate smiled. 'Memories of last week. He'll never forget that.'

'Will you see Connie?' Annie asked.

'No; she wouldn't want me to. And I can't see what I can do for the boy, since the whole tribe from Jarrow will be there. But Mrs Mullen seems to think I should go. It will be difficult to explain to her why I . . .'

'Of course,' Annie put in, 'you'd be expected to go, she's your cousin.'

'Annie.' Kate looked steadily at her daughter. 'I think this will please you as much as it did me when I first heard it . . . Connie Fawcett is no relation of ours.'

'But weren't my granda and her father brothers?'

'Yes, but your granda wasn't my father.'

Annie stared blankly.

'Tim Hannigan wasn't my father, Annie. I didn't know until a month or so before my mother died. She told me during her last illness. My father was an artist who lodged with them . . . Oh,' she said, as the noise of wheels on the gravel came to them, 'there's Blyth fetching the car round, and he must get back to take Rodney to Newcastle. So I must go . . . But isn't that something to be thankful about, darling?' She kissed Annie. 'Don't look so surprised; it is rather a staggering thing to take in all at once, I know. When I first heard it I nearly went wild with joy, I remember dancing round the table. Goodbye, dear. We'll talk about it when I get back.'

As Kate went out Annie sat down slowly on a chair by the open window. She hadn't spoken since Kate had said, 'Tim Hannigan wasn't my father.' What a strange morning. Everything was happening; her joy had been taken away, and now this. And Kate expected her to welcome it. How strange! The world seemed to be upside-down. In a few words she was deprived of a grandfather. Tim Hannigan had been a bad man, getting drunk, beating her grandmother, fighting in the streets and using bad language. All her young life she had been afraid of him; but he was her grandfather, and in some strange way he stood for security. As a child she couldn't say, as the other girls did, 'Me da said this,' 'Me da said that', but she said, with strange pertinacity, 'Me granda said this or that.' Even when he was at his worst, she still hung on to him as a tie, not with any vestige of love, but because he was a form of relationship. And now Kate said, 'This will please you as much as it did me.' But by telling Annie this she had deprived her of her only remaining link of male parentage.

Kate didn't mind being illegitimate. How strange! But Annie, from the time of first being conscious of this stigma, had been haunted by a strange dread, which had taken on a

187

definite shape as she grew older. The dread was with her now and, like a seed nurtured slowly during the years, was bursting forth into actual thought, and crying, Your mother is illegitimate! You are illegitimate! It's in the blood; you'll do the same! The thought grew and burst all bonds: You wanted to, that night by the pool . . . She sprang up, looking wildly around her. It was as if someone had spoken aloud. She put her hand into the pocket where the book lay, and thought: I'm glad I read it; it's a warning . . . Oh dear God, protect me, and never, never let that happen to me . . . Oh, Holy Mary, ever a virgin, watch over me . . .

13

It was unfortunate that Rosie Mullen decided to walk home from the station, and that at about the same time Cathleen should miss the tram to Tyne Dock on her way to visit the Princes. They were approaching each other along the East Jarrow Road.

Rosie was feeling very pleased with herself; her master had praised her, and spoken of great results accruing from the London concert, and tomorrow she was to meet Michael Davidson again. She felt happy and full of self-confidence, which even the sight of Cathleen could do nothing to dispel. In fact, at that moment she was capable of tackling ten Cathleens.

Life was opening up for her. She knew now that Michael Davidson liked her, more than liked her. And she felt safe in the knowledge; it gave her strength to plan the future. When she was established she'd need an accompanist. So why not Michael? He could play really well, and was mad about music. And when she was making money, the first thing she'd do would be to move her mother and father from the fifteen streets – and, of course, try to repay the doctor . . . if he would take it. Life was grand. She had Michael, and her singing; she had her father and mother and friends like Annie and Kate; she could afford to snap her fingers at Cathleen Davidson. There she was, coming along as if she owned the town, with that haughty sneer on her face. Would she stop and speak, or pass on? Well, it didn't matter to her what Cathleen Davidson did.

Cathleen, on her part, was feeling anything but pleased; her taste of Paris had made Tyneside seem quite unbearable, and the people revolting. She was thinking, if only she had some money. It was no use hoping to make money from her work, at least the kind of money she wanted; only painters of the front rank commanded high fees. However, a way lay open to get not only money but position. But she would have to get away from the grubby north. She would have to get a flat somewhere and furnish it. She was confident that her plans for the future could be realised if only she had a place of her own.

John Dane Dee was showing a marked interest in her. Twice during the month she was in Paris he had looked her up. Things would have gone much further if Doris Penell had not been tacked on to her. But perhaps it was just as well, for there was no sense in being too accessible at first. She wasn't giving anything away this time; there was too much at stake. Propriety would have to be her watchword now. There was plenty of time to try on him those enchantments that she had exercised on Steve and Terence; that would come later.

The thought of Terence brought a stiffness to her face. Scary prig! It would be one in his eye if she became Lady Dane Dee! Wouldn't it just! Oh, look what was coming . . . the haybag! Wasn't she a sight? Fancy wearing a striped dress with that figure! She was nuts about their Michael. Good Lord, fancy having that for a sister-in-law! Not if she knew it.

They came almost abreast, hesitated, then stopped, appraising each other, Cathleen's eyes saying clearly, 'The same old haybag.'

They remarked on the heat. Then Rosie, full of her coming concert, could not resist speaking of it. She bragged a little and said something of the glories that awaited her, until she became aware of Cathleen's amused smile, which said plainly, 'How can you hope to become a success on the concert platform with that figure?'

Rosie divined what Cathleen was thinking, for she was conscious of her dumpy figure, and she felt a savage desire to hit back. Oh, if only she could find something to say which would remove that self-satisfied sneer. At this moment she had no fear of Cathleen, and she hunted around in her mind for some weapon to use. And then she had it!

Smiling brightly, she said, 'Looks as if it won't be long before there's a wedding up at Brambleberry House.'

'A wedding?' queried Cathleen. 'What! don't tell me she's having Brian.' She laughed outright.

'Brian? Good Lord, no! It's a friend of yours, Terence Macbane. It sounds as though they're head over heels . . . Didn't you know they were going together?'

Cathleen had a swift desire to push the smiling face against the rough wall . . . The little swine! Just wait, she'd have her own back on her . . . Aloud she said, 'Well, we're only young once.' Her smile was brittle. 'Goodbye.'

She moved swiftly away, not daring to allow herself another minute opposite those small bright eyes . . . So that was it, that was why he had taken flight. She bit into her lower lip . . . Does that anaemic-looking sanctimonious madam think she can get away with it? And does Terence Macbane imagine I can be thrown aside for Annie Hannigan? Mr Macbane, your memory's short! We'll have to see what can be done about it . . . It would have been better for you had

Annie Hannigan not been educated in a convent. It needed only that to make her virginal in the extreme. I wonder how much her sense of propriety can stand. We'll have to see. And as she walked on a smile slowly spread over her face.

Kate returned from the Mullens' house very upset. Her visit had disturbed her more than she thought possible. Against her better judgement she had gone into Connie's house to see the boy. Connie was already dead, and all the relations from Jarrow were there. They treated her with a sort of fawning civility, and were more than willing that she should do something for the boy, since the struggle to feed their own broods was hard enough. But the granny turned on Kate. Holding the stupefied boy to her, she yelled that Kate would be the last person who would have him. Kate had left the house immediately, shaken by the vehemence of the old woman.

In Mrs Mullen's, a neighbour had called for a subscription towards a wreath. The amount was already at £2 5s, and would most likely reach £5 by the time it had gone round the fifteen streets. Gorgeous flowers would lie on Connie's coffin; the insurance money would be ticked for a wake before it was received; the undertaker would get his money in instalments, if he was lucky. And the new black would find itself safely on the pawnshop rack directly the funeral was over. Kate knew it all so well. It was hopeless trying to do anything; by their own efforts only could the people of the fifteen streets emerge from their customary way of living.

She wished earnestly now that she could have done something for Pat's boy, but she knew it was impossible. It saddened her, since but for a slight turn of fate he might have been her son, for had not Connie tricked his father away from Kate many years ago?

Mrs Summers met Kate in the hall. She looked troubled and said, 'I'm glad you're back, ma'am.'

'Why? What has happened? . . . The doctor? He's all right?'

'Oh, yes ma'am; he's got back from Newcastle and had his lunch, and gone off down to the clinic . . . It's Miss Annie. She won't come out of her room; she's got the door locked. I've never known her door be locked in all the years I've been here.'

'Got her door locked!' exclaimed Kate. 'Since when?'

'Well, it must have been straight after Miss Davidson left.'

Kate stood still at the foot of the stairs: 'Did . . . did anything happen?'

'Not a thing that I know of, ma'am. When Miss Davidson came I told her the doctor was down at the clinic and Miss Annie was upstairs starting her packing. She went up, and a while after, when I passed on the landing, I heard her laughing . . . you know, the way she does, ma'am, with that funny deep laugh. Then she comes downstairs and goes off to the clinic. It was Master David who found Miss Annie's door locked. He came to me upset because she wouldn't let him in. But I thought he was only up to his pranks again and took no notice for a time. But when I did go up, it was locked all right. I called through the door, and Miss Annie said she had a headache and was lying down.'

Kate was already mounting the stairs, and Mrs Summers followed, continuing: 'I let her alone for an hour or so, then I told her tea was ready. But she said she didn't want any . . . I was just going to ring the doctor when you came.'

Kate tried the door; it was locked. She called softly, 'Annie. Annie.'

There was no sound for a moment. Then Annie's voice came to her, low and rather muffled: 'I have a headache, I'm lying down.'

'But why have you locked the door, dear?' asked Kate.

'I just want to be quiet.'

The voice was unlike Annie's, and Kate and Mrs Summers exchanged glances.

Kate said firmly, 'Annie, open the door! You can be quiet, but I must see you!'

There was no answer to this.

Mrs Summers whispered, 'There's the doctor coming in, ma'am.'

Kate turned swiftly and ran downstairs, crying, 'Rodney! Rodney!'

'Why! what's the matter?' he asked.

'It's Annie. She's locked herself in her room and won't come out.'

'Locked herself in?' Rodney appeared incredulous.

'Yes. Come up, dear, and see if you can get her to open the door.'

He followed her as quickly as he could. And he too tried the door before tapping gently and saying, 'Annie, it's Rodney. Come, my dear, and open the door.' He stared at the panel, waiting. And when there was no answer he cast a swift glance back to Kate, who shook her head slowly, fear in her eyes.

'Annie!' he called again. 'If you won't open the door I'll have to force it in.'

They waited in strained silence. Then from the other side of the door came Annie's voice, startlingly calm: 'I'm all right, Rodney; I just want to be left alone for a little while. Please let me be.'

He turned and looked from Kate to Mrs Summers, then back to the door again. 'All right, my dear,' he said quietly and, making a motion to the others to come away, he went downstairs. Reluctantly Kate followed him. In the drawing-room, he asked, 'What on earth can have happened? Can you think of anything?'

Yes, she could think of something . . . Cathleen Davidson had been here. She could not keep the bitterness from her voice when she said, 'Cathleen's been here. It was after she left Annie locked herself in.'

'What on earth can Cathleen have to do with it?'

'Everything!' Kate shook with agitation. 'Cathleen doesn't like Annie, Rodney. She's found out about her and Terence, and has done something. I knew she would, I knew it!'

He took her gently by the shoulder: 'Kate, that's unfair, and so unlike you. For some reason or other you don't care for Cathleen, and everything unpleasant that happens you attribute to her. Why, she came down to the clinic to see me after she saw Annie, and she was quite open about Terence and Annie. She said Rosie Mullen told her. And she also said she spoke to Annie about it. You see, she bears no hard feelings at all. And you must realise, Kate, that up to a short time ago she was Terence's girl, and I think she was very fond of him.'

Kate turned away and sat down. What was the use? Cathleen had won again, and her cleverness was frightening. She had been on the point of telling Rodney about Steve, to bear out her accusation of Cathleen, but she saw now it would be Steve, and Steve alone, who would be blamed, and that Rodney himself would take on the responsibility for Steve's behaviour towards the daughter of his friend. She was silly even to imagine he would blame Cathleen. Why was he so utterly blind to her real character?

Rodney said, 'Of course, there must be some reason for Annie acting like this. Do you think she's received a letter that's disturbed her?'

Kate did not reply; she knew the afternoon's mail was still on the salver in the hall. No; the disturber was Cathleen, who was determined to ruin Annie's happiness. But – Kate gripped her hands together – she shan't! I know her, and I'll fight her. We'll fight her together . . . But there was the

195

point: would Annie fight? Kate's hands slackened and drooped in her lap . . . Annie was a composition all her own, an untried composition. She looked at life as black and white, good and bad. As yet there was no middle course for her. If a person or thing disappointed her she was apt to leave them on one side; she voiced no harsh criticism, but with an air of finality that often disturbed Kate she thrust them out of her life.

'It's probably a letter she's had from Terence that hasn't pleased her,' Rodney was saying. 'Love can appear very cruel at her age. She can't imagine that Terence is one of the many she'll have before she marries.'

Her face turned away from him, Kate said quietly, 'From the first moment I set eyes on you I knew I would love you for all time. I may not have been wholly conscious of it from the beginning, but the fact soon forced itself upon me. And it's the same with Annie. I feel that if she doesn't have Terence Macbane she'll have no-one.' She turned towards him. 'Can't you see? Her happiness these past few days hasn't been just ordinary happiness, it's been something beyond the normal. And if it's abruptly snatched from her, she'll sink into the depths as far as she soared into the clouds.'

Rodney came and put his arm about her and drew her up to him; holding her tightly, he kissed her. 'That's for your renewed declaration of love.' He smiled at her. 'And now, my dear, I must really be firm with you. You're taking this much too seriously. Let us give her another hour or so, and then we'll try again. And if she doesn't open the door then, I'll force the lock . . .'

An hour had barely passed when they again went upstairs. Rodney, trying the handle and finding the door still locked, called firmly: 'Annie, open the door!' He gave her sufficient time, then said sharply, 'If you don't open it immediately I'll force the lock.'

There was movement in the room. The key was turned and the door pulled open with a jerk, and Annie faced them.

Kate made a little sound, a suppressed moan, but did not speak. It was as she thought: Annie had gone down into the depths as far as she had been in the clouds. She stared at her daughter's face, which seemed to have changed in a matter of hours from that of a beautiful laughing girl to an expressionless mask, and the paleness of the skin added to this illusion. There was no sign of tears; her eyes were bright and their green so dark as to appear almost black.

Rodney said compassionately, 'What is it, my dear? What's happened?'

'Nothing. I only wanted to rest.' Her voice was level and clipped. She stood straight and her tenseness formed a guard about her.

'Now, now, Annie; there's more to it than that. Come, tell me about it.'

Rodney made to enter the room, but pulled up abruptly when she said, 'I'm not telling you about it, now or at any time, so you can save your persuasion. I just want you to leave me alone.'

She had never spoken to him like this before. All her words to him had been gentle and loving; even ordinary, everyday greetings always held some special tone meant for him alone. The hurt and surprise showed plainly in his face. For a brief second his eyes looked searchingly into hers, then, turning slowly, he brushed past Kate and walked away.

'Annie, how could you speak to Rodney like that! In fact, how *dare* you!' cried Kate. 'What has come over you? What's happened, anyway?'

Annie turned back into her room, and Kate followed her, crying, 'Cathleen Davidson's done this, hasn't she?'

'I'm not going to discuss it, so you needn't keep on.'

Kate was amazed at her tone. Never before had she heard

Annie speak in this fashion. She said: 'I know it's Cathleen Davidson. I warned you.'

'Then tell Rodney,' said Annie. 'Not that he'll believe you.'

'Annie! My dear, my dear,' Kate implored, turning Annie round to face her, 'tell me what it is. Oh, please tell me; you'll feel better.' Then she gave a start of surprise: 'It wouldn't be what I told you before I went out?'

'No, it isn't that . . . although, for myself, I couldn't see anything to be joyful over. But I'm not telling you, Mam.' The coldness of her eyes and the quiet tone held so much firm resolution that Kate dropped her hands and stood away, looking at her daughter. She had always felt there was nothing about Annie she did not know or understand, but this new attitude had a resolution about it and the temper of steel which she could in no way associate with her Annie. This new Annie was strong enough to fight Cathleen Davidson alone. But she wouldn't, for she was turning all her forces upon herself.

Without another word Kate left her. Gone was the fear that Annie would do something to herself, but a greater fear was taking its place, and as yet she could not place it; she only knew that in some intangible way it was connected with the lighted candles on the altar, the open prayer book, and the rosary lying across her bed.

Kate was awake when the phone rang; it was two o'clock, and she found it impossible to sleep. Rodney lay by her side, moving restlessly, his wounded leg jerking at almost regular intervals. The noise of the bell startled her, and she was more surprised still, on lifting the receiver, to hear Peggy Davidson's voice. It came to her full of agitation: 'Kate, can Rodney come up? Peter needs him.'

'Is he ill?' asked Kate anxiously.

'No . . . but he needs Rodney.'

'Just a moment, Peggy.' Kate shook Rodney, saying, 'It's Peggy on the phone, she wants you to go up at once.'

Rodney, sleep gone from him in a matter of seconds, took the receiver, and after listening for a while said briefly, 'I'll be up as quickly as possible, Peggy.'

Handing the receiver back to Kate, he said, 'Get Blyth up. Tell him I want the car immediately.'

As Kate lifted the house telephone she asked, 'What's the matter? Is one of them ill?'

'I don't know. There must be something seriously wrong with either Cathleen or Michael. She wouldn't say on the phone.'

Rodney was half dressed when he exclaimed: 'Good Lord, haven't you got that fellow awake yet?'

'Yes, he's coming.' Kate put the receiver down. 'He must sleep like the dead!'

'More likely he doesn't want to hear. Oh Lord, how I miss Steve! He'd have had the car out by now.'

There was no further conversation between them as she helped him to finish dressing. It was the first time he had mentioned Steve since the night she was told he'd left, and she felt the reference to have been involuntary, slipping out through his annoyance. Nevertheless, after he had gone, she was uncertain in her mind whether it was his allusion to Steve or the urgency to reach the Davidsons' which caused him to leave so coldly. Since he knew her state of mind with regard to Annie, she felt it unfair of him to leave her like that, but she supposed the coldness was just part of the moods into which he had been falling of late, and which were beyond her power to fathom . . .

When Peggy opened the door to Rodney, he could not help the exclamation that escaped him. He saw that she was unable to speak; her small face, red and swollen with crying,

199

was sharpened with grief. She led the way into the sitting-room, and to his astonishment buried her face in her hands and wept convulsively.

Rodney put his arm about her shoulder. 'Peggy, my dear. Peggy, what is it?'

She looked up at him, her eyes weary: 'Oh, Rodney, why should this happen to us? What have we done? We have worked all our lives for them, given them all we could . . .'

'Peggy! What's happened? Tell me . . . Where's Peter? Stop crying now and tell me !'

The sharpness of his voice steadied her and she said, 'Upstairs with Michael . . . He doesn't know I phoned you, but I was afraid for him; he looked as if . . . as if he couldn't bear it, and I couldn't get near him, somehow . . . You see . . .'

'Peggy! What's happened? Just tell me that!' Rodney took her by the shoulder.

'Michael . . . tried to kill himself.'

'My God!'

'He would have done it if Duke hadn't smelt the gas and come scratching at our door. Peter was just in time. But Michael . . . my boy's ill!'

'My God!' muttered Rodney again, as he hastily went from the room.

Peggy remained standing where he had left her. She was in line with the piano, and after a while she was conscious that she was gazing fixedly at the photograph of Cathleen standing on the top of it. Her daughter's eyes seemed to be staring back at her defiantly. Peggy walked to the piano and lifted the picture in her hands and, as she looked down on it, the tears dropped in large blotches on the glass, distorting Cathleen's face into the semblance of a grinning demon. Peggy returned the photograph to the piano again, but she laid it face downwards and, burying her face in her hands, she leant against the wall and continued to cry bitterly.

It was dawn before Peter and Rodney came downstairs, and by common consent they made for Peter's small and untidy study. It was Rodney who went to the little cabinet standing on the bookcase and took out the bottle of whisky which he knew he would find there. He poured a generous supply into a tumbler which he handed to Peter, who was slumped in the leather armchair.

Peter shook his head wearily at the proffered glass, but Rodney insisted: 'Come on, man, get that down you.' He looked with anxious pity on this friend who had stood by him through the great trial of his own life, and now he felt utterly helpless to do anything that would lift the look of acute suffering from Peter's face . . . the face which, during their earlier acquaintance, had annoyed him with its constant smile.

They sat in silence for some time, Peter sipping spasmodically at the whisky, and either passing his hand over the back of his neck or rubbing it hard along his jawbone. Rodney, feeling that it would be better were Peter to talk about the matter, said: 'Have you any idea what made him attempt such a thing?'

Peter's hand moved rapidly over his face. He did not reply immediately, and when he did it was in the form of a question: 'Haven't you noticed the absence of the other member of the family?'

Rodney had noticed Cathleen's absence, but he had thought she must be in another room or with Peggy. Yet it was strange she hadn't put in an appearance, knowing he was there. As he said, 'You mean Cathleen?' there returned to him the memory of Kate saying, 'Cathleen Davidson has been here!'

Peter said suddenly, 'You know us, Rodney; there wasn't a happier family living when the pair of them were young. But these last few years, why . . . !' He shook his head despairingly. 'You wouldn't believe how unbearable life has been at times.'

Rodney said nothing; he was feeling uneasy. For years he had upheld Cathleen's actions. He had at times come very near to losing his temper with Kate because of her obvious distrust of Cathleen . . . But it was Cathleen Peter was referring to now.

Peter heaved himself from the chair and started to walk restlessly back and forward in the narrow space of the room. He talked spasmodically, as though the words were being forced out of him: 'She's a devil! There's something wrong with her; she can't bear peace. I don't blame Michael, he's only a lad, and her taunts would drive a grown man off his head at times . . . She's like no-one I know . . . We can't understand it.'

He stopped and took another drink of the whisky, and Rodney said quietly: 'I can't really believe it.'

'No, you wouldn't!' said Peter with some bitterness; 'you have always thought she was cute. You're about the only one she's managed to hoodwink. But I suppose you're not to blame for believing in her, for she's always kept a special side for you. If you had been here last night, though, it might have opened your eyes.

'When I got in Peggy said she had been at it for hours, taunting, taunting as only she knows how . . . Do you know, she can keep it up for a week. Every meal, every moment, in a thousand and one ways she can allude to the same thing until you have the desire to throttle her.'

'Peter!'

'I'm telling you, man, it's true.' Peter wiped the sweat from the palms of his hands. 'Peggy said she had been at Michael since she came in, at teatime. Michael went out because he couldn't stand any more of it. But when he came back she started on an old trick of hers, making continuous journeys to the bathroom and voicing remarks as she passed his door. She can do this in a penetrating whisper. It's uncanny to hear her. I suppose he could stand it no longer, for he rushed out and struck her. Peggy said Cathleen was aiming the bronze Negro head which stands on the landing table at him. Michael dodged it, and then he pushed her and she fell backwards down the stairs. It's a wonder she didn't break her neck.'

Rodney looked utterly incredulous. He was really unable to believe all he was hearing, yet it must be true. 'Where is she?' he asked.

'In bed with a dislocated shoulder and a broken ankle. And that's what I came home to, after delivering twins that I'd been working on for hours . . . Something like this was bound to have happened, it's the climax of years, but the hell of it is I'll have to send Michael away.'

'But what was it over?'

'Rosie Mullen.'

'Rosie?'

'Yes. It appears Michael's been seeing her. I didn't know anything about it, and I was a bit surprised because . . . well, she's such a little thing and she doesn't appear to be Michael's type at all. Also it's unusual for a lad of his age to take up with a girl older than himself. Anyway, that's what it was about. And I can imagine Cathleen making the most of her material.'

Peter sat down again. He looked tired unto death, and spoke as if he was thinking aloud: 'I'll send him to my brother, he's always wanted him to go out there for a visit. Yes, I'll send him there. I would have sent him a couple of years ago if Peggy hadn't been so against it.'

'You surely don't mean the one that's in Canada?' said Rodney.

'Yes.'

'What! Why, it will break Peggy's heart.'

'Something's got to be done, and he won't stay in this house after what's happened.'

'But Peter! Why not let Cathleen go away? She's been wanting to set up in London or Paris this long while. Why not let me—?'

'No!' said Peter roughly. 'She's not going to Paris. She's not moving further than this house as long as I can keep her here. And that won't be for much longer, for she'll soon be beyond my jurisdiction. But as long as I can keep her under my hand I'm going to. I only let her go on holiday because I was sure of the girl who was going with her.'

'But why, man?'

'Because she wouldn't be on her own twenty-four hours before she'd be on the streets.'

'Peter! Peter!'

'Yes, Peter! Peter! . . . But I know my own daughter. There are things I've found out these past few months that have nearly made my hair turn white.'

In some unaccountable way Rodney's mind at that moment turned to Steve. He had tried not to think of him for months, for he found that his thoughts always reverted from Steve to Kate. He had felt certain that there was some mystery about Steve's hasty departure, and that it involved Kate. He had been torn by unreasonable jealousy at the time. It was only the sure knowledge of Kate's love for him that enabled him to make the effort to stamp it out. But nevertheless it had cast a shadow, and the shadow remained, becoming deeper, as it had done this morning when he mentioned Steve's name and Kate had not replied. Wouldn't it have been a natural thing for her to make some comment on what he said? But no, when he came to think of it, she never mentioned Steve's name; she was as reticent in its use as he was himself.

Peter's voice brought Rodney back from his own minor trouble, startling him with its implications: 'It was only by chance I found she's been on the loose for years. Some little thing she said made me suspect, for you only gain a certain type of knowledge through experience. So one day I ransacked her room. I did it unknown to Peggy, for Cathleen was cute enough always to insist on doing her own room. The drawers were locked, but I soon fixed that. And what I found made me sick . . . It's the only time in my adult life, Rodney, I ever remember crying.'

Rodney could only sit staring at Peter. He was dried of words; there was nothing he could say that would be of comfort to his friend. There was within him, too, the feeling of having been let down, of being hoaxed and made a fool of. He had defended Cathleen for years, looking on her as an impetuous child. How amused she must have been at his loyalty! He had the odd feeling of being young and inexperienced, as if life still held awakenings for him. Only yesterday she had played him again. His mind gave a jolt. What had she done to Annie? Kate was right, she had been right all along. He felt a desperate urge to hurry away home, to both Kate and Annie, and to try to straighten out the tangles. Yes, he must get home, for Annie would start for college in a few hours. And he would ask Kate point-blank what she knew of Steve.

Peter's hand was laid on his knee. 'I feel better being able to talk to you about it. I don't know what I'd have done if you hadn't been here. Will you stay for a while? I need you, man.'

'As long as ever you want, Peter.'

14

⁓

Terence's next letter shook Annie's defences and penetrated the pose of cold indifference she had studiously cultivated. Naturally, it dealt only with the book, and instead of the humility the occasion warranted, the tone of the letter was censorious, and it had evidently been written in anger.

She sat on her narrow bed in the partitioned cubicle and read for the third time:

> *My mother made a mistake in asking you to look for the book, but you too made a mistake when you read it. Opening it must have been quite a business. This alone should have told you it was private. You had no right to read it. Evidently you were shocked by some of the things you read. As the book was meant for my eyes alone I am not going to justify myself to you; but I ask you to try and forget it, and I will forgive you for reading it.*

His tone mollified considerably towards the end, and he finished:

> *Oh Annie, I had been longing and longing for a letter. Then for you to send the book without even a word . . .*

*it was cruel of you . . . You know, a frightening thought
has occurred to me: I think you could be cruel in a puri-
tanical way, because you are so young.*

She crushed the letter into a tight ball. Young! She'd never
feel young again . . . and *he'd* forgive *her*, would he?

She rose from the bed as a bell sounded in the distance, and
walked swiftly through the dormitory, past rows of charac-
terless cubicles. How dare he! How dare he! And, as if
metaphorically striking a blow at him, she added grimly to
herself: I will write to Sister Ann tonight.

Four days later she received another letter. It began in panic:

*Annie, my dearest, you just can't mean you're not going
to write to me because of that silly book. I can explain
every word I wrote and why I wrote such stuff. And I
will when I see you. In the mean time, my Annie, don't
do this to me. I know my other letter was abrupt, and
I'm most sorry for writing in that strain. Oh my beloved,
this is simply hell! I can't get down to work.*

*I kept away from you for years because I was afraid of
what you could do to me. I see now that that fear was
well-founded. I knew that if I once allowed myself to
love you you would consume me. There is no going back
for me now. Annie, for God's sake, write to me!*

She could not read further. She looked wildly around her for
a means of escape. The formal garden of the college lay open
before her, bare of trees but studded with groups of girls. For
a moment the desire to run home, away from all this, assailed
her. She wanted, beyond anything else at the moment, to
escape from the mass of girls, from the routine, from all the
things here that were so cold and impersonal; nothing here
touched the heart. This last thought had a calming effect on

her . . . that was as it should be. That's what she wanted: nothing to touch the heart . . .

The third letter came at the end of a fortnight, and made her cry out: 'What kind of man is he? How can he say such things?'

In this letter he was endeavouring to explain the feeling which had urged him to express himself as he had done in the book. 'Annie,' he said:

The writings in that book were mostly adolescent thoughts. The words didn't mean all they seemed to convey. That book was a sort of safety valve; it was, as it were, part of me that I had to throw off . . . 'self-expression', they call it. Don't you see, the writing was the expression of the phases we all pass through? I suppose it was the one on Cathleen that shocked you. But believe me when I say it meant nothing; it was founded and built up on the merest incident.

At this point, Annie dropped the letter on to her lap. It was impossible that he could lie so. How had she ever let herself love someone who had acted as he had done and referred to it now as the merest incident? She thought back to all the years she had suffered through being 'a mere incident' . . .

She read on: *Talk the matter over with your mother if you like; I know she will understand. You can tell her all that was in the book . . .* He was sure of Kate's understanding because he knew that when Annie was born Kate wasn't married. He would not have dared to say that otherwise. And, she supposed, it was because of his knowledge on that subject that he was surprised that she, too, didn't treat the matter lightly; he was disappointed she wasn't like Kate . . . Oh, dear God, what was she saying? Oh, Mam! Mam! I didn't mean that. She wrung her hands. If only he'd stop writing, if only he'd leave her alone. That was all she wanted, to be left alone. She knew what she was going to do, and she wanted to be left in peace to do it . . .

It was a week before half-term when Kate received the telephone call from the principal of the college. The principal said she was a little troubled about Annie, who'd had a cold and been confined to bed for a few days, but wasn't picking up as she should. Although she was at her studies again, various reports of her tutors were to the effect that she was showing lack of concentration . . . It was suggested she should return home for a rest.

Within four hours Annie was home, full of indignation with the principal and with Kate for their unneccessary fuss. She maintained that, apart from a slight cold, she was otherwise perfectly all right. Did they want her to fail her exams? Why couldn't they all leave her alone?

To Kate's dismay, she found it impossible to get near Annie; her reticence was stronger than when she left home at the beginning of term. Several times Kate tried to penetrate the strange coolness and to draw Annie back on to the old footing that had kept them so near to each other through the years. But with each effort the breach between them seemed to widen. At last she left her to Rodney.

His approach was direct, knowing that she would see through any cautious preliminaries. He put his arm about her and led her into his study. 'Fairy,' he said, using an old childish name, 'there's something troubling you, and it's worrying me and your mother . . . It's to do with Cathleen Davidson, we know, and I want to tell you now that I have found out quite a lot about Cathleen lately. If I hadn't missed you the morning you went back to college we'd have had this talk before. I know she was bent on mischief when she last came up here; she did quite a lot of damage that day, some irreparable.'

For a moment Annie was off her guard. She looked her surprise, then asked, 'Was it through her that Michael went to Canada?'

'Yes, it was. And you'll feel better, my dear, if you'll tell me what she said to you, for whatever it was was prompted by jealousy, and was most likely lies . . . You know, it was also through her that Steve left. But Kate will tell you all about that. For myself,' Rodney went on, 'I think I must have been an utter blind fool.' He shook his head, still unable to comprehend the extent of Cathleen's wickedness.

'How did she make Steve go?' asked Annie, interested in spite of herself.

'Oh, it's a long story. You must ask Kate. That silly woman kept it to herself all this time. If only she had told me I should have been saved a few headaches, and so would you. But there, that's over . . . Now don't you see, my dear, whatever Cathleen said to upset you may have no foundation of truth in it?'

Annie turned from him and, leaning her arm on the mantelpiece, lowered her head on to it. 'It was true, Rodney . . . I know. And it wasn't only what she said, there was something else, something quite different.'

Rodney came and stood beside her and placed his hand gently on her hair. She turned swiftly to him and laid her cheek against his in the old familiar caress.

'Annie, dear . . .' He was greatly touched.

'Don't talk about it any more, Rodney. I can't tell you. It's over and done with, anyway. All I want to do is to forget about Cathleen Davidson . . . and him.'

'Very well, my dear. Very well.' He kissed her gently. He knew it would be useless to probe further; as Kate had said, it was like unearthing a seam of steel where you expected chalk.

*   *   *

210

The following morning Annie made the first decisive step on the road she planned to walk, and went to see Father Bailey. He was a little surprised, but delighted to see her, and it was quite a while before he let her come to the subject of her visit; all his interest and concern seemed to be centred on a canary in its cage by the window. It was a present, he explained, from someone in the parish. 'And you would never believe it, Annie,' he said, 'he sings like a lark . . . Now listen . . . Come on, Sandy. Come on, sing for the old man . . . Aw! come on now,' he coaxed. But Sandy refused to be drawn. 'He's temperamental,' the priest went on, poking his fingers through the bars; 'you wouldn't believe just how temperamental he is. He knows he's good and he plays on it. He has very human traits, has Sandy . . . Come on, boy, come on now.'

'Father,' began Annie from the opposite side of the cage, 'father, I've come to see you about . . . about entering the Church.'

Father Bailey continued to poke his fingers through the bars. He lifted a piece of bacon rind from one bar and wound it round another. He stepped back from the cage and intently watched its gentle swinging; then went back again and, putting his finger into the porcelain bath of sand, he stirred it up. Presently he dusted his hands and walked to the table. Sitting down, he motioned Annie to a seat on the opposite side.

He glanced at her across the broad expanse of the table, then stared down at the brown linoleum, and his eyes followed the dull imprints of his rubber soles on its shining surface, his head nodding as if he were counting each imprint.

'Well,' he said, 'since when have you wanted to be a nun, Annie?'

'Oh, a long time, father,' said Annie, clasping and unclasping her hands in her lap. 'Oh, quite a time.'

211

When had she first thought of being a nun? Was it that day in the convent chapel when she knelt praying beside Sister Ann and experienced a feeling of peace? Yes, perhaps, though she hadn't known about it until that day on the Jarrow road . . . 'Nearly four years, father.'

'Really? And why do you want to be a nun?'

'Because, father, I feel . . . well . . . I can't really explain . . . because the life will be so peaceful, and . . .'

Father Bailey let out a roar of laughter, and Annie's face became tight. 'And of course you want to serve God?' he said, wiping his eyes.

'Yes, yes, of course, father' – her voice was both earnest and indignant – 'and, and I want to teach children.'

Father Bailey leant back in his chair, tucked in his chin, and began to count the buttons on his waistcoat as if he had just discovered their presence. His expression was that of a surprised child. 'So you want to feel at peace and you want to teach?' He did not raise his eyes from the waistcoat.

'Yes.'

'And you think you'll have more peace and teach better if you are a nun?'

'Well . . . yes, father, something like that.'

Father Bailey swung away from the contemplation of his buttons. He leant across the table and thrust a finger at Annie: 'Now I'm going to tell you something, Annie . . . You are one of the majority who think along those lines, and one of the majority that's wrong. Far, far from temptation letting you alone once you become either a priest or a nun, it would seem that God walks out on you entirely, and the Devil has a clear field . . . Yes, Annie, you are very often starkly alone. It's as if God says, "Now I've brought you this far, get on with it," and instead of the "peace" you expect what do you get? A soul torn in agony, temptations that seem to come from the pit itself, and you can see no way out. And mark

212

this, you don't get out!' Father Bailey moved his fingers slowly up and down. 'No, you don't get out unless, in spite of all the Devil can do, you're sure of your road. You must know deep down you're sure of your road. And it's not just wanting peace, Annie, that will make you sure . . . The peace of God that passeth all understanding has to be worked for.'

He sat back in his chair again, and Annie stared at him in hurt surprise. This reception was totally unexpected; she had thought he would be overjoyed, he of all people.

His next remark seemed irrelevant: 'I had a letter from Tim the other day, and it was odd that he should be talking of the grand time he had at Christmas up at your house. A fine lot of people he met there; he had the time of his life . . . Ah! he likes a bit of fun, does Tim.'

Annie exclaimed, tersely, 'If Tim can become a priest, why shouldn't I become a nun, father?'

'Just this, Annie,' he said quietly: 'Tim has a vocation. He has known since he was a very young child just what he wanted to do, and that was to serve God. His laughter, his jokes, his devilment, even that good-looking face of his, are all being used in the service of God . . . But I never heard him say he wanted to be a priest because he wanted peace . . . No, I never heard him say that.'

Father Bailey looked again towards the canary. 'You see, Annie, God has jobs for us all. Some he picks for priests and nuns, others he picks to be mothers . . . That's a great vocation now . . . Ah yes, to be the mother of a family!' He turned and smiled broadly at her.

'Father' – Annie rose abruptly – 'I've made up my mind. I know what I want to be.'

'All right, all right . . .' – the priest got up heavily – 'but, as you know, there's a lot to be done first . . . What does your mother say about this?'

213

'I haven't told her yet,' said Annie quietly; 'I was wondering, father, if . . . if you would tell her.'

'What!' The word came like a pistol shot. 'Me tell your mother that you want . . . ?' He took a deep breath. 'Why, I wouldn't take a bucketful of golden sovereigns to do such a thing! I'm surprised at you asking it; you know how dead against the Church she's been these last years. It always amazed me she let you attend the convent school. I'm sure it was only to prove to herself the pet theory she's worked up about the spiritual freedom of the individual . . . Me, tell your mother you want to be a nun? Not on your life, Annie!'

'Oh, father!'

'Now it's no use, Annie. If you were sure in your own mind of what you want to do you'd not fear telling her.'

'I *am* sure.'

'Then get on with the job. For it will be a job, and you'll find that out.'

'Will . . . will you come up, father, and talk to her after . . . because . . . Because I think she'll be a bit upset?'

'A bit upset! Did you say "a bit"? You're right there. Saints alive! just how right has got to be seen. Very well' – he nodded heavily – 'I'll look in tomorrow. When are you going to see the Mother Superior?'

'I'll go tomorrow, father, tomorrow afternoon.'

'Then I'll be up in the morning.'

Without adding anything further Father Bailey turned back to his canary, and Annie, with a faint 'Goodbye', went out.

It was all so different from what she had pictured. She had imagined Father Bailey, with his hand on her shoulder, expressing his delight and willingly taking on the task of breaking the news to Kate. But now she was alone in facing that task, and the feeling she had at the prospect amounted to terror . . .

On arriving back home she was greeted by a Kate full of

almost girlish excitement about an afternoon shopping expedition to Newcastle. She was brimming over with it; they must have something new, new hats, new dresses; they would have tea in town and go to a film afterwards. Rodney, too, was all for it. And it was patent to Annie it was being done for her benefit.

She wanted to say to Kate: 'It's no use buying me new clothes, I won't be able to wear them.' But at the thought of spoiling Kate's happiness her courage failed her, for she realised that now their concern for her was the only dark spot on their horizon. So she went to Newcastle, and the day and night passed and she still had to tell Kate.

Whatever picture she had in her mind of the scene that would follow the telling of her news could not have been in any way comparable to the one which actually took place. And Father Bailey could not have timed his arrival at a worse moment.

Annie was flying upstairs, away from Kate, away from a wrath whose ferocity staggered her, as he came into the hall.

Father Bailey was prepared for a scene with Kate, but he wasn't prepared for the Kate he saw now, a woman who seemed to have grown to twice her size with the turmoil of her feelings. He put his hat and coat on the hall-stand in a silence that vibrated. Then he was forced to meet Kate's eye as she stood staring at him from the drawing-room doorway with Rodney behind her.

The words seemed to spit from her mouth as she said, '*You*'ve done this! You and your suggestion – bring her up in a convent! Yes, bring her up in a convent, where they can play on her mind and nerves. Catch them young, that's the idea, isn't it? . . . You've had it planned for years! You and that Sister Ann . . . Sister Ann!' she screamed.

Father Bailey's red face paled and a white line showed around his mouth. He seemed to find great difficulty in speaking. 'Don't say any more, Kate, you'll only be sorry.'

'What have I got to be sorry for?' she cried.

Rodney took her by the shoulder and turned her back into the drawing-room, practically pushing her with his body. 'Come in, father, and close the door,' he said to the priest. Although he looked white and drawn he was the calmest of the three.

He tried to press Kate into a chair, but she shrugged away from him and turned again on Father Bailey: 'I'd rather see her dead! . . . Do you hear? dead! . . . Oh my God!' Some of the tenseness went out of her body, and she put her hand across her eyes. 'My Annie in a convent! . . . All her life, never, never to come out. It's wrong, it's wrong.' She dropped her hand and stared at the priest again: 'She's as much fitted for a convent as . . . as . . .'

'As you are,' put in Father Bailey, quietly.

'Yes! as I am,' Kate cried defiantly. 'I know her. I know her, you don't. It's because she's in love . . . She's hurt, and you take advantage. I could have understood Father O'Malley doing it, but not you. I trusted you. You've done this for spite because I wouldn't have David and Angela christened in the Church; I've kept them free from your influence.'

'Kate! Kate!' Rodney cried. 'Don't! Say no more.'

This time he succeeded in pressing her into the chair. 'She's not herself, father,' he said, turning to the priest.

Father Bailey was fumbling in an inner pocket of his coat. He drew out a small tin box which Rodney recognised as a rosary box, for he had just such another upstairs, which Kate had given to him the night he went to France. Father Bailey opened the box and turned out a tiny rosary on to the palm of his hand. The beads had once been coloured, but now they were bare pieces of glass linked by a tin chain. Lifting the rosary reverently, he held it up between finger and thumb and

216

made the sign of the cross over it: 'In the name of the Father, and of the Son, and of the Holy Ghost.

'Look at me, Kate,' he commanded.

She raised her head.

'This is my mother's rosary. It was all she had to leave me. From my early days she set her heart on me being a priest. She died working. She had nothing, she owned nothing, only this. And to me it is as sacred as the Holy Bread . . . and' – his voice rose to a pitch of anger matching hers – 'I swear on it by her and by the body of Christ that the first time I heard that Annie Hannigan wanted to be a nun was yesterday morning.'

The rosary held aloft, he looked, not like the easygoing priest of their acquaintance, but some titanic force of right. They stared at him, surprised out of themselves at the strength and personality of this little man.

As Kate looked at him the stiffness and anger left her, and crying, 'Oh, father!' she turned her head into the wing of the chair and began to sob, great, tearing sounds which brought a twisted anguish to Rodney's face.

When Rodney would have put his arm about her, the priest motioned him away, and in a voice that was still harsh and angry addressed Kate again: 'If you had accused me of conspiring to marry her off to some good Catholic lad it would have been nearer the mark . . . for what good will she be as a nun? The Church doesn't want nuns, it wants mothers, mothers of sons and daughters; it wants families, large families, for God alone knows they are becoming almost extinct . . . Now I ask you, why should I want Annie to be a nun? She's a good, sound Catholic, and any children of hers would be brought up in the Church. There's none of your nonsense about her; the education she's had hasn't made her think she knows better than her creator.' Rodney's brows contracted, and he made to speak, but the priest again silenced him with his hand. 'Now do you believe me?'

Kate was crying more quietly now. She made no answer, and Rodney spoke for her: 'Yes, she believes you, father. This has been such a shock – undreamt of.'

The priest returned the rosary to its box again, and after a space said, 'What we've got to do is to put our heads together and play for time. I'll have a word with the Mother Superior. It certainly won't be my fault if Annie goes into a convent, but I can tell you this, Kate,' he nodded towards her, 'if you want to get her in with all speed, go on the way you are doing now.'

He sat down with a soft *plop* on a nearby chair, and began to rub his face vigorously with a red and yellow patterned handkerchief. Kate had stopped crying and was lying still, her hands covering her face.

Rodney limped about restlessly: 'I should be able to work this out, but I can't, it's beyond me. I've never felt so inadequate in all my life. If she were anyone else's child, something would suggest itself, I would do something definite, but as it is . . .' He threw out his hand in a gesture of hopelessness.

Father Bailey could not resist what he considered a well-merited dig. 'Doctor, I used to hear a lot of talk about spiritual freedom. Where is it now? As I said, I don't want her to go in, but I've been given to understand from time to time that she's an independent human being.'

At the look on Rodney's face, and seeing the writhing of Kate's body, the priest said, 'Forgive me; I shouldn't hit out like that. But it's a long time since I've been so disturbed.' He smiled faintly at Rodney. 'Would it be presuming on your hospitality, doctor, if I were to ask if you had . . . just a little drop . . . ?'

Rodney's face cleared. 'Of course, father. The very thing! I should have thought about it before. That's what we all need.'

He cast a grateful, almost affectionate glance towards the priest and went out. And Father Bailey, moving over to Kate's side, sat down beside her and, taking her hand, patted it gently.

As she listened to the Mother Superior speaking, Annie knew that Father Bailey had been here before her. The Mother Superior was kind. Of course she would like Annie to come in. But shouldn't she pray on the matter? And hadn't she another year to do at college? If she was of the same mind when she finished, then nothing should stand in her way.

The faces of Father Bailey, Kate and Rodney rose before Annie, all asking the same thing, all strangely joined in one force. Six months they asked her to wait . . . She said, quietly, 'Will you take me in six months, if I come then?'

The Mother Superior went through the motion of gently washing her hands. Yes . . . yes, she would take her then.

She rang a bell, gave Annie her blessing, and told the nun who appeared to show Annie out by the west gate.

Annie hesitated; she wanted to see Sister Ann. Then, looking at the Mother Superior's calm and expressionless face, she knew the reason why she was being escorted out: so that she *wouldn't* see Sister Ann.

Why were they all against her? Sister Ann was the only one who would understand . . .

Annie thought it was impossible to be more miserable than she had been at the beginning of term, but now she found there were different grades of misery. During this week, while she had been at home, Kate's effort to act normally pained her to such a degree that at times she nearly cried out, 'All right! All right, I won't do it!'

On this particular Saturday Kate was going about in a state of such high tension that Annie became uneasy. Rising above her own misery was a deep concern for Kate, whose anxiety she couldn't bear to witness. So most of the time she kept to her own room. She was sitting there now, reading a life of Saint Teresa. It was part of the preparation she had set herself, and such books had to be read away from Kate's eyes.

Kate's voice came to her now from the hall, calling excitedly, 'Annie! Annie! Rosie's records have come.' On hearing this, Annie left the room swiftly and met Kate on the stairs, a little of her old eagerness showing again. 'Rodney's putting them on.' Kate held out her hand in the old gesture and Annie placed hers in it. They ran down the remaining stairs and went into the drawing room together.

'Shh!' warned Rodney as he placed the needle in position. Their troubles forgotten for the time being, they smiled at each other and sat down.

The record started, bringing a thin silver wail of violins into the room. Then a soprano voice sang: 'Christe Eleison'. When Rosie's voice answered, 'Eleison', they looked at each other, smiling and nodding excitedly. The voice was clear and full, and conveyed tremendous power. On it went, answering, answering. The bass vibrated '*E . . . lei . . . ison . . . E . . . lei . . . ison.*' One after the other, the solo voices took it up. Then the choir came in, and wave on wave of voices rose to the heavens, forcing acknowledgement, defying death, soaring above it. Gradually the voices sank and became steady, like souls plodding, marching to a known destiny. A trumpet called, gently at first, then louder, as if to blast the gates themselves.

Rosie's voice came alone now, each syllable distinct and beautiful. The soprano joined her, their voices blending. Then, with a strange suddenness, the choir burst upon them for a second, after which all the voices ceased abruptly. Into the silence drifted the tenor's voice, his notes like sun-spangled water falling through space: '*Benedictus . . . benedictus.*' The bass answered, '*Benedictus.*' The violins rippled . . . the voices rose, rose, then fell away, to fall into silence: *'Requiem . . . Amen.'*

The record stopped, and as Rodney turned it Annie thought, I can't stay to hear any more, it's too beautiful, I can't bear it.

But she sat on, crouched in the chair. The writing in Terence's book came back to her; there was a piece which explained this feeling, and she had condemned it as exaggerated . . . How had it gone? *Take from me this beauty I have craved, it is past my power to bear . . .*

The second part of the Mass began. *'Jesu Christe . . .'* The voices came now hopeful and joyous. Annie allowed herself to be borne away on them. *'Sanctus . . . sanctus . . . Hosanna in excelsis . . .'*

This was how it would be in the convent, this was how one felt when one's life was given to God. The voices were like waves of tangible feeling floating about her.

She didn't notice the changing of the records. Rosie sang with the soprano *'Qui tollis peccata mundi'* . . . Drums beat, the sopranos of the choir sang as with one throat, and Rosie broke in sharply with a clarion call. The choir ebbed and flowed about her, the male voices rising to her; but that clear, beautiful bell tone soared above them and was alone. Then, as if at a word of command, it dropped to a whisper. The whisper was repeated, then . . . finish.

They sat quite still. Who would have thought that voice could belong to Rosie Mullen? Through a daze of feeling, Annie heard Kate crying quietly and saying, 'All because you gave her that chance the night you heard her sing "My heart's in the Highlands", Rodney.'

Rosie had something now. She had a career, a wonderful career, before her; but would it make up for Michael? They too would have loved one another had it not been for Cathleen.

Annie had not seen Rosie for weeks, but she'd had a letter from her in which she blamed herself for all that had happened to Michael. And although Rosie didn't know exactly what had taken place between Terence and Annie, she felt that her taunting of Cathleen that afternoon must have had some bearing on it, for she remembered the terrible look Cathleen gave her. Mention of Rosie's feelings was noticeably absent throughout the letter, but, gauged by her own suffering, Annie knew what they must be . . . Why was it everything had gone wrong at once? But why ask such a question when the answer lay in the one word: Cathleen.

Rodney's voice sounded thick as he said, 'Well done, Rosie! It was almost as good as being there.'

'You can understand now, can't you,' said Kate, 'why the old man cried and cried, although it's hard to imagine Mr Mullen crying.'

'It must have been very impressive; it's a pity we couldn't have gone,' said Rodney.

Thinking herself unnoticed, Annie went quietly out and upstairs again. At least Rosie had something sure . . .

15

Usually on a Saturday they all went out together, generally to Newcastle. But today neither Kate nor Rodney made any mention of going. And when David demanded to be taken to see the shops he was told that Mammy had a headache.

As the afternoon wore on, Annie felt she could bear the house no longer. A slight drizzle was falling and the day was cold and raw, but she put on a mackintosh and went out, saying in answer to Kate's enquiry, 'I'm just going to take a short walk along the cliffs.'

Immediately she was gone, Rodney said, 'My dear, you must calm yourself.'

'Oh, I can't. If only he'd come.'

'It's a long journey. Do you think she might suspect?'

'No, no. As he said, she wouldn't expect him, for she would know he couldn't afford the fare.'

'Poor devil.'

'But mind, my dear, whatever you do don't suggest or offer . . .'

'Of course I won't. I wouldn't dream.'

'Well, it's just because he'd be up in arms. I could tell from his letters . . . When I sent the money I told him just how well

223

acquainted I had been with poverty, and I impressed upon him it was merely a loan.'

'I think you should have told him what she intends doing. You were wrong not to prepare him.'

'No . . . It might have had some effect on him; it's better that he shouldn't know, and then he can act more naturally. But his talk about things he wrote in a book puzzles me; I can't understand it.'

Kate, watching from the drawing-room window, saw Terence pass by the main gate. He was looking towards the house, and she rapped sharply on the windowpane before running out. They met half-way up the path and shook hands warmly.

'Oh, Terence, I'm so glad to see you. It was good of you to come.'

'I wanted to come . . . Where is she?'

'She's gone for a walk over the cliffs.'

'Well, I'll drop my case in home and go and see if I can find her. If I can't, I'll come back here.'

'Terence . . . be firm with her. Make . . . make her see that you love her.' Noticing his drawn face, she exclaimed, 'Oh, you look tired! It's such a long journey.'

'It's not that,' he said. 'I've written to her every week . . . twice a week. You'd have thought she would send me some sort of answer. I wouldn't have believed she could be so hard. And all over a . . . some silly writing in a book.'

'What book?' asked Kate; then put in hurriedly, 'Oh, it doesn't matter now. Find her, and put it right, and then come back to tea. Oh Terence,' – she gripped his hand again – 'if you make her see reason I'll . . . I'll never be able to repay you.'

He stared hard at her. 'Is there something else wrong? Is it not just the book? I'm all at sea . . .'

'Go and find her, Terence. Tell her you love her. Make her

see that.' She almost pushed him away; then followed him to the gate, and watched him hurry up the lane.

Terence had been out half an hour when he saw Annie. She looked like a grey smudge against the trunk of the tree under which she was sheltering from the rain, which was now falling steadily. He pulled up abruptly, and shook his head to dislodge the wet from his hair. Then, wiping his neck and face with his handkerchief, he moved over the grass towards her, giving himself time, whispering caution and calmness to the turmoil within.

He was within some yards of her before she saw him. She still leant against the trunk, but her hands came out of her pockets and wavered a second before she put them behind her. It looked a childish gesture, an act of protection used by the young, a survival from her childhood, and it touched him. He approached her more slowly still, his hands hanging limp by his sides.

When he came under the shelter of the tree he stopped, his eyes holding hers, forcing her to look at him. And as he watched he saw their expression change from a frightened, trapped look to a staring cold look of dislike. He made a quick movement towards her, saying, 'Annie! Annie!'

At the same time, she cried out, 'Don't! Don't touch me!'

He halted within a foot of her. They were so close that their steaming breaths wafted in quick gusts about each other's face. 'Why?' he asked flatly.

When she made no reply, he went on, 'I've got to know why. Annie . . . Annie, darling, the writing in that book was just stupid . . . nonsense. If it's that piece about Cathleen that has upset you, why . . . it was just sheer imagination, built up from a little incident. I'll explain it. Look—'

Only inches separated them. She was pressing her body tight against the trunk.

'I love you, Annie. God, I can't go on like this!'

225

His arms were about her and she was pulled from the tree and held against him. Her face was under his, and he cried, 'Don't you see . . . don't you see there's no-one but you? Never has been.'

She grew stiffer, and he cried to her, 'Annie! Annie!' as if he was recalling her from unconsciousness. But she didn't unbend, and for a moment he became mad. His hands moved, pressing her into him as if to infuse life into her body. He kept murmuring, 'Annie, Annie,' but she remained unresponsive. Her head was pressed back from him, and not until his lips came seeking hers did she struggle.

Then, without warning, she went limp; it was not a sign of surrender, it was the relaxing into nothing, into lifelessness. She seemed to shrink and to become small in his arms. With a sudden gesture he let her go, and she lay back against the tree again, not even panting. He shook his head helplessly, pain and bewilderment showing in his face.

She said quite suddenly, in a clear, almost calm voice, 'Do you remember Warrington's field? And the sheltered hollow running down to the river?'

'What?' It was barely a whisper. His brows contracted, and his lips pressed together.

'You used to camp there. Do you remember?'

He became quite still; his hand on the way to his pocket stopped in mid-air.

'You camped there the first week of your Easter vac . . . The weather was fine.'

In the ensuing silence, his hand dropped trembling to his pocket. He took out his handkerchief, and as he passed it once again over his face, he groaned to himself, God! No, she can't know that. She mustn't know that! Cathleen couldn't have been so vile.

Annie stretched herself against the tree. Her hands were now on the bark, rubbing up and down it. 'Cathleen

Davidson stayed there with you one night.'

'Annie,' he groaned aloud, his eyes pleading into hers.

But she went on: 'She explained it to me in detail. And she told me to describe it to you in case she had left anything out.'

'Don't! I tell you, don't!' His face was scarlet; it was as if all the blood in his body had rushed there.

'She said you and she . . .'

She stopped. Her lips formed the words but no sound came. It was an odd sensation. The words were engraved on her mind; she had been determined to say them and, in saying them, to rid herself for ever of their picture.

She looked at him. He stood with his head bowed before her, his face running wet with sweat, not rain, and she knew she could never say, 'You undressed her. You both ran naked in the field. You ran down to the stream and swam together. Then you lay the remainder of the night in the tent . . . not sleeping.'

The rain, weighing now on the leaves, began to fall through in large plops. They could hear the surge of the sea on the rocks.

After a long time, Terence raised his head. 'I understand now.' His voice was tired and lifeless. 'But there's one thing you should know . . . I didn't take her there; she came. And whether you believe it or not, I have never loved her . . . Yes, I know,' he went on as she moved impatiently, 'you can't understand that. You are making the mistake of all youth, you are valuing love in terms of sex . . . Annie, that's only part of one, a small part . . . don't you see?'

She said coldly, 'Don't say again to me that I am young.' Then added, 'Would you have married her if she'd had a child?'

'What are you talking about?' he said heatedly. 'There was never any question of that. It only happened . . . that once; I can swear on that. And . . . and I wasn't the first, by any means . . . she was too well versed . . .'

227

'Then why did you run away?'

He drew his brows down in a questioning frown: 'What?'

'You dashed back to Oxford without seeing her, and she had to go there to you because she thought she might be having a . . .'

'That's a damned lie!' The red drained from his face, leaving it clay-coloured under the tan. 'I went back in a hurry because I wanted to finish with her, for I knew I was in love with you. I wrote and told her it was finished. She took it all right, because she still wanted to keep in touch with me. She already had her eye on John Dane Dee; it was him she came up to see.'

'It doesn't matter,' said Annie; 'it could have been.'

'It couldn't!' He was becoming angry. 'I know I did wrong. But it wasn't with an innocent girl. If there was any seducing to be done, she did it.'

'Stop it!' Annie cried; 'I want to hear no more.'

'You emphasised how grown-up you are, so you *shall* hear. It's a fallacy that men are always the seducers, it's often the other way about. And anyway, if I'd given her ten babies I wouldn't have married her. I am well aware of why you ask that question, so now you know! You lay too much stock on the matter of legitimacy. Do you think your mother would have been happier married to a man who—?'

'Shut up! You . . . shut up!' For a moment she felt she was back in the fifteen streets, yelling and screaming raucously.

The rain pattered about them.

He said softly, 'I'm sorry. Oh! I'm sorry. I know how you feel about it, but I have the greatest respect for Kate . . . the greatest respect.'

Her eyes had taken on the colour of the wet grass, and she was gasping as she said, 'She sent for you, didn't she?'

He made no reply.

'I can see,' she went on, 'that she didn't tell you what I am going to do.'

He remained silent, waiting, watching her as she straightened herself and stood away from the tree. 'She shouldn't have brought you home; it will make no difference, for I am going into the Church.'

She had been looking away towards the sea, but she turned her eyes on him now and saw that he didn't really comprehend her meaning. She added more gently, 'I am going to be a nun.'

As she watched the quick spasms of feeling ripple over his face, she thought he was about to burst into hilarious laughter, as Brian had done. But his features were contorted in pain, and he gasped out: 'No! Annie . . . not because of me. Not that!'

She said, almost with pity, 'It isn't only this. I had thought of it before . . . long before.'

'No!' he said again, taking a step towards her. 'You can't do that just because I . . . Annie, don't let me do that to you!'

His body gave a convulsive twist and he half turned from her, and beat his fists against his temples. He stood like this for a moment, then turned swiftly on her again, shouting, 'Don't be a fool! I'm not worth it. Nobody is. You couldn't be a nun, Annie . . . you *couldn't*!'

Her fixed stare stopped him. 'It's all arranged.'

'Oh my God!' His eyes lifted from her face. 'Your hair . . . You know what they'll do?'

She could stand no more; the emptiness was passing; the feeling of detachment was deserting her. 'That won't matter. Nothing you can say will make any difference.' She backed away as she spoke.

The veneer which his university education had given him seemed to Annie to have dropped from him; he looked once again the boy she had known in the wood, close-mouthed, taciturn and vulnerable. Turning, she ran from him, and did not stop until she reached the main road. The world was empty; there was no comfort anywhere; for the moment, even the convent ceased to be a refuge.

This feeling will pass, she told herself. You knew you would have to see him . . . but it's all over now. And he denied hardly any of it. Remember that, should you be tempted to feel sorry. Yes, remember that.

As she turned from the main road into the lane she saw Mr Macbane coming towards her. He was walking leisurely, his greasy mac hanging open and his black cloth cap planted squarely on his head. He looked at her in surprise, and stopped, awaiting her approach. She had always stood in awe of Mr Macbane, and now she nodded and made to walk past him. But he put out his hand and stopped her.

'Where's the lad?' he asked, looking closely at her. 'Have yer seen him?'

Annie swallowed hard and shrank away from the hand on her arm. He stared at her, his grizzled brows working up and down. 'Yer a fool,' he burst out. 'Yer divn't knaa when yer on a gud thing . . . Luk, lass' – his tone became coaxing – 'he's come all this way, an he's got to gan back termorrer . . . Why divn't yer make it up?'

She shook her head, saying, 'I can't. I've explained . . .'

He drew back from her. 'Yer a bloody fool!' he exclaimed. 'Yes. Gan on, look shocked. Gan on an' tell the doctor what I've said. Ye've been spoilt, yer neck's been broke. Yer making my lad's life a hell . . . Y'always have done, ever since ye wor a bairn scramblin' after him in the woods.'

Her eyes widened, and he went on, 'Aye. Yer can gape. I know. I'm not blind, ne daft . . . An' now he's not gud enough fer yer . . . Alreet fer a bit of sport, but that's all. Hasn't got enough cash, is that it? Let me tell yer, yer'll go farther an' fare worse. An'' – he finished, spilling all his grievance on her – 'his mother's worried to death, the hoose isn't the same.'

She drew herself up and stepped back from him.

'Aye. Yer can get on yer high horse . . .' He wagged his head from side to side. 'Yer can come the fine lady.'

He stopped abruptly, his temper dying away as quickly as it had risen. 'I'm goin' past meself,' he murmured. 'But ye see, it's like this, lass. I know my lad; he's like me in one or two little ways.' It was almost an apology for Terence's inherited traits. 'There'll only be really one fer him, as there was fer me.' He smiled at her, and the blue marks on his cheeks, badges of the pit, seemed to hang from the folds of his skin.

With a catch in her breath, Annie said, 'Oh, Mr Macbane, I'm sorry . . . but it's no use.'

After staring at her for a while, he passed his hand over his mouth, saying, 'Ah weel.' His head drooped and he gazed at the ground.

In an agony of intense feeling, she stood staring at him. At this moment she felt nearer to him than anyone she knew, even Kate and Rodney.

Mr Macbane squared his shoulders and lifted his head. Giving her a level and not unkindly look, he turned away and continued down the lane.

16

〜

'Man, I can't believe it,' Rodney said, looking at Peter in real distress. 'What news to bring on a New Year's Eve!'

Peter took a long drink from his glass. 'I had to come and tell you. We didn't finally decide till last night . . . I don't really want to go, but she's breaking up, Rodney. She's breaking her heart for the sight of Michael. And now, since the other one's gone, there's nothing to stop us.'

'But to sell your practice! Why not put someone in and take a holiday for, say, six months? You'll never settle away from the Tyne.'

'That's what I told her. But she says we can always come back.'

'But your practice!'

'I'm tired . . .' Peter dropped his head on his hands.

Rodney sat staring at him, for the moment unable to realise how defeated his friend was. 'Peter . . . Is there anything I can do?' he said, getting up and going towards him. He gripped Peter's shoulder: 'You can't let this break up your life . . . You can't!'

Peter sat up. His large frame seemed to have shrunk during the past months, and he shifted restlessly in his chair. 'I'm afraid it's got to be. Peggy will fade away if she doesn't see the boy.'

'Bring him back.'

'No. I wouldn't do that. Strangely enough, he seems to like the life, and my brother has taken a strong fancy to him. No. Going there seems the only way out . . . but' – he gave a shadow of his old smile – 'we'll be back.' He looked up into Rodney's grieved face and said, awkwardly, 'I'll miss you . . . Nineteen years. It's been a long time.'

Rodney turned away, incapable of a response. For the first time he was experiencing what he realised many others must have felt, a feeling of hatred against Cathleen. Summed up, the damage that girl had already done was colossal. Kate had almost lost her life . . . Steve had gone . . . Annie and Terence were parted . . . Michael was in Canada . . . Rosie Mullen had undoubtedly received a hurt that even her success could not entirely hide . . . and now this man, who had been his only close friend since he came to the north, was selling up his house and practice. His chest tightened with the feeling of anger. And what had happened to Cathleen? Was she paying in any way? No. Ultimately she had got – from her parents – what she wanted: the money to have a studio in Chelsea. Only four days ago, when she was standing in this room saying goodbye, he had it still in his heart to feel sorry for her. She appeared small and childlike and rather pathetic. It was difficult to keep telling himself that this was a clever and dangerous woman, not the young and appealing girl she looked.

As if following his train of thought, Peter said, 'It's odd, when you think all this has come about through her.' Rodney noticed that Peter never referred to Cathleen by name now. It was either 'she' or 'her'. 'I swore I'd never let her go off on her own until I had to,' Peter went on; 'but Peggy was getting so that she couldn't bear the sight of her. And when she demanded we get the house done up and refurnished so she could ask that Dane Dee there, well, that just finished it. Peggy turned on her. And I saw then she'd have to go before anything worse happened . . . Do you know anything about that fellow?' he asked.

'Not a thing. I've never even seen him. All I know is he was a friend of Terence Macbane's; he was up at Oxford with him, and seemed to have plenty of money. Of course,' he added, 'the last was just hearsay.'

'Oh, that's right enough . . . he's got money. And the title's an old one. That's what I can't understand about it, he's well connected. His people will likely have a big say in whom he marries, yet she's got the idea it's going to be her, because he's motored once or twice to Newcastle to see her. It's not only an idea with her, she's absolutely positive she's going to bring it off. She's banking on it. I've no fear at the moment for the life she'll lead, for this has come to mean so much to her that she'll do nothing from now on to impair her chances. She says he's very keen on her taking the studio, and is going to introduce her to various people who will be likely to buy her stuff.'

'Is there so much need to sell her work if she's going to marry him?'

'Don't ask me,' said Peter, shaking his head. 'Anyway, I suppose she's got to live in the mean time; the money she's got won't last long.'

'Perhaps it will be the best thing that could happen.'

'For whom?' said Peter. 'Not for him. I pity any man who gets her.'

'Oh, Peter!' Rodney's anger was gradually dying, and again his feeling was tinged with pity.

'Yes, you can say, "Oh, Peter!", but you don't know what we've been through; you don't know what she is. Even now I think you're sorry for her . . . she said you would be. When she insisted on coming up the other day, she said that in spite of everything she would enlist your sympathy and would have you on her side again. That's her.'

Rodney stiffened. How nearly right she had been. How nearly right she was. Again he had the feeling of being young and inexperienced. Her knowledge of him and of human nature in general was phenomenal. He was sorry now that he had allowed her to think he was ignorant of the extent of her activities, but from the coldness of his manner she must have judged that he knew something.

Catching sight of Annie throught the study window, Peter exclaimed, 'Ah, there's Annie! You know, I haven't seen her for ages. I thought she would have been up during the holidays. Is she still going with young Macbane? . . . You know,' he added wistfully before Rodney could reply, 'I thought at one time, if that one of mine had got Macbane, it would have been the saving of her. He seemed a steady kind of fellow, with a mind of his own.'

Rodney said evasively, 'No. They've had a tiff. She's passing through a phase . . . they all do. Here, let me fill your glass.'

To his knowledge, no-one outside the house except the priest and Terence knew of Annie's intentions. He could trust Mrs Summers and her niece, Alice. Knowing that Cathleen had had something to do with Annie's decision, he did not want to burden Peter with another revelation.

Coming up the garden, Annie waved to Peter. But when she got inside the house, she didn't go into the study. Instead, seeing Kate in the hall, she said, 'I'm freezing. I'm going up to have a bath. Is there plenty of water?'

'Yes, plenty,' said Kate, and added, 'It's so silly going for walks in weather like this; the mist and damp get into your bones.'

'It was all right,' Annie replied, 'until the wind got up. It's cutting.'

'Have a good soak,' said Kate as she watched her go up the stairs, 'and I'll bring you a hot drink, eh?'

'Thanks.' Annie half turned, and her smile flashed out for a moment.

Kate seemed to hold the smile to her. When the stairs were empty she still stood, saying to herself, 'Oh, my darling. My darling . . .'

Annie lay back in the bath, her eyes closed. The hot water seemed to separate her skin from her body; it oozed beneath it, creeping up from her stiff toes to her shoulders, then into her head, lulling, soothing.

Oh, what delight! To know nothing, feel nothing, only the caressing wonder of hot water; to feel your body, free from every travail, floating, floating . . . Her hands began to move sensuously over her shoulders and down her arms. Oh, it was lovely, lovely! What a marvellous feeling! What more could anyone ask than this ecstasy of hot water loving the body like a— With a start, she was sitting upright. She gripped the rough-haired loofah and scrubbed herself vigorously. She let the water out and turned on the cold tap, and stood under the hand-spray, shivering. Getting quickly into her dressing-gown, she went to her room. And there she found David.

As she opened the door, he sprang round from the altar, hiding his hands behind his back. 'I was only looking,' he said. 'I was only looking, Annie.'

'What have you got there?' she asked.

He brought a hand forward, and dangling from it was her rosary. 'I was only doing the Hailing Mary.' His eyes looked up at her, perplexed yet fearful. He couldn't understand why, all of a sudden, he had been forbidden to go near the altar. He liked Mary's statue: it was pretty, and she had a nice baby, like Angela, and it was fun to talk to her on the beads. He said 'Hail' like the Indian did in his story-book, and instead of 'Mary, full of grace' he sometimes said 'Mary too full of

236

grace', and then he thought the baby smiled. He didn't really know what to say to her, for Annie had begun to teach him, then stopped. It was all a secret; Mammy didn't know. And then Annie wouldn't let him come near the altar, and said she would never love him again if he dared tell Mammy he had been learning the Hail Mary.

Annie took the rosary from him, saying, 'I told you, didn't I?' His lips trembled, and his eyes became wide and fixed. Stooping swiftly, she caught him to her: 'It's all right, darling. It's all right.'

He gulped. 'Don't you love me any more, Annie?'

'Oh yes, yes!'

She knelt down and folded her arms tightly about him. He flung his own about her neck, squeezing her with all his might. 'I love you best in the world, Annie. And I want a little altar like yours. And I want to be called Hannigan Prince, to be like you.'

'Sh! . . . Oh, darling darling.'

Her thoughts tore at her. She would shortly be leaving him. Oh, how could she leave David? And he wouldn't understand. Even when he grew up he wouldn't be able to understand, not being a Catholic. Oh, how wrong of Kate not to bring him up a Catholic, to deprive him of eternal life. She halted in her thinking . . . He was a Protestant. For years, under Father O'Malley's teaching, she believed that no Protestant went to heaven. And although she considered she was now more enlightened, she still believed that Protestants weren't eligible for the heaven of the Catholics. Then where? . . . David, Angela, Rodney . . . all the nice Protestants she knew . . . all the Protestants in the world . . . and then the people who weren't even Protestants . . . what would happen to them all? She would have to talk to Sister Ann about it . . . No! It was a cry from the corner of her mind which was asserting itself more and more, an uneasy, disquieting corner.

237

No, don't talk to Sister Ann about it . . . her answer would be all cut and dried. Only the other day, in answer to Annie's question of why there were twice as many non-Christians as Christians in the world, she had answered that they were put there to be converted! A silly answer which had left her vaguely uneasy.

Sister Ann was lovely, but Annie was finding that her answers to many questions were not satisfactory. So she must think this out for herself; for it was unthinkable that if David were to die at this moment he wouldn't go to heaven, nor even to purgatory . . .

Kate entered unnoticed. 'Here you are; I've brought your drink.' She smiled down on them as if their present intensity was an everyday thing.

Annie scrambled to her feet, embarrassed and annoyed. She knew that Kate would read her own meaning into the little scene.

'Rosie's just been on the phone,' Kate said. 'She wants you to go up tonight for the first-footing.'

'I'm not going!' Annie said hastily. She turned to the mirror and began to brush her hair. 'Anyway,' she added less brusquely, 'I'd rather be at home.'

'I don't know whether we'll stay up or not, for Peter and Peggy aren't coming.'

'Well, it won't matter.'

Kate took David's hand and moved towards the door. 'There was a call from Brian while you were in the bath,' she said. 'He says he'll be up some time this evening.'

Annie swung round from the mirror: 'Didn't you tell him I'd be out?'

'How could I, when I didn't know what you were going to do?' Kate turned at the door and glanced back at Annie. 'Rosie said she'd phone later to see if you were going up.'

Looking helpless, Annie said, 'I'll go up. You can tell her I'll go up.'

When the door had closed on Kate, Annie stood beating the palm of her hand with the back of the hairbrush . . . Wouldn't he ever take a telling? Would nothing make him stop pestering her? . . . But that was it. He didn't 'pester' her, he just came. He talked to Kate and Rodney, he played with David, he made himself agreeable to everyone. Sometimes he hardly spoke more than a few words to Annie. But when she was in the same room with him she could feel his presence like a weight on her body.

She went and stood by the window. Through the bare top branches of the hedge she saw Mr Macbane coming down the lane. She watched him near the gate, pass it, and disappear into the drizzle. He didn't once look towards the house. She was no longer afraid of Mr Macbane, but she was sorry for him, more sorry than she had ever been for Terence. Her sorrow for him was a mature feeling; she understood his disappointment. That Saturday at half-term, when he waylaid her in the lane, was the forerunner of a number of such meetings. Three times last week he walked with her from the terminus. Before, had they been on the same tram, he would have hurried away ahead of her, or lagged behind. But now he made it his business to wait, and to fall into step beside her, even though they sometimes walked in uncomfortable silence for most of the journey home. He no longer swore or got angry, but each time they met he would make a point of mentioning Terence.

The first time he had waited, at the beginning of the holidays, he couldn't keep his news to himself, even for the first few steps of the journey; nor could he keep the pride from his voice as he said: 'The lad's got the job o' maths master at the Fennington Grammar Schul. What d'yer think of that, eh?

239

Only twenty miles from Newcastle. He'll be home every weekend noo . . . Divn't yer think that's a slice of luck?'

She answered his eager conversation with 'Yes, Mr Macbane,' and 'No, Mr Macbane.' And all the while a feeling of pity was growing in her, and the wish to please him. But she knew this to be impossible, for he was working towards one end, the happiness of his son.

Terence had been at home all the holidays, she knew. They hadn't met, but she caught glimpses of him, now and then, in the distance. At these times she would shut down her mind like a steel trap on the thoughts that attempted to rise, with their accompanying feelings of torment. It was quite easy, once you found the knack of doing it. You simply shut your mind for a second, sweeping it bare, then concentrated with all your power on doing something that required action. Yes, it was quite easy . . . during the day.

She turned from the window and began brushing her hair again. Then she stopped abruptly. It was a waste of time. She must get out of the habit; it would prepare her for what was to come.

Mr Mullen was singing 'The Spaniard That Blighted My Life'. Annie stood on the doorstep and listened, and found herself laughing.

'I'll catch that big bounder, I will—' His voice cracked, and was drowned by a chorus of 'Pom-*poms*'.

'The blighter I'll kill;
He shall die, he shall die.'

There was a concerted shout of 'He shall die, he shall die!'

'He shall die, tiddly-i-tie, i-tie-tie,
I-tie, he shall die, he shall die,

240

For I'll raise such a bunion on his Spanish onion,
If I catch him bending tonight . . .'

Annie pressed her hand over her mouth. What was it about the Mullens that always made you laugh? Perhaps because they laughed at themselves. It was odd, but she always felt at home with them. In spite of their roughness, they seemed to be . . . her folk. She hadn't wanted to come tonight, because the thought of meeting people disturbed her and distracted her thoughts from their set course. But now it was like coming home . . . She felt she was going to enjoy herself, and – a sad little thought – it would be her last first-footing party. And another thing, she must take the opportunity tonight to tell Rosie she was going into the convent. Rosie was her friend, and should know. It was ridiculous of Kate to expect her to keep it a closed secret, as if it was something to be ashamed of.

Rosie opened the door and cried, 'Oh, Annie! A happy New Year!' She drew her into the room, saying, 'Listen! The singer's on his feet . . . Have you been knocking long?'

'No. I've been standing on the step laughing . . . That's your father's favourite, isn't it? Remember the night he sang it to us when we were small? He did it with actions, and knocked over the frying-pan full of panhacklety . . . remember? And your mother chased him with the pan yelling, "I'll blight yer life for yer!"'

They hung on each other, laughing at the memory. Through the door leading into the kitchen Annie could see three of the Mullen boys and their wives arranged tightly along one wall. She waved to them, and they shouted, 'It's Annie! Hello there, Annie. Happy New Year.'

As Annie returned the greeting, Rosie ran to the intervening door and closed it. She came back, saying, 'Give me your things.'

'What have you done with the bed?' Annie exclaimed, looking round the front room.

'It's upstairs,' Rosie laughed. 'The back room is now a correct illustration of a "bed"room . . . Annie' – Rosie turned and poked the fire – 'Annie, promise you won't be vexed with me.'

'Vexed? Why on earth should I? What do you mean? I can't ever remember being vexed with you.'

'I've done something, and now I'm a bit afraid.' She turned from the fire, her face serious and pleading. 'Oh, Annie, I want you to be happy. You above all people. And I reckon it this way: one of us should be.'

Annie stiffened; the hand that was arranging her hair remained still, and without moving she seemed to withdraw from Rosie. What did she mean? . . . Terence? She couldn't mean Terence, Rosie hardly knew him . . . Then what?

'I thought if you . . .' Rosie was saying when the door opened and Mr Mullen yelled:

'What yer hidin' in there for? Come on oot of that . . . Why, Annie lass, I've been waitin' fer ye all the neet.' He put his arm about her waist and pulled her into the kitchen, crying, 'Best-lukking lass on the Tyne! What d'ye say, lads?'

In the kitchen were the four married sons and their wives and children, together with Nancy, Jimmy and Florrie. And, in the corner of the horsehair couch near the fireplace, sat Terence.

He rose slowly to his feet and, as the Mullens chaffed and shouted, and Mrs Mullen said, 'There's no need to introduce you two, you're neighbours,' he stood looking at her, not shyly or fearfully, but squarely, his grey eyes steady.

After the first trembling shock of seeing him, Annie was filled with anger against Rosie. How could she place her in such a position? And Kate had known! They were all in it. What did they think she was? An imbecile who didn't know

her own mind? Someone who could be led and turned by their combined efforts?

It was all she could do to stay in the room. But if she were to go now, besides making a spectacle of herself, he would likely follow her . . . Well, she would show them just how futile was their planning. She would be calm. She would laugh and talk as if nothing unusual had occurred. She would play them at their own game; calmness was the hardest of all weapons to fight . . . What business was it of theirs, anyway? Why couldn't they let her alone? Why? No. Don't probe, she said to herself. Don't argue; keep calm.

'Sit down, man,' John Mullen said to Terence. 'What ye on yer feet for?'

Terence sat down beside John again.

'Luk,' went on John; 'Aa'm interested in what ye wor saying just a while ago.' Terence looked at him questioningly. 'About miracles, ye know. We was just gettin' warmed up when me da decided to render.'

'Don't start talkin' about religion,' said Mrs Mullen, 'else I'll throw you out.'

'Aw shurrup, Ma! We're not . . . t'aint religion.'

'Let's have a drink,' cried Mr Mullen. 'What's it fer you, Terry me lad?'

'Nothing, thank you, I've already had one.'

'Weel, have another to keep it company. We may not be together like this fer a long time again.'

'No,' put in George, the family Jonah; 'likely be on the road with the other blokes this time next year . . . down to two shifts noo. How do they expect you to live?'

'My God, he's off again!' cried John. 'Give him a stiff un, Da.'

'But he's right,' said George's wife. 'How do they? How *do* they think we're goin' to get through? With bairns, dole . . .?'

'Give her a double too,' chimed in Harry.

'Here,' said Mr Mullen, handing George a glass of whisky. 'Get that down yer kite! It'll help to keep yer strength up fer when ye get on the road. What yer worryin' aboot, anyway? Our Rosie's gaan buy a castle, and she's gaan take us all in . . . ain't yer, lass?'

Rosie, helping her mother with the food, turned and grinned at her father. But her eyes slid from him to Annie, and a sigh of relief escaped her when she saw that Annie was engaged in conversation with Hilda, John's wife.

'Let's have another song!' cried Mr Mullen. 'What about it, lass?' He put his arm affectionately round his daughter's waist.

'Shurrup a minute, can't yer!' cried John; 'I can't hear a word Terence is saying.'

Out of deference to the visitor, a hush came over the kitchen. And Terence laughed, and said, 'It was nothing . . . We'll have a talk about this another time, John.'

John had married a Protestant, who hadn't 'turned' – he was the second of the family to commit this 'error' – and Annie knew that it was about religion that he was talking, and was getting Terence to air his views. No doubt he was hoping they'd coincide with his own. Although she was listening to Hilda, she was also straining to hear what those views were. She was sitting a few feet from Terence, with her back half turned towards him, and in the general buzz of conversation and shouting of the children she could only catch odd sentences.

John was saying, 'But what was that ye were saying aboot faith, Terry?'

Looking intently at Hilda, but shutting her mind to her voice, Annie keyed her ears to hear the reply.

'Well, faith itself is a miracle, John. Apply faith to anything and you get results. There you have the basis of the miracles in your religion. The faith of a particular person can be so strong that the mind is affected in the way desired; and in the mind's action on the body is the miracle.'

'Then you don't believe in God, Terry?'

'Well, not the one with the beard,' laughed Terence. 'Nor the one divided up into three persons. I see God as Mind, operating in everything.'

The awe in John's voice conveyed itself to Annie, as he said, 'Ye don't believe in Jesus then, Terry?'

'Yes, John. I believe him to be the greatest man ever to be born on this earth, and that he was in closer contact than anyone else with Him whom you think of as God and with what I think of as Mind. But they both mean the same in the long run, John.'

The last vestige of anger against Rosie and Kate fell away from Annie. This had to be: it was ordained that she should be sitting here tonight. They had contrived to get her here, and it had been for a purpose . . . but not the one they supposed. The purpose was that she should hear his views. It was all so plain now. She saw it as another example of the workings of God to ease her mind. How had she imagined for one moment that there could be anything between him and her! She never even thought of religion in connection with him. Or, if she had, it was as a foregone conclusion that he would convert. But what did he say? . . . God was Mind. In other words, each of us was a little god unto himself, and you created your own miracles. She was staggered at his audacity, and trembled at the blasphemy.

It seemed strange to her now that she had expected him to fall in with her ideas, to be in harmony with her way of life . . . Oh, things would be much easier now. There was less and less to regret. She was not losing anything. It was no wonder he was immoral and behaved as he did.

Others had now joined in the discussion, and the stronger Catholic element amongst them, with the help of the whisky, was becoming a little heated, when Mr Mullen clinched the whole matter with a crude but profound truth when he stated that morbid introspection on religion was generally a case of constipation, and that a well-regulated bowel made God much more understandable. To put it in his own words: 'Eat plenty o' cabbage and gan to the lav three times a day, and God nor nebody else'll worry ye.'

This remark was greeted as all truth is greeted until it is proved – it was howled down by the entire family.

'Da, talkin' like that, an' people here!'

'Da, ye get worse. Shut up!'

'Make him stop, Ma.'

'I hope ye don't mind him, Terry,' said Mrs Mullen; 'Annie there's used to him, ain't ye, lass?'

Annie, a little red in the face, said nothing, but Terence laughed and said, 'He's right. There might never have been a Lutheran church if Martin Luther hadn't been troubled that way; it was a trial to him. It's a point that needs debating.'

The name 'Luther' made no impression on the Mullens, but to Annie, in her present frame of mind, Martin Luther was in the same category as the Black Mass and witchcraft. Luther and all his followers were the enemies of the Catholic Church, and Terence Macbane had laughed. Oh, she was glad she had come! Yes, indeed!

The evening passed swiftly. More than once their eyes met, and she returned his look steadily. After two glasses of whisky and the same of beer, he became amusing to everyone but her. His characterisation of particular schoolboys brought roars of laughter from the Mullens.

It was close on a quarter to twelve when they decided he should be their first-foot in place of Mr Mullen. He was dark and, as young Nancy Mullen said through her adenoids, he was 'nearly nansom'.

Terence was standing in the middle of the kitchen, with a lump of coal and a bottle of whisky in his hands, ready to leave by the back door, when the knocker of the front door banged so loudly that he and all the others in the kitchen started.

'Who on earth can this be?' cried Mrs Mullen. 'Close on twelve, too! You go and see, Father.'

'Some bloke three sheets in the wind, got to the wrong door!' exclaimed Mr Mullen, shambling through the front room.

'There'll be two of them when they meet, then,' laughed Harry.

Mrs Mullen cried, 'Sh! the lot of yer. Listen!'

As Annie listened, the blood slowly mounted to her face. She heard Mr Mullen say, 'Yes. Yes, she's here. Cum in, whoever ye are, and welcome.'

When Brian stood, filling up the room doorway, he faced a solid battery of eyes, which in no way perturbed him. He looked straight at Annie, and said thickly, 'Hello there! It's like being in a circus chasing you around. Why couldn't you let a fellow know?'

Annie could make no reply; she could only stare at him. A nameless dread was asssailing her. She felt that she would never, ever be able to get away from Brian. Others she could ward off, but never him.

'Funny Kate didn't know where you were,' said Brian.

There was a moment of uneasy silence, which Mrs Mullen broke by exclaiming, 'Well, well, now ye're here, come and sit down so we can get on with the first-footing. This is my son Harry, and this is his wife. And this is . . .' She went the round of introductions, after which she gave him a seat on the other side of the room from Annie. Then, going into the scullery, she encountered Rosie, so furious she could hardly speak.

'*Him!* He would have to come! And he's nasty drunk, Ma. He means trouble.'

'I'll see to him, never fear . . . Oh, are you off, lad?' She turned to Terence on his way out.

Rosie caught Terence's arm. 'Oh, Terence, I'm sorry; he's spoilt everything.'

Terence said nothing but, patting her hand, smiled ruefully and went out. He groped his way down the back yard and into the back lane, his thoughts as black as the night about him. Blast Brian! Acting as if he owned her! If he dared to touch her . . . as much as to lay a hand on her, he'd . . . Well, what would he do? he asked himself. What could he do? Oh, God, it was maddening! He had wanted things to go quietly, smoothly. If he could have taken her home, just spoken to her ordinarily, shown her there was no need to shun him, got on a friendly footing! But now what would happen? . . . And she was afraid of Stannard, he could see that. Well, she needn't be afraid.

He shook his head violently, trying to chase the muzziness away. Why did he have that whisky? He was a fool to take it when he wasn't used to it . . . Trying to work up Dutch courage?

He was now one of a group of men standing at the corner of the street. Similar groups were standing at the ends of all the fifteen streets. Many of the men were already drunk. Nevertheless, they were quiet, talking only in loud whispers and laughing with restraint, as men do in a house where there are sleeping children.

Someone said, 'A minute to go.'

A silence fell on them, which was punctured by a hiccuping drunk, and someone else cautioned, 'Quiet there, lad.'

Then the ships' horns, the dock hooters and the church bells all spoke at once. There was a swelling of voices: 'Here they come!', 'There they go!', 'Happy New Year, lad,' 'Same to ye. Many of them,' 'Full shifts, full bellies,' 'Happy New Year.' They dispersed, still calling to each other. Knockers

248

were banged briskly and fists were beaten on doors, which opened to laughter and muffled greetings.

Terence rapped the knocker smartly. Endeavouring to fall into the role of a first-footer, he called, 'A happy New Year!' as the door was opened.

They were all crowded into the front room now; the men shook his hand and the women kissed him as if he were a long-lost relation.

In the surge of greetings, his mind was still on Annie. He noticed she wasn't in the front room; nor was Brian. He made his way through the throng to the kitchen, apparently to get rid of the lump of coal he was carrying, Mr Mullen having already relieved him of the bottle of whisky.

Annie and Brian were in the kitchen, but Mrs Mullen was there too. She said, 'A happy New Year, lad . . . Here, give me that coal.'

Brian ignored Terence. He was leaning with his elbow on the high mantelpiece, looking down on Annie, who was sitting, with her head lowered, staring into the fire. 'I wonder where you and I'll be this time next year, Annihan?' Annie did not reply, and Brian turned to Terence as if only now becoming aware of his presence: 'A happy New Year, Macbane.' His tone was insolent and full of threat.

Terence answered coolly, 'I wish you exactly the same.'

He looked at Annie. Her face was turned from him, but the strain she was under was evident in the whiteness of her cheeks. He went and stood near her, having to stand almost in front of Brian to do so. 'A happy New Year, Annie.'

She looked up, startled, and stared into his eyes. They were soft and kind and, as on that day when he took her hand and led her through the arches, they were telling her not to be afraid.

The words would not come; she had to force them out: 'A . . . happy New Year.' They were drowned in Mr Mullen's shouts and the bustle of the family trooping into the kitchen again.

'Cum on noo,' Mr Mullen was crying. 'Get yer glasses! Drink in the New Year! And wor George an' the wife an' bairns gannin' on the road!'

A roar of laughter greeted this sally, and George said dolefully, 'Aye, there's mony a true word spoken in a joke,' which sent the family off into hysterics.

Rosie busied herself in getting the crowd seated again and handing out the food. But do what she might she couldn't separate Brian from Annie, who sat crushed in the corner of the horsehair couch.

The kitchen was stifling and full of the smell of beer and spirits, tobacco fumes and breath . . . The evening had turned into a nightmare for Annie. If only it were one o'clock and the car were here, and she could leave . . . Brian's flesh seemed to flow over her; her thigh was lost in his. It was impossible to ease herself from him. If she got up and went into the front room the Mullens would think it was odd, and anyway she would only have to come back again. And Brian would see that her place was kept for her. The combination of smells that was wafting from Brian, a mixture of spirits and the peculiar body smell that was distinctly his own, sickened her.

She was conscious of Terence's eyes fixed, not on her, but on Brian. He was sitting opposite, and when anyone came into the line of his vision, which was often, he would shift his position, which made him appear to be swaying.

For the most part, Annie kept her head half bowed, talking at odd moments to young Jimmy, who sat at her feet. Brian said little; he seemed to be talking with his body, moving it slowly this way and that, until she thought, wildly: I don't care, I can't stand it, I'm going.

The room became unbearably hot. She lifted her head, and

250

the picture on the wall opposite began to sway. She heard Terence say, 'No, no. Definitely no more for me, Mr Mullen, I've had enough.' She felt Brian pressing closer to her; his hand, hidden by their bodies, began to rub the small of her back. She felt his breath on her neck; his mouth touched her ear, and he whispered thickly, 'Come on, we're going . . . I've had enough of this lot.'

Unable to resist the nearness of her, he caught the lobe of her ear in his lips. The room whirled and, involuntarily, a cry escaped her. There was a tremendous bustle in the centre of the room; the Mullens seemed to be scattered to either side, and Terence was standing over her and Brian.

Before she could struggle to her feet, Brian was lifted bodily off the couch, and in the faintness and humiliation that assailed her she was conscious of thinking, Terence couldn't do that, he's not strong enough!

John Mullen was shouting, 'Steady, Terry lad! Steady!'

'Here! Here!' Mr Mullen's voice boomed. 'We're havin' none o' that.'

The men were between them, loosening Terence's hands from Brian's collar and restraining Brian's fists.

Mrs Mullen cried, 'My God! On a New Year's morning too!'

As Annie gained the front room Rosie caught her: 'Oh, Annie, what have I done? I did it for the best.'

Annie pushed her aside. 'Leave me alone! I'm going.'

'But you can't, the car isn't here. You can't begin to walk all that way.'

Annie grabbed up her coat and, as she pulled open the front door, gasped, 'It's all right, I'll meet the car.'

Once outside, she ran blindly down the deserted street and into the main road. The stinging night air and drizzle swept away the faintness and cleared her mind, leaving it empty to receive the flood of mortification.

She couldn't bear much more, she couldn't! If only they would let her go . . . if she could fly to Sister Ann this minute . . . if she could only get within the quiet greyness of those stone walls . . . Terence had fought like some drunken docker – like her grandfather, who wasn't her grandfather. He had spoilt the Mullens' party. But it was her fault. She should have got up sooner; she should have turned on Brian. But how could she? Even when he was sober she couldn't make any impression on him . . . She musn't wait another four months! She must get away quickly from Brian. If she didn't . . .

Her feet flew faster, her breath tore at her chest. She imagined she could hear running footsteps behind. Oh, if the car would only come!

She saw lights approaching, and stopped, gasping, under a streetlamp, and hung on to it for support. As the lights drew nearer she made out the shape of a lorry. Her own breathing was loud in her ears, but above it she heard clearly the sound of running feet. She started to run again, faster than she had done before. If only she could meet someone. She couldn't go on much further, there was a stitch in her side . . . If it was Brian! She made an extra effort, the pain tearing at her. If she could reach the Jarrow slakes she would throw herself in if he touched her . . . Oh God! Where was the car? It must be nearly one o'clock.

The steps were on her now; she could even hear the gasping breath of the runner . . . Oh, Mother of God! She stopped abruptly and flung herself against the wall, her hands outspread.

The running figure loomed out of the dimness, stopped, and gasped, 'Don't be afraid, Annie . . . it's me, Terence.'

She was in the pool again, and struggling with him. And he was saying comfortingly, 'Don't be afraid, Annie . . . it's me, Terence.' But there was no comfort now.

He was standing before her, supporting himself with one

arm stretched out, the hand pressed against the wall by the side of her face. He spoke in jerks: 'Oh Annie, I'm sorry . . . I wouldn't have had this happen for the world . . . believe me. Don't be afraid, don't look like that . . . Annie, won't you be friends? Won't you just speak to me?' He waited, then drew in his breath. 'If Stannard touches you again I'll kill him!'

Still she made no sound.

He took deep gulps of air, and when his breathing was easier he said, 'Annie, have you still got your mind made up about . . . the other thing? Won't you give me another chance? . . . Oh, for God's sake!' he cried. 'Answer me!'

She moved her head wildly.

'I didn't mean to ask you. I meant things to go differently . . . I'll not ask you again, not after tonight. Oh, Annie—' his voice shook, and he made to draw her from the wall. But she shrank from him, putting her hands before her to ward him off. 'All right. Don't worry, I won't touch you . . . But won't you let us try again? Annie, please! Just be friends; I'll ask nothing more.'

In the dim light from the streetlamp a few yards off, he saw each feature of her face strained to its utmost. She was standing as stiffly as though she had become part of the wall. With a feeling of hopelessness he turned from her and walked to the kerb.

She stared fixedly at the dark blur of his back . . . If the car did not come soon she would faint. Her head seemed to be swelling and disengaging itself from her body.

Two lights approached swiftly from the distance. To her they appeared to dance hectically as they came nearer. She stumbled past him into the road, and when the car was still some distance away she recognised it and waved her arms wildly.

The car pulled up almost opposite to where Terence was standing, and before the chauffeur had time to get out,

Annie had opened the door and was getting in.

The man stood uncertainly on the road. Then, putting his head inside the car, he asked, 'Is the gentleman with you, miss?'

'No! No!' she cried. Her voice sounded strange, as if she hadn't used it for a long time.

The chauffeur got in and began to turn the car. As he backed, the headlights shone full on Terence, and their glare seemed to awaken him.

Before he swung round and stalked away his face showed up clearly before her. It was as if she were staring at a picture, and the picture showed him crying. It wasn't the rain – though his face was wet with that – but his eyes were full and blurred with tears. It's the whisky, she said to herself. It's the whisky. Men never cry otherwise. It's disgusting! But she felt no disgust. The feeling she had was one of remorse, which was ridiculous, for what had she done that she should feel remorse?

17

There was a new crispness about the garden. Groups of daffodils edged the lawn; beds of tulips, their colours just beginning to show, bordered the paths; the herbaceous borders were thick with a variety of greens; among them were already showing sprinklings of tall, star-faced yellow dorontiums. The house was newly painted, black and cream. There were fresh light curtains at all the windows, some blowing gently out into the bright sunlight. Everything had a prosperous, well-ordered appearance.

Kate, standing in the greenhouse slowly arranging daffodils into bundles and tying them with bass, kept looking up over the garden towards the house. With each uplifted glance she murmured the same words: 'Oh God, make something happen.' She murmured them so often they seemed to become part of her regular breathing. She had ceased to see the garden or the house as they were. The house was merely the place from which Annie would emerge when she returned from church, where she had spent most of this Good Friday, and the garden a piece of ground over which she would walk.

This was the last holiday Annie would spend here. In two weeks' time this would no longer be her home, and never,

ever again would she belong to her. Oh God!

Kate pulled the binding too tight, and it snapped, scattering the flowers on the floor. As she knelt down to pick them up she was hidden from view by the racks, and for a moment she pressed her head against the wooden support, and the tears she was continually restraining welled up and ran down her cheeks . . . It can't happen! Is this a punishment on me for denying the Church? Oh God, don't punish me this way. Anything else! Anything else!

Rodney's voice, calling her name, came to her from the garden. She carefully dried her eyes, and as she gathered up the flowers she thought, with sudden intensity: Something *must* happen! I'll will something to happen. Anything! Anything! The words seemed to be screamed inside her.

Rodney, looking round the garden, caught sight of her when she straightened up, and hurried towards her, his limp becoming pronounced in his haste. 'I didn't see you there,' he said as he opened the door.

Kate saw at a glance that he was excited, and her heart leapt. He's got news, she thought, he's heard something.

'Who do you think I've been talking to?' he said. She shook her head, her eyes wide and staring. 'Steve.'

She felt her body collapse like a pricked balloon.

'I caught a glimpse of him in Grainger Street, in Newcastle. I got out of the car and caught him up. He's had a rough time, Kate.'

She smiled at him, covering her disappointment, for she knew that this meeting was something he had been hoping for since he had learnt the real reason for Steve's departure.

She said, 'Oh, I'm glad you've seen him. How is he?'

'In rather low water; he's only been in work a couple of months since he left here . . . He didn't really have a brother to go to.'

'But surely Steve could get a job anywhere?'

256

'Yes, if there were jobs to get. But as he said, and not without some truth, it's the ex-majors and -colonels who are being taken on as chauffeurs these days . . . You know, Kate, I think he's missed us as much as we've missed him. He got a post with a family in Jesmond directly after leaving here. But he gave it up, which he regretted after a while, for he's done nothing since.'

'Where's he living?' asked Kate.

'He didn't say, but I've got an idea it's a lodging-house.'

'Oh no! Poor Steve.'

'Kate . . .'

'Yes, darling?'

'Would you mind if I have him back?'

'No, no, of course not. Not at all!' Kate said spontaneously. 'You know, I never blamed him. It was her . . . that –' her voice choked – 'that devil! She's caused all this.' She turned from him, unable to control her tears.

'Oh, darling, don't—' He pulled her round to him. 'For a moment I forgot . . . Don't. There, my dearest. There.' He stroked her hair.

'I'm sorry,' she said. 'But oh, Rodney, what can we do?' She leant back within the circle of his arm and looked into his face, her eyes beseeching him to give her hope.

He shook his head: 'I can't see any way out, bar taking it to law, since she's not yet twenty-one. But I've never heard of anyone going to law to stop their daughter entering a convent. And Father Bailey has done his utmost. I wouldn't have believed he would try so hard to persuade her against it . . . But you know, my dear, it's my belief, and it's rather late in the day to start thinking this way, that there's been too much persuading done in one way and another. If we had ignored the whole matter, it might have been better, for she seems more set now than ever. It's that damn calm manner she's assumed. You can't get beneath it. If you could, you'd let

257

loose all the torment she's going through, and then there'd be some hope of getting her to change her mind. But as it is, there's no way out I can see. My dear,' he said, gripping her shoulder, 'with every pore of my body I hate the thought of her going in there, but I'm afraid we'll have to make up our minds to it. As Father Bailey caustically pointed out that day, you always wanted her to be free to choose. Well, you'll have to look at it that way: she's made her choice.'

'No, she hasn't! She hasn't!' Kate burst out. 'I know how she feels inside. She still loves Terence, and that . . . that witch told her something about Terence that day. I know it! I know it! And the tragedy is, it may not be anything of importance. But she's so young that she thinks it's unforgivable! If she could keep this attitude up for ever I wouldn't be afraid for her, but she'll wake up . . . and then . . . Oh! I don't know what will happen. Sometimes,' she ended, 'I feel there is no justice in the world. Here's Annie's life broken before it begins, and we're all unhappy, while that monster who started it all is enjoying herself in London.'

'Come,' said Rodney quietly, taking her by the arm, 'I want to show you something.'

As they went up the garden he said, 'Getting back to Steve, he won't return unless you agree, for he feels responsible for what happened to you.'

'Oh, that's silly!' said Kate. 'It wasn't his fault. When is he coming to see you?'

'He's not coming at all unless he's sure of your attitude. He's going to phone me about three-thirty.' He looked at his watch: 'It's nearly that now.'

'Oh, tell him to come. Tell him to come down and have some tea with us. It may take our minds off things for a time. And you'll have to give Paynter notice as soon as possible, won't you?' she asked.

'He was going anyway, he's only on a month's trial. You

know,' he laughed, 'I'm getting a bad name as a boss; Paynter is the third in six months. Steve spoilt me for any of these time-keeping johnnies. And I know someone else who'll be glad to see him . . . old Summy; she's always on about him.'

They went into the study, and Rodney took a paper from his desk. 'Look at that,' he said, pointing to an announcement. 'The mills of God are starting to grind for her.'

Kate read:

The engagement is announced between Lord John Dane Dee, only son of Eustace, eighth Earl of Halstead, Essex, and Maud, Countess of Halstead, and Patricia, youngest daughter of Lt-Col R. A. C. Fanshawe MC and Mrs Fanshawe, of Fenton Manor, Surrey.

She turned to Rodney: 'But hasn't he been going after Cathleen? Didn't she think . . . ?'

'Yes. He may have done, but apparently not with marriage in view.'

'I can't feel sorry.' Kate looked squarely at Rodney. 'I think it's only what she deserves. Now she will know what it feels like to be hurt. The only thing is, she'll likely make someone else pay for it; she'll never suffer alone.'

Rodney turned to his desk and began to arrange his papers. That was true. Cathleen would always take payment for her frustration and disappointment . . . But she was alone now, in London. For a moment the old feeling of sympathy for her returned. After all, she was really very young, and completely on her own, for there was no place now to which she could return. He shook himself. What a hold that girl had on the emotions! His common sense told him she wouldn't be alone for long, and Peter's words came back to him: she'd be on the streets within twenty-four hours. It sounded terrible, but that seemed her destiny.

Would he ever see her again? He hoped not. It wasn't likely she would return to the north now that her defeat was made evident in the papers. He felt a sense of relief that his family was out of the line of her retaliation. But had she not already done her worst here? He turned to where Kate was sitting staring wearily out of the window, her kind eyes shadowed with pain. His conscience smote him . . . that Cathleen could have had the power to make him doubt this woman, even for a moment. His love should have been strong enough to withstand a thousand Cathleens. His love *was* strong, it was like a rock. Then Cathleen's power for evil must be even greater. In this moment his last vestige of sympathy for her vanished.

Annie had her back towards Kate when she said, 'I'm going to the clinic to see the children. I'll have tea with them, and if David's down there I'll bring him back with me.'

'But Annie, I've just told you, Steve's coming to tea . . . Surely you want to see him, don't you?'

'No.'

'But you can't blame him. You know as well as I do—' She stopped abruptly, then said sharply, 'You must stay to tea, Annie!'

'I'm not going to . . . After all, there's no need for me to see him. When he comes back, I'll . . . well, there's no need for me to see him if I don't want to.'

'When will you grow up?' Kate said, almost angrily. 'Your trouble is you put the wrong value on things!'

Annie turned and looked at her coldly. Why did everyone think she was still young? The 'things' Kate was referring to were sex, of course – almost the same words as Terence had used. She said evenly: 'Well, you taught me nearly all my values.'

She would not allow herself to be touched by the pain in

Kate's eyes. She would not allow herself to be touched by anything.

She walked past Kate, through the hall and out into the garden by the side door. It wouldn't be long now, just a matter of days, and then she'd have peace. No more strain . . . it would be done. She wouldn't have to face Kate's and Rodney's eyes and feel them forever watching her. Kate had expected her to meet Steve as if nothing had happened, after all she had told her. Didn't she see that it took two to do . . . to commit sin? The word struck a false note in her mind, but she could think of no other to replace it. If she could overlook Steve's action she could overlook . . . She wasn't going to dwell on the matter. She would dismiss it from her mind.

On the way to the clinic she decided instead to sit in the tennis pavilion and read. The sun was quite warm and she would be quiet and undisturbed there.

Annie had only just left the house when the doorbell rang. At the sight of Brian Kate experienced a strange apprehensive feeling, followed by a surge of hope . . . wild hope, which found instant opposition in her mind. Well, far rather she married Brian than that the other thing should happen, she argued. But there was only a fortnight, no time at all, left. Yet if she told him of Annie's intentions anything could happen in that time. He was domineering and tenacious, and his conceit, she knew, had never yet allowed him to recognise failure of any kind . . . and he wanted Annie so much.

'Do come in, Brian,' she said, forcing herself to smile at him. 'Come into the drawing-room.' Brian looked at her sharply; her manner was more pleasant than usual. 'Do sit down.' She noticed his face wore a stubborn, petulant look.

'Where's Annie?' he asked. 'Now don't tell me she's out,' he said, raising his hand warningly and giving a grim smile.

261

'Well, she is,' said Kate; 'she's down at the clinic.'

'Oh. Well, that's different. She's been avoiding me, you know . . . Or don't you? Look, Mrs Prince' – he leant forward, his elbow on his knee, his hand moving in time with his words – 'I'll come to the point. I want Annie – you know that – I want to marry her.'

Kate stared at him. All the turmoil of feeling she was experiencing was replaced by one great wave of sickness . . . her Annie, and him! He was huge now, but he still had some shape. A few more years and he would be a gross hulk . . . Oh no, no! She couldn't will that.

She heard herself say, 'You'd better know, Annie has set her mind on becoming a nun.'

His laugh startled her. 'What! Still that old yarn?'

'Did you know?' she asked in surprise.

'Nearly a year ago,' he answered.

Kate sat back limply in her chair.

'You don't take any notice of that, do you? Why, you're her mother; can you imagine Annie a nun?' He looked at Kate with a knowledgeable stare. Then he got up from the chair with surprising agility for one so big, and came and stood over her. 'Annie's the only girl I've ever really wanted, and can you imagine me not getting what I want?' His laugh rumbled deep in his chest. 'The trouble with Annie is she's been spoilt and pandered to; she doesn't know her own mind. Well, I'm going to show it to her. That is, if it's all right with you.' He smiled ingratiatingly, his face close to hers.

Kate blindly nodded her head.

'You don't want her to end up as a nun, do you?' His hand came down on her arm, and she stared at the reddish-brown hairs on the back of it. She noticed they thickened towards the wrist and that no bones showed in his hand. Again she nodded. 'When I bring her back we'll be engaged . . . you'll see.' He squeezed her arm. She looked up into his great face, and he slowly lowered one thick eyelid. Kate shuddered; and he went on, 'Don't you worry. Just leave it to Brian, and get the house ready for a wedding.'

He chucked her chin familiarly, saying, 'Well, here I go, Mother-in-law. I'll be back to tea . . . I suppose I'm invited?' Laughing boisterously, he went out through the french window and into the garden with the air of already being one of the family.

As Kate watched him go, her whole being cried, 'Stop him! Don't let him go near her!' But she sat on, powerless to move . . .

He found Annie quite by accident. He had been to the clinic, and finding she wasn't there had walked through the wood. He was on his way back to the house when he thought of the pool. She wouldn't be bathing, he knew, but she might be around there. But, coming away, he happened to glance towards the tennis court and the pavilion beyond. On the off-chance he went towards it.

He approached the pavilion from the side, his footsteps making no sound on the grass, and he came upon her sitting in a deckchair within the doorway. She was too surprised to speak, and gazed up at him with startled eyes. Placing a hand on each side of the door, he smiled down at her.

With a sudden scurry, she tried to rise to her feet. But, lifting one hand, he pressed her slowly back, saying quietly, 'Sit where you are.' He sat down on the step, his back resting against a stanchion of the door, one leg drawn up and the other stretched out on the grass. His hand gripped his knee, and his forearm pressed against her legs.

'What are you reading?' he asked quite casually, and without waiting for a reply he took the book from her lap and said, 'St Francis of Assisi? . . . mm! Have you read Renan's *Life of Jesus*?'

She didn't answer, and he went on, 'You don't believe

I've read it, do you? I have. There's a book that gives you the life of Jesus as a historian would describe the life of a king or a period . . . no sentimentality . . . You look surprised, Annihan; you don't know your old Brian. We must get down to exchanging ideas,' he laughed. 'What's your favourite author besides this stuff?' He tapped the book and waited.

When she didn't reply he said, 'Have you lost your tongue?'

She gave a perceptible gulp, and gasped, 'I must go, I've got to get back for tea.'

'There's no hurry,' he said; 'Kate knows.'

She scraped back the chair by digging her heels into the floor.

'Now, don't rush things, there's plenty of time. You'll make me rush, and then . . .' He gave a throaty laugh. 'Look, I have something to show you.' Bringing from his pocket a small box, which he snapped open, he said, 'It's yours. Put it on.'

She stared down at the ring lying on its bed of white satin. The rays of the sun caught the half-hoop of diamonds and glinted into her eyes.

'You said seven was your lucky number. Well, there's seven of them.'

With a great effort she gained her feet. 'Let me out!'

He threw the book on to the grass and slowly got up. With one hand he pressed her back into the pavilion, and with the other slung the deckchair outside, saying, 'There's not room for all of us.' Then he closed the door with his foot.

She flew at him, tearing at his coat. But her efforts were as fruitless as if she were trying to move the pavilion itself.

Laughing, he held her at arm's length. Then swiftly his mood changed and he said roughly, 'Listen, Annie. I'm asking you again to marry me.'

She glanced towards the window which was slightly

ajar; it was no use trying to get out that way. There was no way out, only past him. She suddenly began to plead.

'Brian, I can't. Please let me go . . . Brian, Mam should have told you, I'm going into the convent in a fortnight's time. I told you last year, remember?' She gave him a weak, placating smile. 'Oh, Brian, let's go up and have tea now. Please, Brian!'

She made to shrug his hands from her shoulders, and he pulled her into his arms. 'Are you going to become engaged to me?'

'No, no, I can't . . . I've told you . . .'

'Stop struggling and listen! You're going to marry me in any case, you won't be able to get away from it. I've always said you were my girl, haven't I?' His voice was soft again, and one hand slipped down to her hips.

She strained away from him, her eyes wild with terror. 'I'll scream,' she panted, 'I'll scream if you don't let me go!'

'Don't be silly, there's no-one to hear you. But I'll see you don't scream. Come, be sensible. You know I love you . . . I'm mad crazy about you, I always have been. And you like me; I know you do, only you're afraid to let yourself go. What are you afraid of?' His voice had dropped to a whisper.

'Brian,' she pleaded again; 'oh, Brian, let me go . . . Please, please!'

'Not this time. But don't worry, we'll both be back in time for tea.' He stared at her mouth, and his head moved lower.

She stood as one fixed in a trance. Then his mouth dropped on hers as if a supporting stay had been suddenly removed from his head. Her head jerked back with the weight, and his hand came behind it, pressing it upwards again, and her mouth into his. His lips moved like an animal at a meal; but they never freed her. And her body, for a moment, became limp against his.

265

Still with his mouth on hers, he lifted her off her feet and, as she felt herself being lowered to the floor, she flung all her strength into tearing her face from his. The air rushed into her lungs, and she screamed, a shrill, penetrating scream.

He dropped her with a flop, thrust his hand over her mouth and put his knee across her thrashing legs. Then he remained still, waiting.

There was no sound, no voice calling, no running steps. He heaved a sigh and looked down at her. 'You're a fool. Do you think you wouldn't get any of the blame if we were found like this? Remember that old saw, "The woman always pays"? Well, it still applies . . . Look, Annie. I've tried to get you fairly, but you wouldn't have it. Now this is the only way. But don't worry, I'll stand by you.'

Jesus! Oh Christ! Mary, Holy Mother! This was the accumulated fear of all her life. This had happened to Kate. This had happened to her grandmother. It seemed as if she had been waiting from the beginning of time for just this moment. Her grandmother had loved the man; and Kate . . . Kate had never said. But it couldn't have been like this, for she would not have lived on. This meant death in any case.

'It won't hurt.' His hands touched her flesh.

Jesus, Jesus, save me, save me . . .

Pretend, relax . . . It was like a voice speaking from some cavern in her head.

As her body went limp he sighed. 'That's a girl! . . . All right?' He looked down into her eyes, and she closed hers against the horror of him. He took his hand from her mouth, and his weight eased for a moment from her body. It was then that she called the name. She screeched it twice before his hand slapped across her mouth and his body crushed the breath out of her . . .

*　　*　　*

266

Mrs Macbane stood cutting bread on the scullery table, whilst, with his back almost touching hers, Terence cleaned a tie on the wooden lid of the wash boiler.

'Your da will leave that door open, and there's such a draught!' remarked Mrs Macbane.

'Well, I'd better not close it,' said Terence, 'he's bringing in wood.'

'Terry, lad!' Mr Macbane called from outside.

Terence went to the door, saying, 'What is it?'

His father was standing near the wood pile, which was built against the hedge separating the garden from the Princes' grounds. His arms were full of logs, and he asked, 'Did ye hear owt?'

'What do you mean?'

'I thought I heard somebody scream.'

'It's likely the magpies.'

'It wasn't a magpie, that!'

'Bring in that wood or close the door!' called Mrs Macbane.

'Shurrup, woman! Listen, lad, I don't like it. I'm sure somebody screamed from over there.' He nodded in the direction of the hedge.

'Likely the youngster,' said Terence.

Mr Macbane walked reluctantly to the door, and there he paused again, his head on one side, listening.

'Come in or out,' Mrs Macbane was saying when, like a whisper on a breeze, came the terrified call: 'Terence! Terence!'

'It's the lass!' Mr Macbane dropped the wood and ran down the garden after the flying figure of his son.

When Terence came to a stop above the clear, still water of the swimming-pool, he heard his father's laboured breathing as he struggled up from the stream, and he called to him, 'There's nothing here!'

He looked wildly round him. Then, through the narrow belt of trees that separated the pool from the tennis court, he saw the deckchair lying on its side. Within seconds he was at the pavilion. He had the door off the latch and partly opened when a weight was thrust against it. He put his foot into the opening and levered his shoulder into the upper part.

Mr Macbane, wet from the waist down, came running up and, taking in the situation, he stepped back a few yards. Then, running, he hurled his weight against the door.

They were inside, asprawl the stacked deckchairs.

'What the hell do you mean?' yelled Brian.

Terence righted himself, and pulled his father to his feet. He looked from Brian to the inert figure on the floor. His eyes became focused on a brown piece of felt, with a red heart in the centre, attached to a cord and lying on Annie's bare breast. He made an odd noise in his throat. And his father said, 'Not in here, lad. Get him ootside. And,' he added, 'kill the bugger!'

Brian's neck began to swell. The veins stood out like red ropes. Throwing off his coat, he rolled up his shirtsleeves, saying, 'You've been asking for this! Now you'll get it. I'll teach you to mind your own bloody business.'

Terence, too, threw off his coat, and said to his father, 'Get them.' He cast one swift glance at the seemingly lifeless body of Annie, then went outside, where Brian's fist met him almost before his feet had touched the grass.

Mr Macbane, shouting directions to his son, ran towards his own hedge. Mrs Macbane was on the other side, waiting. She called, 'What's up, lad?'

'Run up to the hoose an' get them down here at once,' cried Mr Macbane. 'It's the lass . . . Summat's happened.'

When he reached the clearing again, Terence was just evading a blow aimed at his head. Brian's arms lashed the air

268

like huge pistons, but now they rarely reached Terence, who wove and ducked and was just that fraction out of reach when the blows fell. They were fighting in spurts, stalking each other round and round like animals, their teeth bared, hate glaring out of their eyes. They completed circles without aiming a blow. Then Brian would make a swirling rush, and it would seem impossible for Terence to keep his feet.

Mr Macbane cautioned, 'Tha's it, lad. Keep calm, keep yer heid an' ye've got 'im; he's nowt but wind.'

With a sudden rush, Brian aimed low at Terence's body, bringing a flow of invective from Mr Macbane: 'Ye dirty swine! Ye lily-livered waster! Go fer him, lad. Knock his teeth oot.'

As if obeying instructions, Terence darted in between the flailing arms. There were two swift blows, and he was out again. Brian's head jerked back, his heavy lids closing over his eyes for a moment. The blood trickled from his mouth, and he spat on to the grass.

'That's one of them,' cried Mr Macbane.

Infuriated, Brian bore down on Terence. His hairy arm shot out from the dangling shirtsleeve and caught Terence full on the side of the face, making him reel. Dazed, his evasion too slow, Terence received a hail of smashing blows on his body before he slipped free again.

In their rushes and retreats they reached the belt of trees, and, as Mr Macbane cautioned once again, 'Steady, lad, steady, keep clear,' he heard Kate's voice calling, 'Where are you? Where are you?' He saw her racing down the pathway to the pool. He shouted to her, and she turned towards him.

'Oh, Mr Macbane! What's happened? Where is she?' She stood gasping, her hand held to her side and nodding towards the fighting figures, now amongst the trees. 'What's . . . what's happened? Why are they . . . ?' She gripped his arm. 'You must stop them. Brian will . . . he'll kill Terence. He's strong, like an animal . . .'

'Not him, missis. Don't ye worry aboot the lad. Ye'd better go in thor,' he said, nodding back towards the pavilion, 'and see the lass.'

As Kate ran on, Mr Macbane turned to meet Rodney, who came limping hurriedly towards him, accompanied by Steve. There was sheer amazement in Rodney's eyes when he saw the battling figures. He looked to Mr Macbane for explanation, and his face darkened as he listened. He clenched his teeth, and swore at Brian as he swiftly made for the pavilion.

Steve said quietly, 'If he doesn't finish him off, I will.'

'Aye, ye will after me,' replied Mr Macbane, without taking his eyes from his son. 'And where've yer sprung from?' he added.

Before Steve could reply, Rodney called from the door, 'Will you come here a minute, Steve?'

Steve went inside, and came out again almost immediately, carrying Annie in his arms. Kate walked by his side. She seemed to have grown old in a matter of minutes. Her hair had not turned white, nor had her face become lined, but she walked like an old woman and her eyes held the look of countless age.

Mr Macbane allowed himself time to look at them before turning his gaze back to his son. The blood was running freely from a cut in Terence's cheek and dripping on to his shirt. For a moment he was locked in Brian's arms, as if in a passionate embrace. They swayed like drunken men, supporting each other. Then, as if in disgust, they thrust each other away. Panting and moving heavily, they started their circling movements again. They were now near the pool, and as Brian made a sudden rush Terence retreated, almost coolly, it would seem. Brian, not to be worn out by this strategy, dropped his rush tactics, and again they circled round each other, their eyes glaring, full of loathing and destruction.

A passion of bitterness burning within him, Rodney gave a withering glance at the stiff, uncreased shoe on his foot and the limply hanging arm by his side. Never before had he wished for the use of his limbs as fiercely as he did at this moment . . . or, he thought, a gun. If I had a gun I would use it without compunction, he said to himself.

Mr Macbane cried, 'That's it, Terry lad, wear him oot. Go steady, an' ye've got 'im.'

For a moment, Rodney wondered at the confidence of this man in his son, who looked like a lath beside Stannard. But evidently the lath was made of steel. Terence was boxing, if anyone so tired could box; he was using his head as well as his hands, whereas Brian's arms were just flailing. They were on the grassy bank by the side of the pool. Terence was closing in; his teeth bared, he hammered through Brian's arms to his face. His fists were covered with blood, and he struck with renewed force. Then his tactics were discarded, he was attacking with all the remaining strength he possessed. He backed away for a moment to regain his breath, and in doing so tripped and sat down, almost ludicrously, on the stone coping of the pool. Brian was quick to seize his chance. His foot came up, and in a flash Terence was kicked backwards into the water.

Almost before Terence hit the water Mr Macbane and Rodney hurled themselves simultaneously on Brian. So quick and heavy was the impact that they were borne to the ground with him. Mr Macbane's fists never stopped lashing, and Rodney, with his one good arm, pounded the great body beneath him until he realised that Brian was not moving. The blind rage clearing from his mind, he saw that Brian's head was lying on the coping in a spreading pool of blood. He pulled Mr Macbane away, and pointed.

Mr Macbane, rubbing his hands across his mouth, spluttered, 'Aa hope to God it's finished 'im.' He stood swaying above the prostrate figure. Then, as if coming to himself, he exclaimed, 'The lad!' He turned to where Terence was endeavouring to climb out of the pool, and helped him on to the bank.

Terence threw himself down on the grass. His ribs, where Brian's foot had made contact, felt as if they were broken, his body ached, and his heart was like lead within him. He had fought with a blinding hate, which the sight of Brian's inert body did not lessen. All he wanted to do was to kill Stannard, to kill him with his own hands . . . It was no satisfaction to know he was out if he hadn't been the means of putting him out. Not even his father's voice saying, 'Don't worry, lad, he's finished; ye would have had him in any case,' brought any comfort, for he was experiencing the primitive desire to kill his enemy, alone and unaided . . .

Kate walked into the drawing-room like someone blind. She groped at a chair as she sat down. Rodney had forced her out of the bedroom. Now she would have to wait to know if what she willed had come to pass. For she *had* willed it. For months past she had tended to think, Far better she should go the way I did than shut herself up for life. She writhed in mental agony. Would this feeling of anguish and remorse ever lessen? Always she would know that she could have prevented Brian. She had seen the lust in his face; and, knowing, she had let him go in search of Annie. She should have killed him rather than let him get out of the room. He was lying in the clinic now. His scalp was cut open, but he was far from dead. She had the terrible urge to go and drive a knife into him. She had always loathed him, yet, for a space, she had been willing that he should take Annie . . .

She suddenly gripped her hands together on her breast: Oh, God forgive me, she prayed. I was mad. Only let there be nothing wrong with her and I will reconcile myself to her going into the convent. Grant me this, and I will do anything, anything.

The old bargaining she abhorred was in her prayer, but she was past scorning any means of intercession. She dropped on to her knees and beseeched God to hear her. All she wanted now was that Annie should be in a fit condition to enter the convent.

Yet her prayers that something should happen had been granted! She beat her head with her closed fists. He could do anything, anything, only don't let her have a baby by Brian, for it would seem there was a curse on the three generations.

It was like this that Rodney found her. He lifted her to her feet, saying, 'It's all right. It's all right.'

She gazed at him, unable to believe what she heard. Her voice sounded cracked as she murmured, 'Are you sure?'

'Perfectly.'

Slowly she began to cry, painful, heavy tears. She shook her head from side to side. 'The mills . . . the mills of God are grinding for me.'

He drew her tenderly to him. 'Then if they are they'll grind nothing but good.'

'Oh, you don't know! You don't know!' she sobbed. 'I've been willing something to happen . . . do you understand? . . . *willing* it! And I've been punished. At the bottom of me I've always been afraid I'll be punished for deliberately going my own way. But that it should be taken out on her! . . . She's done nothing.'

'Now, now,' he said firmly. 'All that fear and superstition is behind you. Why, you've been free of it for years.' But he knew, as he spoke, that the seeds of fear planted during her earlier life would periodically burst forth in this way, and she would imagine God was punishing her. It was no use appealing to her reason. She could use her reason better than anyone he knew, but this went deeper than reason. So he just held her and said soothingly, 'It might be all for the best . . . somehow I think this is the turning-point.'

18

The thick, muzzy blanket was lifting. Annie clung on to it, pulling it around her, for once she let it go she would stand exposed in an immeasurable space, filled with fear and terror, with truth unvarnished. The space held a new self, a self she must wear if she were to live. She couldn't face it. She tried to grip the intangible muzziness, but it evaded her, and, like driftwood, thoughts began to flow into her mind, a queer jumble of events which seemed to have happened in another life.

Steve was again carrying her up the garden. She had the odd idea she was still the young girl he had carried up the same path years ago. The idea was strengthened by Kate's voice murmuring over her, but it was abruptly shattered when Summy held her arm and the needle was thrust in. She became startlingly aware of why Rodney was doing this. She wanted to cry out, but she was beginning to float away ceilingwards. On the bed lay somebody who was like her, and tears were falling on to her face. She didn't know whose tears they were, or who kept chanting, 'Thank God. Thank God.' She had her ear on the ceiling and was straining to listen, and although she couldn't hear what was being said, she remembered experiencing a feeling of dizzy relief. Then the ceiling opened abruptly and she passed through into nothingness.

It seemed but a minute until she was back again on the bed. She heard the clock striking one and Rodney's voice saying, 'Drink this, my dear.'

She raised herself straight up and drank, then flopped back on the pillow again. His voice came, insistent, 'Annie! Listen to me. You are quite all right . . . You are quite all right. Do you hear?' He left her, there was another movement in the room, and Summy was leaning over her, saying, 'You're all right, hinny . . . you're all right. Just have a good sleep.'

She waited; there was someone else to come and tell her she was all right. Why didn't Mam come and say, 'You're all right. You're all right'? Because Mam knew that she wasn't all right. Never again would she be all right.

The protecting blanket was dragged from her mind. She opened her eyes and stared about the room. She was alone, and a night-light was burning on the side table. It was night . . . no, morning. Another day. It was tomorrow now, and she was standing in the great space and her thoughts, untram-melled by the sleeping-draught, were terrifying in their starkness. She remembered what Brian had tried to do, and was horrified by the fact that she felt no disgust. She was right out in the open now, but she was not alone. There was another being, who looked like her. She came quite close and began to talk, saying dreadful things, yet things she seemed to have heard before: 'You wouldn't have minded if it had been Terence, would you?'

Her own mind screamed her denial.

Then the other Annie's voice came back, 'Then why did you call for him?' The figure was pointing at her, stabbing each word into her brain: 'You called for him because you thought: If only this was Terence.'

No, no, I didn't.

276

'Then why did you compare it with the night by the pool, and then again at the cave?'

I didn't compare it. You are mad!

'Oh yes, you did. And why were you so horrified by what Cathleen told you? Ask yourself why.'

No, no; I won't. She stared at the girl with the fair hair, and shouted at her: 'I am going into the convent. Do you hear? I am going into the convent!' She held her head in her hands and rolled across the bed. Her head was going to burst, she was going mad.

The girl began to laugh. 'Escape? You won't escape that way; you've got to take your mind into the convent with you. You've been longing for Terence to do something desperate to stop you going.'

Be quiet! I haven't, I haven't!

'Look at me. You can't face the truth. You know you'll never make a good nun . . . There's plenty of time left to turn back.'

I can't. Oh, I couldn't possibly say I wasn't going in. There'd be nothing to live for.

'Do you still love Terence?'

I won't answer you.

'Well, whether you do or not, you can't go into the convent . . . you can't keep up a lie to God.'

The space began to close in. It rolled in swiftly from the edges, becoming smaller and smaller. The other girl moved nearer until, with a rush, she entered her body. Annie flung herself on to her face, burying it into the pillow, crying, 'I know I can't go into the convent. I know, I know! . . . But I can't tell them. I couldn't face them all now . . . I can't live . . . I won't live!'

Terence lay with his hands across his chest, staring into the darkness. He would try no more to court sleep, for it must soon be dawn. He switched on a torch which was on the table by the side of his bed and looked at his watch. Only three o'clock! The night was endless.

As he lay down again he felt his cheek tenderly; it was sore, like his hands and ribs. That swine! If only he had fought cleanly he could have finished him! At least there would have been some satisfaction in that . . . Was she asleep? Yes, she would have had a sleeping-draught. What would happen when she came round? What would she do? He turned impatiently on to his face. The same old circle, round and round.

The pressure of the palms of his hands on his eyes made a black background, against which the picture of Annie as he last saw her showed up. If only he could have killed Stannard!

Although he knew now that Brian hadn't accomplished what he set out to do, the desire to tear him to shreds had not lessened, for he knew that had Brian achieved his end Annie would have married him. Even before she had proof of any necessity she would have made sure there would be no more Annie Hannigans.

As it was, this would surely drive her into the convent with added momentum. He accused himself of having been the instigator in turning her thoughts in that direction in the first place . . . What a fool he had been! What an utter, utter fool! That one night with Cathleen had wrecked their lives. What would happen to him and Annie because of it? For himself, there would be work. And for her? What would there be behind those walls? . . . Oh God, why had he let Cathleen stay that night? Why did he become infected with her madness? And who would have thought she would have been so vicious as to speak of it! The remembrance remained a hot shame in his mind.

He realised now that he had been clinging to some obscure hope that at the eleventh hour Annie would change her mind. But Stannard had put paid to that. He turned on his back and again looked at his watch. A quarter past three. If he wasn't so stiff and sore he'd get up and go for a walk.

As he moved his knuckles in an endeavour to lessen the stiffness, he heard a quick series of bangs on the front door. He didn't stop to ask himself who it could be, but was out of bed, down the ladder and at the door within a few seconds. His father was calling, 'What's oop, lad?' but he didn't answer, for he was staring at Kate. The wildness of her appearance was intensified by the swinging hurricane lamp she held.

'Terence! Terence!' she cried. 'Come and help find her, she's gone!'

Mr Macbane, arrayed in his vest and long drawers, came into the gleam of the lamp. 'What's that?' he blinked down on Kate. 'Come in, missis, what's oop?'

'She's gone; we can't find her anywhere.'

Without a word Terence dashed up to his room again, and pulled on his trousers and coat over his pyjamas. He hunted madly for his shoes. And when he found them, he did not stop to fasten them until he reached the kitchen again. His mother had just lit the lamp, and his father was struggling into his clothes. Kate was leaning against the jamb of the door.

She said, in answer to Mr Macbane's question, 'We've searched all the grounds and the pool.'

'What about the stream?' said Terence, speaking for the first time.

'Rodney's gone up there. And Paynter's gone back into the woods.'

'I'll go downstream.'

His mother said anxiously, 'Be careful, lad, in the dark. It drops steeply down Butcher's Gulley . . . Here, put this coat on.' She forced him to take his overcoat. Then she turned to Kate. 'Do come and sit down, you look dead beat. I'll make you a cup of tea.'

'No, no,' said Kate. 'I must look for her.'

'Stay here with my mother, Mrs Prince,' said Terence. 'Da, where are you going?'

'Aa'll go along the main road towards the cliffs,' said Mr Macbane, putting on his mackintosh.

As Terence went out, he said to Kate, 'Don't worry; we'll find her.'

The stark pain in Kate's eyes took the assurance from his words, and, as he stumbled along the bank of the stream, flashing his torch over the water, he wondered in an agony of doubt just how they would find her.

Before he had gone far, he tripped over a root and fell headlong. The torch flew from his hand, and he swore softly to himself. Picking himself up, he recovered the still-shining torch and stumbled on, cursing his stiffness.

The ground became rougher and steeper as the stream narrowed and dropped towards the gulley. Terence stopped. Unless Annie had a torch she would never have got this far. And if she came out with the intention of . . . His mind would not form the word. Anyway, in the state of mind she must be in, would she have stopped to get a torch? The night was black now, but there had been a bit of a moon earlier on. It was more likely, if she was making for the cliffs, she would have gone by the main road, taking the cut by the farm. Had she gone over the cliffs? . . . God! . . . Well, if she had, there would be an end to the search, for they dropped sheer all along their line until they came to . . . Davy Jones!

The words struck him with the force of a blow. He switched off the torch and stood in the darkness. The cave! Had she gone there? Why should he think she would go there? He remembered describing it to her as a death-trap. But surely she wouldn't . . . Why not? If she had it in her mind to finish it, that would be as good a place as any.

Throwing caution to the wind, he started to run. He'd need

280

a rope; he'd have to see the time of the tide; he'd get his mother to send his father along, for if he had to go down the cliff and over the shelf he'd never get up again without help.

The cottage door was open, but there was no sign of Kate, nor of his mother. Running out the back way, he shouted, but received no answer. He rushed back into the kitchen and searched feverishly for the previous evening's paper. 'High tide: 5.10 a.m.' It was now twenty-five to four. Already the only way into the cave would be cut off.

He ran out on to the road and yelled. No answering shout came back to him. For a moment he became panicky. If he got down the cliff and reached the cave by the sloping roof, how would he get her back? His usual level-headed coolness returned, and he told himself: Meet the obstacles when you come to them. He was strangely convinced now that she was in the cave. There was nothing for it but to go alone. He would soon find out if she were there by shouting down the fissure. That is, if she would answer him. And if she did, well . . .

He ran to the shed and snatched up a coil of rope, then through the kitchen to the road again and down to the stream. By going this way he'd save time, but he'd have to jump the stream . . . the water was flowing almost to the top of the bank. He made his way to the narrowest part, but was handicapped in his jump, as there was no running distance on the bank because of the scrub. He missed the far bank by a fraction and, although he clutched at the grass to save himself, he was wet up to the thighs before he got out, and the weight of his sodden clothes impeded his running.

About a quarter of a mile before he reached the cliff above the cave, he stopped and flashed his torch along the rough edge, searching for the ledge by which he had descended once before, when he first found the fissure in the rock. It was dangerous in the daytime, and he asked himself whether he was being foolhardy now in tackling it in the dark and without help. But the sea slapping against the rocks below gave him his answer.

He found the place and, after tying the coil of rope round his waist, he cautiously lowered himself on to the narrow ledge that ran along the face of the cliff, and began the descent. Pressing his back against the rock, he focused the torch on his feet. The light showed him the black void below, and the sight was an added strain on his nerves. Step by step he edged himself along. Sometimes his toes would overhang the ledge where it narrowed, or a bulge in the rock would make him bend forward, almost precipitating him into the depths below. He chided himself for his slow rate of progress. The tide must already have reached the sand under the shelf. But he knew that one false step would be the end. So he kept his pace. It seemed an eternity before the ledge widened, telling him he was approaching the shelf. He flashed the torch sideways, and saw with relief the long, black fissure running through the circle of light on the sloping rock. Now the ledge became part of the slope, and he was leaning back on it, his legs across the gap and his heels wedged against the further wall of the fissure.

He lay for a moment, listening. The sea seemed distant from here; only the faint lapping of it could be heard on the beach below. The night was fine and there was no wind to cut through his wet clothes, for which he was thankful. He slid his body nearer the gap. Bringing his knees up and dropping his head between them, he listened. The crevice in the rock formed a kind of amplifier, but it brought no sound to him. His mouth was dry, and he wetted his lips and called, 'Annie!' Then he waited.

The rocks re-echoed, 'Annie! Annie!' but there was no other answer. A startled seagull, which must have been roosting near at hand, flew close above his head, its wings making a wind about his ears.

As he called again, 'Annie! . . . Annie, are you there?' a gasp like a giant's breath came up between the walls, and he called louder, 'Annie! . . . Annie!' He waited, his breath held tight in his lungs, and again there came to him a broken moan and a gasp.

He straightened up and took in great draughts of air. He felt a momentary faintness with relief. Then he smiled to himself in the darkness. He was right. Bending again, he called, 'Don't worry, I'm coming down.'

He waited awhile, but there was no reply. He turned on his face and flashed the torch over the slope. It took him a matter of seconds to find a piece of jutting rock around which to tie the rope. It wasn't what he would have chosen as ideal for a safe descent, much less for a safe return, but it was the only thing available. Divesting himself of his overcoat, he gripped the rope and started down the slope. He was amazed at the short time it took to reach the edge of the shelf and drop the twenty feet from there to the beach. Standing still a moment, he listened. There was no sound, only the rhythmic lapping of the waves. He flashed the torch towards them. The running rim of foam was no more than a foot from where he was standing. Turning swiftly, he ran up the beach towards the cave, calling softly, 'Annie! Annie!' He squeezed through the aperture and she came immediately into the full beam of the light.

She was standing pressed against the far wall, and the anguish in her eyes tore at his heart; they were staring wildly out of her dirt-smeared face. Her hair was hanging in lank, damp streaks, and a sleeve of her coat hung torn from the shoulder. Never had he seen her looking like this. For a terrifying moment, he wondered if the strain had unhinged her.

He swung the light away from her, and said, 'Come on, Annie.'

She gave a whimper like a child.

'It's all over now; come along,' he coaxed.

She made an inarticulate sound, and when he went to take her hand, she slid away from him along the wall. His fear of a moment ago seemed confirmed.

'Annie, the tide's rising; there isn't much time. Listen to me.' He followed her, but she kept moving away from him, her eyes fixed in a dull, unblinking stare. She moved the whole way round the cave until she came to the slit that formed the exit, and there she stopped. He came close to her and said gently, 'If you stay, I stay, Annie.'

For a moment his words seemed to penetrate the mist surrounding her. She moved her head from side to side and the expression of her eyes changed. Her lips parted and formed words, but with no sound.

He said eagerly, 'What is it? Speak to me, Annie.'

For answer, her expression changed, and again he was confronted with the blank stare.

Panic seized him; he could do nothing with her like this. His idea had been to tie the rope about her and haul her on to the ledge. In a little while they would be caught like the proverbial rats in a trap. Even if he should manage to swim around in the bay until the tide went out, which was most unlikely as the water was icy at this time of the year, she could never hope to survive. Unless she could be shaken out of her apathy they were both doomed. Gentleness had failed; as a last resort he must try the other way.

He rapped out harshly, 'Snap out of it, Annie! Do you hear? You won't be so apathetic once the water starts swirling round your neck.' He saw a shiver pass over her, and he went on, 'Have you thought of Kate and Rodney up there, nearly mad? I'm telling you this, if anything happens to you, Kate will go mad, and I mean literally mad. Can't you stop thinking of yourself for a minute and see what chaos you are going to leave behind you? It's always the cowards who take this way out, through pure selfishness. And don't forget, you who believe so much in God, you'll go over to him just as you are now, for that's your belief, isn't it? You see, you won't be able to get rid of yourself.'

He paused for breath, and in the pause the wash of the waves came to him, conveying a sense of immediate urgency. Talking, he saw, was having no effect on her, for she still stared at him with that blank look. He put the torch down on the sand at a convenient distance from them, and as he went towards her again its light played about her feet, showing them wet and mud-caked. He thrust aside the pity the sight of them aroused; pity was lost on her at present.

As he gripped her firmly by the shoulders, she started and tried to draw away from his hands. But he pressed her back against the rock, saying, 'Listen to me . . . I'm going to pull you up on to the ledge. Do you understand?'

With a quick and surprising movement she shook herself free from his hands, and she was half-way through the opening before he realised her intent. He flung himself at her and pulled her back into the cave. Now there was no need to pretend anger; it was in his voice and his hands as he shook her and cried, 'Snap out of it! Do you hear?'

Momentarily he forgot the strain that had led up to her present condition, and in the forgetting he broke through the barrier that would have destroyed them both, for as her head wobbled wildly to his shaking she began to gasp out words.

The word 'convent' brought him to an abrupt stop. He stood still; his hands, gripping her shoulders, supported her. She seemed almost on the verge of collapse, and he thought frantically that that stage would be worse than this. He said firmly, 'Listen, Annie; we're going home. Do you hear?'

She opened her mouth wide, taking in deep gulps of air as if she had been suffocating. Then the sobs came, tearing cries that made him feel helpless. He could do nothing but hold her up while his own body shook with the force of her emotion. Then again words came: 'I . . . I . . . can't go . . . into convent. I . . . I can't go . . . not now.'

He said softly, 'You're all right, Annie; you can go into the convent if you want to.'

The sobs slowly subsided, and she muttered incoherently, 'Not now . . . not now.' She sagged under his hands and would have fallen had he not put his arm about her. She made no move to repulse him, for she seemed hardly aware of him now. He led her to where the torch lay, and bending her with him he picked it up, then led her unresisting out of the cave.

As he tied the rope firmly about her waist, he talked to her, saying, 'Don't be afraid. Keep tight hold of the rope and you'll be all right. And when you come to the ledge, shout. Will you shout? Do you hear, Annie? If you shout I'll stop pulling, and you can ease yourself on to the roof. Do you understand?' As a double precaution against her untying the knot, he left a long loose end and tied it behind her back.

In the second before leaving her he shone the torch in her face. Even the sudden glare only caused her to blink her eyes slowly, and for a brief moment he thought: If she's lost her reason it would be better we stay here. But again he was instructing her, saying, 'Try not to be afraid. When the rope tightens you'll be pulled a little way into the water.' She gave no answer and made no move, and he forced himself to turn from her.

How he reached the fissure again was never really clear in his mind. When he later recalled the climb, he remembered the agony of the rope burning his hands as he laboriously pulled himself up to the shelf, and his knuckle bones seeming to force their way through the already grazed and torn skin. After lying for a second on the slope to regain his breath, he fixed his feet in the fissure and began to pull on the rope. It came easily, without any resistance, and wildly he thought: She's untied the knot. Then it seemed to stiffen in his hands, and setting all his weight against it, he pulled hand over hand. The weight brought his back off the rock, almost pulling him down the slope. Again he pulled, and this time the rope seemed to come alive. A scream came up to him, followed by another and another. They were so shrill and petrifying that he almost loosened his hold. In his mind's eye he could see her swinging dizzily out over the water, then in under the rock. Seagulls, which had been perched on the cliff, began to fly over his head. One after another they came, confusing him, their wings making a flapping canopy above him. He continued to pull until the agony of his hands blotted out everything else from his mind. The rope was tearing the skin from his palms; they became sticky, and he was wondering how much more he could bear when his misted eyes saw her face; it was upturned to him; she was on the ledge. The torch, set in a crevice, shone full upon her; she was like an apparition. He hadn't thought she could be near the ledge yet; she must have pulled herself on to it very quickly.

He realised the strain on his hands was lessening; she was helping herself with her feet. Their hands touched; then hers gripped his arms. She was beside him and he was wedging her feet into the fissure and gabbling, 'You're all right. You're all right.' His relief was so great that he felt a choking in his throat. He lay back on the slope and, pulling his coat towards him from the jut of rock, he placed it over her, saying, 'You mustn't move; we'll have to stay here until it's light. It won't be long.'

He waited for some word, but none came.

Lying staring up into the heavens, waiting for the first

streaks of light to appear, he thought: If she's lost her mind completely I swear I'll finish Stannard.

As if in answer to this he felt her hand groping by his side. He remained still, waiting for the next move. It came when her hand found his. The fingers touched his torn palm, and their contact was agony. His hand was lifted and carried to her face; the torture of her flesh against his was exquisite, the straightening of his palm to cup her face almost unbearable. He shivered, partly with cold and partly with a feeling of blinding happiness. He did not caution her to be careful as she turned towards him and lifted half of the coat over him. If he needed any further assurance of her return to sanity, it came when her hand tucked the coat around him; it was such an ordinary action, yet a loving, maternal one. Again her hand cupped his, gently, soothingly.

He could bear no more. He turned and put his arms about her, crying, 'Annie. Annie.' He buried his head on her shoulder and her hand began to stroke his hair. And as he felt her lips press hard against his temple, in some strange way he knew that the girl Annie Hannigan had gone, and it was a woman he was holding closely to him.